"It's Rare to Meet Someone With Such Zest for Her Work,"

Doug teased softly.

Cassie knew she'd almost given herself away. Her face was flushed, but the room was a little too dark for her color to show. Pretending to be the cold-hearted Vonda was difficult when Doug Hunter started kissing and caressing her.

She figured she had two choices, and going to bed with Doug wasn't one of them. Choice number one was to carry the charade through as planned, and choice number two was to tell him who she was and say a polite good-night. She didn't have to think about it for more than two seconds.

Dear Reader:

Nora Roberts, Tracy Sinclair, Jeanne Stephens, Carole Halston, Linda Howard. Are these authors familiar to you? We hope so, because they are just a few of our most popular authors who publish with Silhouette Special Edition each and every month. And the Special Edition list is changing to include new writers with fresh stories. It has been said that discovering a new author is like making a new friend. So during these next few months, be sure to look for books by Sandi Shane, Dorothy Glenn and other authors who have just written their first and second Special Editions, stories we hope you enjoy.

Choosing which Special Editions to publish each month is a pleasurable task, but not an easy one. We look for stories that are sophisticated, sensuous, touching, and great love stories, as well. These are the elements that make Silhouette Special Editions more romantic...and unique.

So we hope you'll find this Silhouette Special Edition just that—*Special*—and that the story finds a special place in your heart.

The Editors at Silhouette

BROOKE HASTINGS
Hard to Handle

Silhouette Special Edition

Published by Silhouette Books New York

America's Publisher of Contemporary Romance

SILHOUETTE BOOKS
300 E. 42nd St., New York, N.Y. 10017

ISBN: 0-373-09250-4

First Silhouette Books printing July 1985

10 9 8 7 6 5 4 3 2 1

BROOKE HASTINGS

is a transplanted Easterner who now lives in California with her husband and two children. A full-time writer, she won the Romance Writers of America's Golden Medallion Award for her Silhouette Romance, *Winner Take All*. She especially enjoys doing the background research for her books, and finds it a real challenge to come up with new plot twists and unique characters for her stories.

Silhouette Books by Brooke Hastings

Silhouette Romance

Playing for Keeps #13
Innocent Fire #26
Desert Fire #44
Island Conquest #67
Winner Take All #101

Silhouette Special Edition

Intimate Strangers #2
Rough Diamond #21
A Matter of Time #49
An Act of Love #79
Tell Me No Lies #156
Hard To Handle #250

Silhouette Intimate Moments

Interested Parties #37
Reasonable Doubts #64

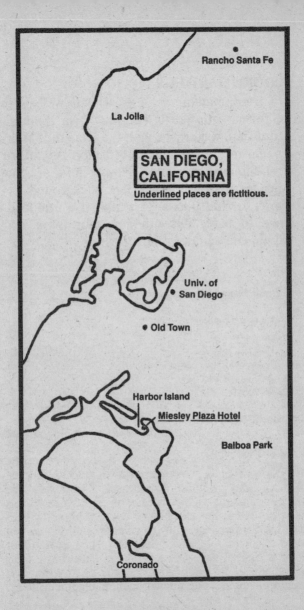

Rancho Santa Fe

La Jolla

**SAN DIEGO,
CALIFORNIA**
<u>Underlined</u> places are fictitious.

Univ. of
San Diego

Old Town

Harbor Island
<u>Miesley</u> Plaza Hotel

Balboa Park

Coronado

Chapter One

As bachelor parties went, it was a pretty tame one. There was a Padres game on the television set—they were losing again—and beer cans littered almost every available surface. Bowls of pretzels, nuts and popcorn had appeared on various tables, replacing the Mexican food Horace Miesley's cook had served for dinner.

The absence of orgiastic activities was in keeping with the personality of the bridegroom. It wasn't that Dr. Edward Kolby was a prude. It was just that the only curves that had ever managed to hold his interest for more than a couple of months at a time were the sweeping currents of the oceans he had dedicated his life to studying. Put him in a roomful of his colleagues from the Scripps Institution of Oceanography, and you heard a lot of talk about fish and very little about women. Kolby's two older brothers were doing their best to change that by plying him with beer, with a fair amount of success. He'd never been much of a drinker.

His best man, a friend of twenty-odd years' standing, was watching the scene with a mixture of boredom and weariness. Douglas Hunter had had a very tough week and an even tougher couple of months. He gave Edward's marriage till fall, which was as long as it would take for Edward's bride-to-be to finish her work on the movie she was shooting in San Diego and drift back to New York. As far as Doug could see, Melanie Ford and Edward Kolby had absolutely nothing in common. Even worse, the lady was a two-time loser in the matrimonial sweepstakes. But would Edward listen to reason? No way. He was enchanted. Bewitched. *In love.*

At the moment, Edward was also rather intoxicated. Urged on by his older brothers, he got up from the couch and crossed the room, planting himself squarely in front of the television screen. "This is the dullest bachelor party I've ever been to," he complained. "Dammit, Doug, you're the best man. You're hosting this party. So where are the dirty movies? Where's the cake with the naked woman inside? I deserve a night of debauchery before I settle down to respectable married life."

"Debauchery? *You?*" Doug smiled and reached for his beer. "Edward, my friend, if a frosting-covered naked woman suddenly materialized in this room, ran up to you and begged you to lick her clean, we would probably have to call in the paramedics to scrape you off the rug. And as far as dirty movies go—"

Doug never got a chance to finish the sentence. He was interrupted by his stepfather, Horace Miesley. "You're blocking my view, Eddie. You want skin flicks, you go out and rent them like everyone else. You can play them on the VCR in the game room. But move your bloody carcass, because that's thirty-five million dollars' worth of cattle on the screen. *My* cattle, by God. I paid for every man on that team and I'm going to watch them, even if the idiots are losing again."

"There's a beer commercial on at the moment, Horace," Doug pointed out.

"Hmm?" Horace Miesley peered at the screen. "Oh, so there is. How do you expect me to know what's going on when Eddie's legs are in the way?"

"There's always the jingle. . . ."

"It's insipid. Nobody writes good advertising anymore, Douglas. I'm going to get myself a different sponsor next year." Horace picked up a half-empty can of beer, drank deeply, and then grimaced in distaste. "This stuff stinks. And it's gotten warm."

Horace was right. Dudweiler beer *did* stink. Nobody else was drinking it. The only reason Horace had it around the house in the first place was that the sponsor provided it gratis. If he drank it warm, it was because he couldn't bear to throw anything away. The man had his quirks, not the least of which was a deep-seated streak of stinginess.

The ball game came back on, and Edward moved out of Horace's way. One of the Padres promptly belted the first pitch into the seats to tie the score. That didn't make their owner happy—*happy* was not a word one used in connection with Horace Miesley—but it made him a mite less cantankerous.

He reverted back to form as soon as the doorbell rang, bellowing, "Chris! Where the hell are you? Get the damn door!"

"Chris" was Chris Patterson, Horace's houseboy, a twenty-six-year-old former pitcher whose persistent rotator-cuff problems had forced him into retirement. He'd left the house after dinner, but Doug didn't bother reminding his stepfather of that. He simply got up to answer the door.

The house was huge, so that by the time he'd made his way through the family room and front gallery to the door, whoever was on the other side of it had rung twice more. Doug found that annoying. Anybody who showed up uninvited at eight-thirty on a Friday night *deserved* to cool his heels for a while. He reached for the knob, then hesitated. On an average night it would have been impossible for anyone but the family to drive onto the Miesley estate without being buzzed through the locked gates, but they were open tonight because of the party. There were a lot of fruits and nuts in the world: salesmen, religious fanatics, even burglars and kidnappers. The doorbell rang again, so loudly that he winced.

"Who is it?" he called out.

The reply was breathy, lazy and decidedly feminine. "Vonda, sweetheart. Let me in."

Doug didn't know anyone named Vonda, but judging by the lady's voice, the Vonda outside was definitely worth meeting. He opened the door a fraction and looked outside.

The house was Spanish styled, with white stucco walls and a red-tiled roof. It had two courtyards. The first was in the center of the house, and contained a pool and patio. The second was in front, and consisted of a garden enclosed by high white walls and bisected by a flagstone path leading to a set of gates.

When Doug didn't see anybody right by the door, he opened it wider and looked into the garden. A woman was leaning against a magnolia tree, one hand raised languidly above her head to clasp a convenient branch, while the other swung a sequined red purse back and forth. A little taken aback, Doug walked outside for a closer look.

Her legs were splendid: long, shapely and tanned, with silver spike-heeled sandals and silver panty hose that sort of sparkled. She was wearing silver lamé shorts that hugged her hips and a red sequined top with narrow straps that tied at the shoulders. There were dangling silver-and-rhinestone earrings tangled into her hair, a pair of silver slave bracelets on her upper arm, and a red velvet ribbon tied around her neck. Her toenails and fingernails were painted the same bright red as the ribbon.

The outfit adorned the kind of body that sailors dream about. Doug made a quick mental estimate—35-22-35—and then raised his eyes.

What you noticed first was the hair. There seemed to be tons of it, all blonde and wild and curly. Doug knew something about women's hairstyles because his eleven-year-old daughter, Lisa, had recently taken an interest in the subject. Sometimes she braided her hair when it was soaking wet and combed it with her fingers once it dried, coming up with an effect like this. The difference was that on Lisa, the style looked cute, while on Vonda, it looked as hot as the chilis Doug had had with dinner.

The second thing you noticed was her mouth. She was giving Doug a lazy smile, the sensuality of her full lower lip accentuated by the crimson red lipstick she was wearing. Her nose was small and freckled and her chin dimpled. Doug couldn't see her eyes, though, because they were hidden by enormous silver-framed sunglasses.

He stared at her, trying to figure her out. Obviously she was a hooker, but the looks didn't go with the clothes. She was far too beautiful for all that trash and flash. Walking over to her, he extended his hand and said, "I'm Doug Hunter."

She held on to it a little longer and a little more intimately than your average dressed-for-success executive type would have. "Nice place you have here," she said. Her voice was little-girl breathy, like Marilyn Monroe's.

"Thanks," Doug answered. "It belongs to my mother and stepfather." He reached up and removed her sunglasses. It was an intimate sort of gesture, but she didn't object or flinch away. He assumed she was used to being touched without permission.

Her eyes were a clear light-blue. Now that Doug was closer, he could see how heavy her makeup was: a generous amount of blusher, false eyelashes, dark brown eyeliner, and eye shadow that ranged from a grayish blue to an iridescent silver. Scrub it all off and she'd be spectacular. Hell, she was spectacular even *with* all that junk on her face.

There were no wrinkles or lines, so she could have been anywhere from her late teens to her early thirties. Forced to guess, Doug would have said about twenty-five. He'd never been to bed with a pro, but he knew as much about the different types as the next guy. A beautiful blue-eyed blonde like Vonda commanded top prices. She didn't have to prowl the streets looking for pickups, but arranged her appointments over the phone. Her customers would be well-heeled business-men who understood that an evening with a girl like her should include dinner in a nice restaurant and maybe even some dancing before they took her off to bed. The Vondas of the world wore expensive if provocative clothing, had nice manners, and knew how to flatter a man. It didn't add up.

When Doug didn't understand something, he gener-ally tried to get answers. "That's an interesting outfit you've got on," he remarked.

"Don't you just love it?" Vonda's smile got a little broader. "The customer requested it."

"And who would the customer be?"

"Trade secret, Doug Hunter." The girl straightened up and hooked her arm through his. "You can take me inside and introduce me to the prospective bridegroom. Edward Kolby, isn't it?"

Doug was finally getting the message. Vonda had been ordered up and paid for, right down to her style of dress, by one of the guests at the party. He couldn't imagine anyone at Scripps hiring her, so that left Horace and Edward's brothers.

He played around with the possibilities. As a boy,

Edward had been a frequent visitor at the house. Horace had known Edward almost as long as Doug had, and had teased him right from the start. Edward had been small as a kid, a year ahead in school, and indifferent to organized sports. Even worse, he'd been so wrapped up in science that he hadn't noticed women till he was almost out of high school.

Given Horace's personality, it was inevitable that he would delight in tormenting Edward, but he'd been smart enough to rein in his more malicious instincts. The reason was simple: Horace Miesley was just a little bit afraid of Douglas Hunter. Doug had been hot tempered as a teenager and, even at fourteen, could have left his stepfather bruised and bloodied if it had ever come down to a physical fight. Where Edward was concerned, it had been a small step for Doug to become protector as well as best friend. Edward was almost as big as Doug now, a well-built six-footer and expert sailor who could look after himself very nicely. But a part of Doug Hunter would always feel like his protector. So Horace was a definite possibility. And there was no question that he knew women like Vonda. Back in the days when he'd run the Miesley Development Corporation on a day-to-day basis, he'd offered them to important out-of-town business contacts as a matter of course, along with parties at his Rancho Santa Fe mansion and tickets to local sports events.

Tom and Joe Kolby were equally likely suspects. They loved their younger brother but were convinced he'd never learned how to have a good time. Doug had never been able to figure out how a sensitive, intelligent man like Edward Kolby had ever wound up with a pair of brothers who thought that Dudweiler beer commercials depicted the ultimate in gracious living; but the relationship was undeniable. In the end, he decided that maybe all three of them were in on the deal.

Doug was so preoccupied with the matter that he scarcely noticed when Vonda led him up the front path and into the house. When he took back his arm to close the door, the lady kept right on walking. It wasn't hard to figure out where to go, because in the short time Doug had been gone the party had gotten louder. He could hear the televised cheers of the baseball crowd and, at the same time, the slightly muffled punchline to a joke. There was a burst of appreciative laughter, and then, drowning out everything else, Horace's cranky demand that everyone shut up so he could listen to the play-by-play.

Doug hurried over to Vonda and took her arm before she could reach the family room. She stopped and turned around, curious but not startled. "Did you want something?" she purred. She didn't have to add, "Like *me*, for example?" because her suggestive tone did it for her.

"I'm sorry," Doug answered, "but you'll have to leave. I'm afraid Edward isn't your type."

She pursed her lips, pouting up at him, and moved so close that her breasts almost brushed his chest. Gazing into his eyes, she said in her little-girl whisper, "Mr. Hunter, *everyone* is my type. I promise you, I'll show your friend a real good time."

Doug didn't doubt it for a minute. He preferred his women more subtle and sophisticated, but on a purely animal level this girl attracted him very much. He wouldn't have wasted his time *talking* to her, but he could easily picture himself spending the whole night in bed with her. "I'm sure you could," he said, "but Edward doesn't go in for that kind of thing. He's very conservative. . . ."

"*All* men go in for that kind of thing, *especially* the conservative ones," she interrupted with a giggle. She put her hands on his shoulders, massaging them in a way that made him want to pull her against him and sample the merchandise. "Unless they're gay, that is. Are you gay, Doug Hunter? Is that why you don't like me?"

Doug glanced down, encountered her cleavage, and hastily looked away. The civilized gentleman in him was a little embarrassed by the whole situation, but the raw male underneath would have loved to touch her. Instead, he took her hands off his shoulders and firmly placed them at her sides. "No, I'm not gay. I like you fine, Vonda, but you really don't belong here." He put a hand at the small of her back and urged her toward the door. "Why don't I walk you to your car. . . ."

"Why don't we get together later?" she countered. "You may be a little uptight, but you're also kind of cute. Consider it on the house, honey. My pay for taking care of your friend was *very* generous."

"I'll bet it was," Doug muttered. He was beginning to get flustered, which wasn't like him at all. He found it unnerving, that he actually wanted to sleep with this girl. She was a pro, for God's sake. Obviously it had a lot to do with the week he'd just had and the amount of beer he'd consumed, but knowing all that didn't help any.

When he wanted to, he could use his voice like a verbal whip to intimidate people—or so he'd been told. Somehow, though, when the girl dug in her heels and refused to budge, his "We're leaving, Vonda. Right now!" lacked the proper ring of authority. She simply slid him the kind of smile that said he had to be joking and slipped away from him. A moment later she was halfway to the family room.

Doug had no idea what his next move was going to be, but it didn't matter because he never got to make it. He was turning around to go after Vonda when Edward's brother Tom walked into the hall. Tom's reaction was entirely in character. He took one look at Vonda, broke into a big smile and drawled, "Well, well, *well!* Hello there, sweetheart. What did I do right today?"

Vonda walked up to him and took the hand he was holding out, allowing him to escort her toward the party. "I'm Vonda, honey. I'm looking for Edward Kolby."

Tom winked at her. "I'll show you a better time than Edward ever could, baby."

Doug followed them, resigned to letting the sideshow play through to its conclusion. The girl giggled and murmured something to Tom about business before pleasure, but she also took back her hand and walked briskly on ahead. Doug thought she seemed uncomfortable, and that puzzled him. Tom Kolby might be a classic case of arrested development, but he was also entirely harmless.

Vonda's appearance in the family room caused something of a sensation even among Edward's more scholarly friends, all of whom had had enough beer to revert to the locker-room mentality so typical of these occasions. When she asked who Edward Kolby was, half a dozen fingers pointed toward the couch. Even Horace joined in, his attention temporarily diverted from the ball game. Vonda sat down next to Edward and, amidst a chorus of laughter and ribald comments, put her arm around his shoulders.

Doug looked around the room, studying each man's face. There were plenty of amused smiles but only one smirk. It belonged to Horace Miesley, whose eyes were lit by an accompanying telltale gleam. Tom and Joe Kolby were exhorting their little brother to take the girl down the hall, telling him it was his lucky night, but they seemed genuinely surprised by her arrival. Edward, meanwhile, was shaking his head and blushing.

The laughter and joking abruptly stopped, as though somebody had punched a button to switch off the noise. For a few seconds the only sound in the room was the voice of the baseball announcer, but then Horace pressed the "mute" button on the remote-control device. Everyone stared at Edward, waiting to see what he would do.

It wasn't the first time in Doug's life that he'd felt like

killing his stepfather, and it wouldn't be the last. The man had put Edward into a no-win situation. The general atmosphere reminded him of a high-school locker room after a triumph, or maybe even a bar full of sailors on shore leave. If he displayed anything less than macho bravura, Edward was in for some merciless needling. A real man would have known what to do with a tasty little morsel like Vonda.

The problem was, Edward Kolby wasn't a real man, at least not in the Hemingway or Mickey Spillane sense of the phrase. He would no more have retired to the nearest bedroom with Vonda than he would have run naked through the winding lanes of Rancho Santa Fe. At the moment he was staring at her with a kind of appalled fascination, as though she were a strange-looking underwater discovery he'd just made.

With Edward at an apparent loss for words, Doug automatically charged to the rescue. "I hate to deprive you of the lady's company," he said, "but my mother will be back with Lisa soon. I wouldn't want her to see Vonda in the house."

"Nothing to worry about there." Horace gave a loud cackle. "They decided to go to a double feature, Doug. Can't possibly be back before eleven-thirty or twelve."

Vonda snuggled closer to Edward and tiptoed her fingertips across his chest. "They didn't tell me how cute you were, honey. The bride-to-be is a lucky gal."

"Miss, uh . . ."

"Just call me Vonda. Everyone does."

"Vonda," Edward repeated. He ran a distracted hand through his hair. "You're terrific looking, Vonda, but, uh, I'm not in any shape for this kind of thing. I've had too much beer, for one thing, and, uh, I'm an engaged man." He trapped her wandering fingers underneath his palm. They'd been tickling his chest, among other things. "If you wouldn't mind . . ."

She gave him her best hurt-little-girl expression. "You don't like me."

"Sure I do. It's just . . ."

"What's the matter, Edward? Afraid of her?" his brother Joe interrupted.

His brother Tom made a beckoning gesture with his right hand, almost knocking over his can of beer in the process. "If you don't want her, send her over here!"

Vonda, meanwhile, was nuzzling Edward's neck, stopping every few moments to murmur a breathy but perfectly audible compliment about his virility. He wasn't any more immune to that than Doug would have been. He mumbled a strained protest about fidelity, only to be told that he wasn't married yet and that until he was, he was entitled to have a little fun. Edward's two brothers loudly agreed, while his friends merely smiled and awaited further developments.

Doug gave Horace a dirty look, but if it penetrated even the topmost millimeter of his hide it didn't show. He simply sat back, crossed his arms in front of his chest, and grinned. Turning his attention back to Edward, Doug said, "If you want me to get rid of her for you . . ."

The girl was nibbling her way down Edward's chest. "She's persistent, I'll give her that," he answered with a laugh. Ignoring his brothers' teasing remarks, he grasped Vonda's head in both hands before it could dip any lower and coaxed it back where it belonged. "Vonda, honey, this hurts me more than it hurts you, but I'm going to have to insist—" He cut himself off and stared at her. Doug saw puzzlement on his face and then growing self-confidence. It was the look Edward got when he was totally in control of a situation. "On the other hand," he went on, "you *are* beautiful, and I *am* still single. It would be a shame to let such enthusiasm go to waste."

He pulled Vonda onto his lap, leaving Doug all but flabbergasted. The only explanation he could come up with was that Edward was even drunker than he looked. Edward's next move, which was accompanied by laughter and whistles, was to kiss the girl on the mouth. She seemed relieved when he finally lifted his lips, but her expression segued into sheer astonishment when he rose from the couch with her in his arms. He winked at Doug and carried her out of the room, presumably to one of the vacant bedrooms down the hall.

It took Doug a full ten seconds to realize that Edward had to be playing along, that he would take the girl into one of the guest rooms, spend some time talking to her, and then reemerge, the picture of the satiated stud. What it went to prove was that Edward Kolby could take care of himself very well.

A look at Horace's face told Doug that Edward had scotched the man's glee; he was almost comically disappointed. Under other circumstances Horace might have turned on the intercom system and listened in on Edward's lovemaking, but he had to know that Doug would never have permitted such a thing. So he turned the television sound back on and started grumbling about the Padres instead. The rest of the men went back to their beers, and amidst a couple of sly remarks about Edward's true character finally emerging, the party resumed.

Chapter Two

$\mathcal{V}$onda the Call Girl wasn't Vonda at all, much less a call girl. Her name was Catherine Ford Valkenberg, she was a respectable widow, and at the moment she was suspended somewhere between disbelief and panic. She was also suspended in the arms of a very drunk Edward Kolby. He just *had* to be drunk, if Melanie knew the man even half as well as she thought she did. There was no other way to explain his behavior.

"You'll have your hands full just to drag him away," Melanie had said. "He was so proper on our first few dates that I finally had to seduce him. But let me tell you, there was nothing proper about him once I got his clothes off!"

Cassie was more than happy to take Melanie's word about Edward's behavior when naked. She only hoped he wouldn't insist on giving her a personal demonstration. As he carried her into a long hallway, it occurred to her that Melanie's knowledge of her fiancé might be a trifle sketchy. They'd only met each other six weeks before. A man didn't reach the age of thirty-two and become a fabulous lover without having known a few women along the way, in the biblical sense of the term.

"Edward, listen to me!" They passed another couple of doors, but Edward didn't stop. He didn't even seem to hear her. His destination was a large bedroom midway down the hall. There was a vase filled with fresh flowers on the dresser but no other sign that the room was occupied: no cosmetics on the dressing table, no clothes in the closet, no books or magazines scattered on the night tables. Once they were inside, Edward slammed the door closed and turned the lock. Then he switched the television on, turning it up full blast.

Bemused, Cassie tried again. "You don't understand, Edward. My name isn't Vonda." She would have said more, but Edward had just tossed her onto the queen-size bed, temporarily knocking the wind out of her. The bed, at least, was across the room from the TV, so she could hear herself think. And what she thought was, *Just get a grip on yourself, Cassie. You've been in worse spots than this one.* But not with a highly intoxicated groom-to-be. And not decked out in an outlandish getup that marked her as fair game. Still, it wasn't anything she couldn't handle.

She began to feel less confident when Edward followed her down, slid fully on top of her and pinned her arms above her head. The grin on his face should have clued her in about his real intentions, but she was too incredulous to notice it.

"For God's sake," she sputtered, "I'm Melanie's sister, Edward. I'm Cassie!"

"I know," he answered calmly.

He *knew?* And he was still practically assaulting her? When he didn't release her, she sniffed at his breath. "Are you stinking drunk," she asked, "or only a little bit sloshed?"

"The latter. Well, more or less, anyway." He

frowned. "How about you, angel? Been hitting the bottle lately?"

"Unlike you, Edward—"

"Gee, Cassie, Melanie told me you were a writer, not a hooker." He released her wrists and ran a finger down her cheek. "You're beautiful, though. Far be it from me to look a gift horse in the mouth. . . ."

"I *am* a writer, Edward. If you would just get off of me—"

"Doing a little research, then? One of your famous first-person articles?" He recited a few of the titles, then went on, "And the most recent: *San Diego Call Girl,* or *How to Earn a Good Living and Still Keep Your Days Free for the Beach.*" Starting to laugh, he rolled off her and grabbed a pillow, which he fluffed up and placed against the headboard. Then he lay back and laughed even harder.

Cassie promptly joined him. It went on like that for a whole minute, the two of them like little kids sharing a private joke who can't help giggling every time they look at each other. When Cassie finally found the self-control to stop, she said, "I don't understand how you knew. I thought I was wonderfully convincing."

"The earrings," he answered. "I nearly cut my lip on one of those things once."

They were Melanie's earrings. Cassie had borrowed them because they were so totally perfect for the role of Vonda. "You're very observant," she said.

"Umm. Must be all those years of identifying fish. And then there's the family resemblance. So what are you doing here a day early, and in an outfit like that? Or is it your usual way of dressing?"

"I'll have you know, Dr. Kolby, that it took me most of the day to find these clothes, do my hair, and plaster all this makeup on my face. Melanie was nothing short of awestruck when I stopped by her location to show myself off."

"Were they still filming?" Edward asked.

Cassie nodded. "Uh-huh. They were trying to finish up a scene, but don't worry, Edward. The director promised Melanie that he'd close down in time for her to make it to the wedding tomorrow. Can you turn down the TV?"

"Not a chance. There's an intercom system in this house that lets you listen in on any room you want."

Smiling, Cassie said, "Then maybe we should moan and pant and bounce on the bed." She hugged herself, feeling a little cold in the skimpy clothing she was wearing. Edward noticed and went off to get her a sweater.

There was a sitting room connected to the bedroom, so Cassie went inside, turned on a lamp, and sat down on the couch. Edward returned a minute later with two cans of beer and a white cashmere sweater—Valerie Hunter's, he told her. He clicked on a radio and joined her on the couch.

He'd been out on the *Melville,* one of the institution's vessels, for the last couple of days, so Melanie hadn't had a chance to tell him that Cassie was flying in from San Francisco a day and a half early. In the normal course of events, Cassie and her future brother-in-law would have met for the first time on Saturday afternoon, when he took her and her family to lunch. But the normal course of events hadn't obtained.

As Edward draped the sweater around Cassie's shoulders, she explained that she'd finished up some work ahead of schedule and managed to slip away. Then she took a sip of beer and went on, "Melanie was mad enough to spout lava when she picked me up at the airport last night. You know how volatile she can be, Edward."

"Volatile? Melanie?"

His ingenuous look said that he knew it all too well. "Ah, I see that you do," Cassie observed. "Anyway, Melanie was in her trailer changing yesterday afternoon when one of the other actresses in the film stopped by.

The woman's name is Lynn—she's a local with a bit part. She admitted to Melanie that she turns a few tricks on the side when she needs some extra cash. Somebody had called her about coming here tonight, for you, and she'd agreed. But then she'd found out that you were Melanie's fiancé and started feeling funny about the whole thing. She asked Melanie what she should do."

Edward was shaking his head. "I don't believe this. I assumed it was something you and Melanie had cooked up, probably to check out how wild the party had gotten. She's told me you'll do almost anything for a good story, and then there's your new book. . . . What's the title? *A Hundred and One Nights in Union Square?*"

"Right." The subtitle, *An In-depth Look at San Francisco's Most Exclusive Call Girls,* said it all. "I'm an absolute expert, Edward, but I'm afraid I've had to skip the usual on-the-job training for this one. Until tonight, that is. Did Melanie tell you I'm going to do a book tour?"

Edward said that she had, and also that she'd given him a copy of the manuscript to read. "It was fascinating, Cassie. Now that I think about it, I can pick out the ones you based Vonda on. But who hired Lynn?"

"She wouldn't say. Melanie figured it was your friend Doug, seeing that he's doing his best to talk you out of marrying her. But I don't think she's right. He tried too hard to stop me."

"It couldn't have been Doug. He doesn't deliberately embarrass people, especially not his friends. But it had to be someone at the party." Frowning, Edward started to drum his fingers on an end table. Cassie could almost see the mental wheels turning as he considered the alternatives. According to Melanie he was absolutely brilliant. After fifteen or twenty seconds of silence, he started to think out loud, mumbling something about macho games and men who equated monogamy with terminal wimpiness. Finally, with a slow nod of his head, he said, "It had to be Miesley. The only other possibility is one of my brothers, but they only turn into complete idiots when they've had too much to drink."

From what Cassie had heard about his brothers, she wasn't entirely sure that liquor was wholly to blame when they acted like jerks. Still, Edward knew them better than Melanie did. She turned her thoughts to Horace Miesley.

Edward had pronounced the name "Mizely," whereas Melanie had referred to the man as "Measly," obviously with tongue firmly in cheek. Cassie knew how the name was spelled because the hotel she was staying in was called the Miesley Plaza. She knew that San Diego had a brand-new downtown office building called the Miesley Tower. And she knew that Miesley was Douglas Hunter's stepfather, that he was the principal owner of the San Diego Padres, and that her sister didn't care for him.

"But why would he do something like that?" she asked Edward.

He shrugged and said that he was an old friend of the family. "Call Miesley a childhood antagonist, for both me *and* Doug. There were times when I wanted to kill him. A stunt like hiring Lynn would be right up his alley, believe me, but I've learned I can put up with a lot in a man who gives a hundred grand a year to my favorite cause—Scripps, of course—and who's earmarked two million for the institution in his will. I assume you decided to take Lynn's place."

"It was too good an opportunity to pass up." After calming Melanie down, Cassie had been quick to sketch out the possibilities. "Melanie and I figured that all I had to do was get you alone and then you and I could turn the tables on whichever imbecile arranged this.

And on the rest of your mentally defective friends out there, for that matter. And to think they call themselves scientists!"

Edward gave her a sheepish look. "Give them a break, Cassie. It's supposed to be a bachelor party. Put a bunch of men together, give them enough beer, and throw in a woman who's dressed like a hooker and looks as good as you do, and even the ones who are normally straight arrows are going to cut loose a little."

"I suppose so," Cassie said, "but it doesn't change my plans. We'll wait another twenty minutes and then go back to the party. Just leave everything to me—I'll stick around for a while and put on a first-rate show. Miesley expected you to turn down what a *real man* would have accepted? Well, fine, because he's going to be very disappointed. And he's going to feel like a total fool when he sees me at the wedding tomorrow."

In the normal course of things, Edward Kolby had little use for revenge. He was a gentle, generous man who believed in turning the other cheek and going about his business. But Horace Miesley had been pricking at him for nearly twenty years now, and he'd had a little too much beer. And then there were Miesley's numerous other victims to consider. He told Cassie he liked her style.

Cassie Valkenberg had never been one to talk a subject to death. Once Edward agreed to her plans, she moved to a topic that interested her far more than Horace Miesley did: Douglas Joshua Hunter. Melanie had outlined the basics for her, so she knew that Doug was a year older than Edward, that he was the son of actress Valerie Hunter and a long-dead stuntman, and that Valerie's refusal to marry the man had been one of the great Hollywood scandals of its time. Which only went to show how much things had changed in the ensuing thirty-three years. Every actress and her sister seemed to have out-of-wedlock babies these days, with scarcely a batted eyelash from anyone.

Valerie had eventually settled down with Horace Miesley, a wealthy San Diego-based developer whose tentacles reached from Phoenix to Seattle to Las Vegas. Miesley was sixty now, but still handsome, dynamic and virile looking. Doug had taken over the family business a few years before, but that was only because Miesley was more interested in baseball than in building these days.

According to Melanie Ford, Douglas J. Hunter was straighter than a desert highway and smoother than a mountain lake. He was single with one child, an eleven-year-old daughter named Lisa who was the product of his marriage to local socialite Buffy Saint-Simon. Ironically, Buffy had died at just about the same time as Cassie's husband John, also with swift, horrible violence. In Melanie's opinion, Buffy must surely have gone straight to heaven upon her untimely demise, her reward for having put up with somebody as stuffy and judgmental as Douglas Hunter.

"You've probably noticed," Cassie said to Edward, "that my sister has very little use for your best friend. But don't let it worry you. She'll eventually come around, assuming he's not as horrible as she makes him out to be. She knows she makes up her mind too quickly at times."

"It's entirely my fault. I was much too honest with her." Edward gave Cassie a pained look. "It was just that I'm so crazy about Melanie that I wanted to share everything in my life with her, the good as well as the bad. So I told her how Doug felt."

"Maybe you should have kept your mouth shut, but where does he get off, trying to talk you out of marrying her?" Cassie demanded. "It's *your* life, Edward."

Edward slumped down on the couch and clasped his hands together behind his head. He looked completely sober and a little pensive. "Doug used to watch out for me when we were kids, Cassie. He's had a hard time

breaking the habit. Maybe he's a little stiff and cool
with people he's not close to, but if you'd had his
childhood you'd be the same way. It's a defense against
humanity's propensity to step on people who are
already down. It wasn't easy being Valerie Hunter's
bastard. It was probably almost as hard being Horace
Miesley's stepson."

"I can appreciate that," Cassie said, "but according
to Melanie, he didn't even give her a chance. He was
cold as ice from the word go."

"She's an actress with two bum marriages behind
her. Those aren't the best credentials, especially to a
guy with Doug's background." Edward suddenly
smiled. "And let's face it, Cassie. Melanie is almost as
ditzy as you are."

"Ditzy? *Ditzy?*" Cassie repeated the word in mock
indignation. "What have I ever done to merit the
adjective 'ditzy,' Dr. Kolby?"

"Well, for one thing, you're sitting there in skintight
silver lamé shorts and a top that shines like a beacon.
And for another, there are the things you'll do for an
article, like posing as a lady umpire or signing on as the
cook on a freighter with an all-male crew."

"That's not ditziness," Cassie retorted, "that's creative journalism. You think it was easy to learn umpiring? Or to cook so well that those animals kept their
distance for fear of offending me and getting lousy
food? In my opinion, this outfit was a stroke of genius.
The joke wouldn't have been nearly as effective if I'd
shown up dressed for the theater, now would it,
Edward!"

Edward insisted that her objections only illustrated
the point he was trying to make. "Both you and your
sister are willing to do crazy things if it suits your aims,"
he said. "You know how Melanie and I got together?
They were shooting an action sequence out on the ship,
the part in the movie where something first goes wrong
with one of the experiments. But the director had

changed the story to make things more exciting. What he wanted to do was scientifically implausible, almost impossible, so I started to argue. I figured it was part of my job as the technical adviser. The director had very little patience with my objections, but what could he do? He couldn't confine me to quarters or make me walk the plank. So he stood there and tried to explain the concept of dramatic license, only I wasn't listening. By the time he shut me up and started shooting, things were so tense that everything went wrong. I was standing there watching when, out of nowhere, a grip who looked like his first cousin was King Kong picked me up and started to the edge of the ship. I caught Melanie laughing at me and realized she'd put him up to it. By the time I hit the water I was furious, because it isn't exactly warm this time of year. I came up to the surface, ready to resign, and saw her diving off the ship, fully clothed except for her shoes. She threw her arms around me, told me I was beautiful when I was angry, and asked me out to dinner. I didn't know if she was serious, but everyone was watching and laughing, and I knew I'd look like twice as much of a fool if I didn't go along with her. So I told her I'd hold her to the dinner date and swam away." Edward gave a soft reminiscent laugh. "The director yelled at her for messing up her hair and makeup, but I thought she looked incredibly beautiful. Her prank broke the tension, and it taught me to take my role a little less seriously. Unfortunately, there was a reporter from the San Diego *Times* on the ship, and the whole business wound up in the paper. They've managed to follow us on most of our dates. Doug can't believe I'd have anything to do with a woman who would deliberately embarrass me, much less put up with reporters trailing after me, but the truth is that Melanie's spontaneity is precisely what I'm so attracted to. I have a better time with her than with anyone I've ever met. She's worth giving up some privacy for."

Maybe to Edward, but evidently not to Doug Hunter. "Doug and Melanie are obviously totally different types," Cassie said, "but even so, I'm surprised she can't win him over. She's usually so good at loosening people up."

"I doubt that Doug is loosenable right now," Edward answered. "He's had a tough couple of months, and it hasn't helped his mood. His company is trying to get a major downtown project off the ground, and it's been nothing but aggravation for him. The city officials have kicked him one way, the environmentalists another, the unions a third, and other special-interest groups a fourth and fifth and sixth. Meanwhile, Miesley keeps hassling him for results. By now he feels like a football after double overtime."

"So why doesn't he just forget it?"

"Two reasons. First, the potential profits are enormous. And second, he believes in the concept of a vital, growing central city."

"In that order?" Cassie asked.

"Probably," Edward said. "First and foremost, Doug is a businessman. He has to pay attention to the bottom line."

So Douglas Hunter was a pragmatist with a streak of idealism. It was an appealing combination, but then, a lot about Hunter was appealing. The man's good qualities started with his blond-streaked brown hair, which made him look as though he spent a lot of time outdoors. If he did, he obviously did more than stand around giving orders, because his build was trim and solidly muscled, yet another good quality. And then there were his sherry-colored eyes, which met your gaze with no-nonsense directness, and his movie-star handsome looks, obviously inherited from Valerie Hunter.

In fact, Cassie had only one complaint about his appearance: he was much too proper outwardly. His hair was too short and too meticulous. Unlike the other men at the party, he was dressed in slacks and a long-sleeved shirt rather than jeans and a T-shirt or tennis shirt. His sole concession to informality had been to roll up his sleeves to the elbows, revealing the same even tan on his arms as on his face.

In Cassie's opinion, it was too bad that Hunter's character dovetailed so closely with his ever-so-straight appearance. She liked men who shared her sense of the amusing or ridiculous, the way John had, and who had John's childlike capacity to enjoy whatever life had to offer. She missed sharing her life with somebody who could be open and easy and even silly, but she didn't make a habit of dwelling on what she'd lost. When the bad times hit, as they did every so often, she thought about how lucky she was to have Jessica and about how satisfying her career was. She picked herself up, pushed away the loneliness, and tried to look forward to the future.

She checked her watch, deciding to wait twenty more minutes before returning to the party. She and Edward filled the time by talking about his work. Cassie's interest was professional as well as personal. She was between projects at the moment, had occasionally written about science, and considered oceanography a good possibility.

The decibel level in the family room gradually increased during those twenty minutes until they could hear the commotion all the way down the hall. Cassie nodded her understanding of something Edward was explaining, sipped her beer, and casually told him to take off his shirt.

He frowned. "Take off my . . . ?" There was a quick shake of the head. "Oh, no, Cassie. I'm not going back there naked. . . ."

"Only half-naked," Cassie corrected him. She grabbed a handful of material and started to yank the shirt loose from his jeans. "Come on, Edward, you've got to get into the spirit of this. Hands over your head, that's right, now we'll just get this off and take a look underneath."

Utterly bemused, Edward allowed her to pull the shirt over his head. "You've got a terrific tan," she remarked.

"It's from being on the ship." He gave a startled jerk when Cassie put her hands in his hair. "Cassie, what on earth are you doing?"

"Messing up your hair. What does it look like I'm doing?"

When his hair was suitably tousled, she grasped his shoulders and turned him around so that she could take a look at his back. "Hmm. How's your tolerance for pain?" she asked.

"For pain?" he repeated, sounding dazed. "For pete's sake, Cassie . . ."

"Relax, Edward. I'm only going to scratch you up a little. Vonda's had so many men she's jaded, but *you* were so terrific in bed she totally lost control of herself. Aren't you flattered?"

"Enormously," he answered with a sigh.

Cassie took that as permission. She proceeded to engrave a splendid pattern of scratches on Edward's back, something he endured with a mumbled, "You're even crazier than your sister is." Afterward she went into the bathroom adjoining the bedroom and took off her sandals and panty hose, wiped off some of her makeup, and pushed around her hair until it was even more sexily unkempt than before. On her way back through the bedroom, she stopped to turn off the TV and mess up the bed, leaving Valerie's sweater on a convenient chair. She was still barefoot when she sauntered into the sitting room, her right index finger hooked around the straps of her sandals.

So far, so good, she thought, but she had to give Edward a plausible reason for showing up stripped to the waist. Her eyes lit on his shirt, which she'd tossed onto the couch.

You know the thrill of
escaping to a world where
Love, Romance, and
Happiness reach out
to one and all...

Escape again…with 4 FREE novels and

get more great Silhouette Special Edition novels —for a 15-day FREE examination— delivered to your door every month!

Silhouette Special Edition novels are written especially for you, someone who knows the allure, the enchantment and the power of romance. Romance *is* alive, and flourishing in these moving love stories that let you escape to exotic places with sensitive heroines and captivating men.

Written by such popular authors as Janet Daily, Donna Vitek, Diana Dixon, and others, Silhouette Special Edition novels help you reach that special world—month after month. They'll take you to that world you have always imagined, where you will live and breathe the emotions of love and the satisfaction of romance triumphant.

FREE BOOKS

Start today by taking advantage of this special offer—the 4 newest Silhouette Special Edition romances (a $10.00 Value) *absolutely FREE,* along with a Cameo Tote Bag. Just fill out and mail the attached postage-paid order card.

AT-HOME PREVIEWS, FREE DELIVERY

After you receive your 4 free books and Tote Bag, every month you'll have the opportunity to preview 6 more Silhouette Special Edition romances— *before they're available in stores!* When you decide to keep them, you'll pay just $11.70, (a $3.30 savings each month), *with never an additional charge of any kind and no risk!* You can cancel your subscription at any time simply by dropping us a note. In any case, the first 4 books, and Cameo Tote Bag are yours to keep.

EXTRA BONUS

When you take advantage of this offer, we'll also send you the Silhouette Books Newsletter free with each shipment. Every informative issue features news about upcoming titles, interviews with your favorite authors, and even their favorite recipes.

Get a Free
Tote Bag, too!

**EVERY BOOK YOU RECEIVE WILL BE
A BRAND-NEW FULL-LENGTH NOVEL!**

She gestured toward it with her sandals. "Edward, do you have any special affection for that particular item of clothing?"

"My shirt?" It was white with blue stripes and not especially new, but Edward had always liked it. "Are you telling me I have to sacrifice it to the cause?"

"I wouldn't dream of being so pushy," Cassie answered. "It's only a suggestion. But don't you think Vonda would have torn it off in her haste to possess you?"

"No question about it." Resigned by now, Edward picked up the shirt and started ripping. When it was tattered enough to suit Cassie's taste, he tossed it over his left shoulder and stood up. "Shall we?"

"I'll follow you in. Now don't forget to swagger, Edward. And for God's sake, try to look a little happier. You've just experienced life's greatest pleasure with San Diego's premiere sexual athlete, and you're still drunk enough not to feel any guilt about it."

Edward said he would do his best and started walking. They were greeted by a spate of off-color remarks, with Edward blushing and grinning at the same time. Cassie, meanwhile, affected a look of almost feline self-satisfaction. She'd eavesdropped on enough of John's poker games to know that boys would be boys. One of Edward's brothers raised his hands over his head and started clapping, and everyone else joined in. Douglas Hunter was smiling, but the smile had a wry edge to it, as though he meant to distance himself from what was going on around him.

Cassie decided that Edward was the perfect man for her sister when he grabbed her by the wrist to pull her down on his lap and announced that "Vonda" was going to stick around for a while. "Get the lady a beer," he said to nobody in particular, "and not that crap that Horace gets for free. Make it a Budweiser."

Nobody moved. They were too busy leering at Edward's bare chest and Cassie's bare legs. Doug

Hunter told himself that he was probably the only one sober enough to recognize a can of Bud when he saw one and glanced around the room. There wasn't a fresh Bud in sight.

"I'll check the kitchen," he said, but nobody was paying the slightest attention. He was still shaking his head in disbelief as he opened the refrigerator. The scene in the family room had about as much connection to everyday reality as the soap opera Melanie Ford acted in when she wasn't making movies.

Doug peered into the refrigerator. Edward's sexual strutting, the torn shirt on his shoulder, the fresh scratches on his back, the panty hose trailing out of Vonda's purse, the sexual glow on her face and the sensuality of her unruly hair and bare feet . . . none of it jibed with anything Doug knew about Edward Kolby. The man would have made love to a fish before he'd cheat on his fiancée with a call girl. Honor was his middle name.

So what was going on? Was it a setup? Was Vonda a friend of Edward's whom Doug had never met? He rummaged around inside the refrigerator. There was a six-pack of Bud on the bottom shelf, buried under some bags of fruit. He pictured his stepfather's face as he pulled out the beer and decided that if the incident was a setup, it wasn't *that* kind of setup. Horace had been much too delighted when Vonda walked in and much too disappointed when she and Edward went off together. True, he'd barely reacted to their reappearance, but then, the Padres had just blown another ball game and he was probably thinking about whom to fire next.

Doug fell back on his original theory, that Edward had talked the girl into forgetting Horace's game and playing one of their own. The only obvious flaw was that the two of them looked so much like they'd spent the last forty minutes in bed. If they had, Doug only hoped that Melanie Ford never got wind of it. The lady was tough as nails, but Edward couldn't see that. He was so infatuated with her that she could have walked all over him, and he would have smiled adoringly and thanked her for the footprints on his back.

Doug opened a can of beer and drank down half of it. He'd exceeded his usual limit and could feel himself slipping, but for once he didn't care. He didn't have to drive anywhere tonight. It was a relief to unwind a little and forget that on Monday, it would be back to business as usual.

Chapter Three

*H*orace had left the family room by the time Doug got back, and somebody had turned off the television set in favor of the stereo. There was an old Rolling Stones number playing, and Chris Patterson, having returned from wherever he'd gone, was dancing with Vonda. She held out her hand for the can of beer, giving Doug a coy wink. He pulled the tab for her and slid the beer into her waiting fingers, then sat down next to Edward to watch the show.

The more Doug saw of Vonda, the more intrigued he was. The heavy makeup and bubble-brained cheeriness didn't fit. There was an incongruous freshness there, an underlying sharpness. He was tempted to drag Edward out of the room to find out what was going on, but it smacked too much of two teenaged boys disappearing into the school bathroom to talk about whose date had put out more the night before. He decided it could wait.

Cassie took a sip of beer, thinking that she was tired

of giggling incessantly, talking in a breathy voice, and wiggling around like a starlet. She'd made her point and hammered it home by now, and she wanted to go to bed. When the song ended, she thanked Chris for the dance and started to walk away, only to have him grab one of the ties that held her top in place and give it a playful tug. Luckily she'd had the foresight to double knot it.

She was curious about Chris Patterson. When Edward had introduced him as Horace's houseboy, a onetime pitcher with the Padres, her first thought was, *He could have done better.* He was a green-eyed blond in his mid-twenties with golden-boy good looks that he should have been able to parlay into a career in modeling or television. Instead he spent his days waiting on Horace Miesley, who by all accounts was a singularly unpleasant man.

Cassie had no particular desire to embarrass him, so she giggled and asked, "Did you want something, honey?"

He gave her the answer she'd expected. "Yeah, baby. You."

It was easy enough to handle him. All she had to do was remove his fingers from her strap and say that she was sorry, but she'd only been paid for Edward. "A girl has to think about her bills," she added.

"I've got plenty of money," he replied, showing off a little.

Cassie had expected *that,* too. She dropped the little-girl voice and airheaded giggle, becoming the image of the hard-nosed businesswoman. "All right, Chris. I can give you a little time. It will cost you three hundred dollars up front. In cash."

Chris was visibly intimidated. Maybe it was the price tag, but more likely it was the voice. Cassie figured he'd never run into girls of Vonda's particular type before, but she knew them well. They stayed away from pimps and dope, did exactly what they pleased with their lives, and often saved up enough money to buy themselves legitimate businesses. Chris reached into his pocket, but Cassie was sure he didn't have the cash. He was only stalling, trying to think of a way to save face in front of a group of older, more sophisticated men.

Maybe the beer had mellowed her out, but Cassie felt a little sorry for him. The world had once been his oyster, but a torn-up arm had ended all that. He pulled out his wallet and checked inside, then mumbled something about being a little short. Cassie managed to look acutely disappointed as she ran a finger down his cheek and said, "Gee, Chris, I wish I could wait for you to get the money, but I have another appointment. Can I give you a rain check? At a discount, of course, to make up for the delay."

He picked up a cocktail napkin and held it out to her. "You've got yourself a deal. Here. Give me your phone number. I'll call you next week."

Cassie wrote down the number to call for the time of day, hoping it was the same in San Diego as in San Francisco. Chris shoved it into his wallet without looking at it, patted her on the fanny, and walked away with a smile on his face.

Very nicely done, Doug thought. Just as he'd guessed, Vonda was a lot more clever than she liked to let on. And then there was Horace's behavior to consider. He'd paid top dollar for the girl. By all rights he should have stuck around to inflict a little more embarrassment however he could. Why had he lost interest so fast?

Vonda blew Edward a kiss and said, "Thanks for the memories, honey. Have a nice marriage." Then, waving and smiling, she started toward the door.

Doug got up and followed, telling her he would walk her to her car. He wasn't motivated so much by politeness as by a desire to get a better look at her.

Cassie hesitated. She hadn't missed the way Doug

Hunter kept studying her and was smart enough to realize that he didn't quite buy her act. He seemed a little more sober than the rest of them, but that didn't mean he hadn't had too much to drink. He probably had. He was no pushover like Chris Patterson, and she had no intention of tangling with him.

Nothing on her face gave away her thoughts. Her manner as open and cheerful as ever, she said, "No thanks, Doug. I'll be fine."

"I insist," he replied. "It's dark out there, and your car must be at least halfway down the driveway, beyond the range of the outside lights. I'd feel personally responsible if you hurt yourself."

Cassie squared her shoulders, switching on the businesslike crispness she'd used so successfully on Chris Patterson. "I said I'd be fine, Mr. Hunter. What I really meant was, I don't want your company at the moment. Now if you would excuse me . . ."

She didn't finish the sentence, but turned on her heel and strode briskly out of the room. Tom Kolby called out, "Guess you're not her type, Hunter!" and everybody laughed, but Cassie didn't allow herself to react.

Doug knew he couldn't go after her, not after such an explicit set-down, so he ceded her the victory and returned to the couch. Edward's shirt was still draped carelessly over his left shoulder; Doug picked it up and shook it out, displaying front and back in turn.

"If Vonda was fighting a battle with your shirt, I think the shirt lost," he said, and dropped it in Edward's lap. "I take it the lady turned out to be a regular wildcat in bed."

Edward looked around the room. Everyone was waiting for his answer. "More playful than dangerous, Doug. She tends to get a little carried away."

"You . . . are . . . in . . . b—i—g . . . trouble, little brother!" Tom Kolby stretched out every word. "What are you going to tell Melanie about those scratches?"

There was an awkward pause before Edward dismissed the problem with a wave of his hand. "I'll tell her I was diving and scratched myself on some coral."

"Coral?" A colleague from Scripps gave him an incredulous look. "You were nowhere near any coral. It'll never wash."

Edward shrugged. "Melanie doesn't know a reef from a fissure, Sam."

Doug found the exchange revealing. Edward should have been swimming in guilt by now, not to mention worried about Melanie's reaction. The fact that he wasn't produced a dazzling insight. Maybe he wasn't worried because Melanie Ford was in on the whole business. It wasn't hard to picture her sending a friend to check out the party and report back. As for Miesley, one look at Vonda and he would have started to relish the situation, even if he hadn't arranged it.

Wanting to get Edward alone, Doug said, "I'll get you another shirt. In the meantime, maybe you should make some coffee to sober up your friends. Otherwise they're liable to crash into the front wall or drive off a hillside."

Edward looked at Chris, who immediately jumped up and offered, "I'll take care of the coffee, Doug. It's my job, you know?"

"Right. Thanks, Chris." Doug gave it one more try. "Edward, you want to walk to the cottage with me?"

Edward yawned and made himself more comfortable on the couch. "Not really, Doug. It was a tough forty minutes. I'm too exhausted to move. Chris can lend me something of his."

In other words, Doug thought, *Forget it, buddy, I'm not saying a word.* It was a hell of a way to treat your best friend. Defeated, he muttered, "No, I'll get you a shirt. I feel like taking a walk outside."

"In that case, thanks." Edward grabbed a can of beer and started talking to one of his brothers.

The shortest route to the guest cottage where Doug

was living temporarily would have been out the sliding glass door and across the central patio. The cottage was behind the main house. Instead, Doug went out through the front. He wanted to see if Vonda had left yet, although he had no idea what he would do if she hadn't.

He heard the sound of an engine turning over and dying as he pushed open the courtyard gates. Walking down the driveway a bit, he saw Vonda sitting in a dark-colored American car that was parked on the left-hand side of the road, facing the house. The headlights, he noticed, were off. A brief silence was followed by the sound of the engine coughing, even weaker now than before.

Inside the car, Cassie flicked off the ignition and yanked out the keys. She hated the idea of going back to the house, especially after the splendid exit she'd made. She thought about walking to the nearest neighbor and asking to call a taxi, but the nearest neighbor wasn't all that close. Dressed like this, anything could happen, even in a respectable upper-class neighborhood. Irritated by the idea of another fifteen minutes of giggling and wiggling, she picked up her purse and reached for the handle on the door.

It was halfway open when she noticed Doug Hunter approaching the car. She stifled a groan and thought about throwing herself on his mercy. For all she knew, Edward had told him everything by now.

He opened the door the rest of the way and held out his hand to her, saying, "You see, Vonda? I should have insisted on walking you to your car. Of course, if the thought of my company is still so objectionable, I suppose I could always leave you here."

The look on his face was too damn amused, and his tone of voice was exaggeratedly innocent. He couldn't have known who she was. The sister of the woman he so disliked would have received no more than a stiffly polite offer of assistance from him.

Cassie took his hand and let him pull her up. Touching him sent a jolt of sexual awareness through her, but she relegated it to the back of her mind as she removed her hand from his grasp and closed the car door. Slipping into the role of Vonda again, she pouted. "That's the last time I put my lights on till it's really dark outside. I forgot they were on and the stupid battery must have been half-dead to begin with and then the dumb car didn't even *talk* to me! I mean, it told me to fasten my seat belt when I got in earlier tonight, so why did it clam up when I left the lights on? Talking cars, talking cameras, talking elevators . . . what's the world coming to, Doug?"

Doug stayed right where he was, so close that a short step forward would have brought them into physical contact. "I know what you mean," he said. "When you pay all that money for the latest technology, you expect it to work." Cassie might have put more credence in his sympathetic tone if it hadn't been for the grin on his face. "Judging by the car, business must be terrific, Vonda."

"Terrific," she agreed. "But I *do* have another client tonight, so if you would give me a jump . . ."

"That's the best offer I've had all day," he interrupted, laughing openly now.

So the man made bad jokes in addition to everything else! Cassie swallowed back the dry retort she was itching to make and giggled. "A jump *start*, honey. Do you have some jumper cables around?"

"Sure. They're in the trunk of my car, in front of the garage." Doug didn't have a problem with giving the lady a jump start, but he wasn't in any hurry. Maybe it was the beer and maybe it was the moonlit night, but she looked even more beautiful now than she had inside.

Whoever she really was, her ability to stay in character amazed him. He was deliberately blocking her way, but instead of showing the annoyance she had to be feeling, she gave him the same fluff-headed smile he'd been watching all evening. It made him wonder just how hard he could push before she'd lose her temper and tell him to get lost.

"Before we get the cables," he said, "I want a few words with you."

She crossed her arms in front of her chest and hugged herself. "Sure, Doug, but could you make it quick? It's getting cold out here."

Doug wasn't about to let an opening like that one slip by. Putting an arm around her shoulders, he murmured, "You should have said something sooner, angel. Is that better?"

Cassie was at a temporary loss for words. The man was making a pass at her, and she wasn't sure what to do about it. His body was warm and firm against her side, his hand felt wonderful around her shoulders, and he smelled absolutely marvelous. All in all, he was much too attractive. The moment he touched her, she forgot about the nighttime breeze and began to wonder where the nearest air conditioner was.

"You were supposed to offer me your jacket. That's what a real gentleman would have done." She giggled. "Too bad you're not wearing one, honey."

"It's not too bad in my opinion. I'd rather warm you myself than let a jacket do it."

He hugged her even closer. She could feel him watching her, but she kept her eyes focused straight ahead. She knew all about the way he was looking at her, just as she knew about the heat in her own blood. A handsome man, a susceptible woman, the right sexual chemistry—one wrong move and the situation could be much too hard to handle.

He caressed her shoulder. "Your skin is so damn soft. . . ."

To Cassie, her skin felt hot, not soft. "Thanks for the compliment," she said, "but I've really got to get moving. What did you want to talk about?"

"Talk? Oh, right." Talking was the last thing on Doug's mind. He didn't want to talk. He wanted to work his hand under her top and cup her breast, kiss her hair and nibble his way lower, tease her till she pressed herself against him and clawed at his back. He put a firm hold on his baser instincts and said, "It's Edward. He's getting married tomorrow. . . ."

"Yes. He told me all about her. She sounds terrific."

"He's entitled to his opinion," Doug mumbled. "The point is—"

"It's not *your* opinion?"

"No, but then, I'm not the one who has to live with her." Doug felt the girl stiffen slightly and realized that she would have liked to pull away. Given her response, he no longer had the slightest doubt that she was connected to Melanie Ford, probably through the movie they were making. A fellow actress would have been the logical one to carry out this little charade.

Deliberately goading her, he went on, "Melanie is the type who's never had a serious thought in her life. She collects husbands like other rich women collect exotic pets. Edward is a novelty to her, *homo scientificus,* but the moment something else catches her eye she'll forget all about him and flit off after it."

"You must know her very well to be such an expert."

"You can meet her for an hour and know her very well. With someone like Melanie, there's nothing under the surface to probe."

Doug paused, waiting to see if Vonda would snap at the bait. Her tone hadn't been quite so casual the last time she'd spoken, and the tense feel of her body reminded him of a novice skier trying desperately to loosen up. His guess was, she was flat-out furious with him by now.

"Like you said," she finally replied, *"you* don't have to live with her. So?"

"So Edward is my best friend." Doug jabbed as hard

as he could. "He thinks he's madly in love with the woman. He won't listen to reason . . . well, sometimes you have to find things out for yourself. In the meantime, I want to make sure that you won't contact him again, Vonda. His future wife is hard as nails. She'll make his life miserable if she ever finds out about tonight."

If Doug Hunter meant to play the protective best friend, Cassie was less than impressed. She only wondered how Edward could have failed to notice that Hunter was arrogant and judgmental in addition to being a closet Don Juan. She was just about to pull away from him and stalk off to the house when logic caught up with emotion. According to Melanie, Doug Hunter was always a perfect gentleman, so much so that it drove Melanie crazy. He wasn't the type to make nasty comments about his best friend's fiancée to a total stranger, unless . . .

Unless he suspected that the total stranger was connected in some way to the best friend's fiancée, and was doing his level best to provoke her into admitting it. *So you want to play games, do you?* she thought. *Okay, Mr. Hunter. Just deal me in.*

It hadn't escaped her notice that he wanted her. His arm was tight and possessive around her shoulders, and he couldn't seem to keep his fingers still. They kept stroking her upper arm. She trapped them under her hand and smiled up at him. Unlike her earlier smiles, this one wasn't forced. It was all she could do to keep a straight face. "No problem there, honey," she said. "I don't want to seem conceited or anything, but I've got them standing in line. If Edward calls I'll tell him I'm all booked up."

"You do that." Doug slid his arm off Cassie's shoulders. For a moment she thought he'd lost interest, but then he wrapped his fingers around her upper arms and pushed her against the car. Only inches separated their bodies.

"You're going to cancel your other date," he said. "You're spending the night with me."

Cassie took a quick surprised breath. When the man decided he wanted something, he didn't waste any time going after it. "Am I?" she asked.

Doug took a step forward, trapping her between his body and the car. "Yes. Don't argue."

Cassie had no intention of arguing. Things were going exactly as she'd planned. The only problem was, when he bent his head to nuzzle her neck she started to forget about her plans and think about him instead. He nibbled his way to her ear, and for a few crazy moments there was nothing in the world but the feel of his mouth, sucking and probing, and the hardness of his body pressing her against the car. He dropped his hands to her buttocks and gently lifted her against him, making the physical contact hotly intimate. Closing her eyes, she raised her arms to his shoulders and swayed in time with the erotic movements of his hips. It had been so long—too long.

She was just about to turn her mouth in search of his lips when she remembered Vonda. Vonda wouldn't have taken this for a minute. She was a hardened pro who never gave it away for free.

And then there was Cassie herself. More than one editor could have told Doug that Cassie Valkenberg was a total professional who never backed off on a commitment. And at the moment, her commitment involved a delightfully creative practical joke.

Giving Doug a no-nonsense push, she sidestepped his embrace and said, "Okay, Mr. Hunter, that's enough of the free samples. If you want it you're going to have to pay for it, just like everyone else does."

Doug was so startled by Vonda's brusque withdrawal that he never even tried to stop her. He had been turned on to begin with; the uninhibited response he'd felt had been enough to make him ache like a virgin on his wedding night. He studied the expression on her face, thinking that maybe he'd made a mistake. Maybe she *was* a call girl. God knows she'd sounded as tough as one.

"That's not what you said before," he reminded her.

"That was before. This is now. The terms are the same ones I gave Chris. Three hundred up front."

"I don't have that much cash on me," he said slowly.

Cassie hoped she had the nerve to pull this off. "That's *your* problem, Mr. Hunter, not mine."

It only took Doug a few moments to start wondering what she would do if he actually came up with the money. "Will you take a check?" he asked.

"In *my* line of work?" She laughed at him. "No way. You might stop payment."

"Not if you're as good as Edward says you are." When there was no reaction to that statement, Doug went on, "I'll tell you what we'll do, Vonda. First I'll jump start your car, and then you can drive me to an automatic teller. The trip should recharge your battery enough for you to restart the car later on. Agreed?"

Things were going better than Cassie had anticipated. Doug had just suggested what she'd expected to have to propose herself. She pursed her lips and pretended to think it over. "Well, I guess I *could* call my client and ask to reschedule. . . ."

"There's a phone by the ATM," Doug said.

Cassie held out her hand. "Then you've got yourself a deal, honey."

Doug wasn't about to settle for a handshake, and besides, there was still that troublesome question buzzing around in his head. This time, though, he wasn't going to let the lady off the hook until he had the answer. He took her hand, but instead of shaking it he gave it a quick, strong tug. The movement was so abrupt and, to Cassie, so unexpected that she stumbled forward and fell against him. Before she knew quite what was happening, a strong male arm was around her back and a possessive hand was tangled into her hair.

Doug caught a couple of strands in his fingers and gave a gentle but firm pull, forcing her to look up at him.

She felt a sharp stab of excitement when his mouth came down to hover just above her lips. The look of naked passion in his eyes was so seductive that it could have induced a woman in traction to try to follow him out of her hospital room. "I said *in advance*," she began, only to have him interrupt.

"I never buy blind, angel. Let's check out the compatibility factor."

He didn't bother coaxing, but then, he didn't have to. Cassie gave up fighting with the first light movement of his lips, the first taste of his tongue. She opened her mouth and let him kiss her, then sighed and put her arms around his waist because it felt so good. He alternated deep, dominating thrusts of his tongue with teasing nips and kisses, and she couldn't have said which she found more arousing. She felt him shudder and breathe in sharply when she slid her tongue into his mouth and started to kiss him back. It went on like that for too many long, lazy seconds to count, the two of them taking turns leading and following. And when he slipped his hand under her top and worked it up her midriff to cup her breast, the fingers that played with the hardened nipple were just as skilled as his mouth had been. She remembered Melanie's line about Edward—that he was proper till you got his clothes off—and hazily decided it also applied to Doug Hunter. She didn't want him to stop.

Doug had even less desire to stop than Cassie did but preferred a warm, comfortable bed to standing around in a driveway. He'd found out what he wanted to know, and it was so intriguing that he eased himself away in order to study her. She stared back, regarding him with a kind of glazed passion. Then she raised a hand to his cheek and whispered, "Doug . . ." The next thing he knew, she was curling her fingers around the back of his neck, just at the hairline, and kissing him wildly. Either she was an incredibly good actress or she was too worked up to help herself.

He had as much of an ego as the next guy, enough to think that she wasn't acting, but not enough to believe that a three-hundred-bucks-a-shot hooker would lose control of herself just because he'd kissed her. There was only one possible conclusion: she wasn't a hooker. She was a friend of Melanie Ford's, and she'd decided to play a little game with him. That was just fine, since he was playing a game of his own. Both of them were enjoying it, so there was no good reason not to go the full nine innings.

A part of him wanted to toss her over his shoulder and haul her off to the cottage, but thirty-three years of experience had taught him that there was ultimately more pleasure in waiting. The preliminaries had a charm all their own.

It wasn't easy to let her go when he was dizzy with the feel and scent and taste of her, but he wasn't the type of man who ever lost control of his emotions. "It's rare to meet someone with such zest for her work," he teased softly. "Are you sure you want to waste time visiting banks?"

Cassie knew she'd almost blown it. Her face was flushed with chagrin, but it was a little too dark out for the color to show. It was hard to think about her sister or the fictitious Vonda when Doug Hunter started kissing and caressing her. She put it down to too much beer, knowing very well that the little she'd had wasn't enough to affect her.

She figured she had two choices, and going to bed with Doug wasn't one of them. Choice number one was to carry the joke off as planned, and choice number two was to tell him who she was and say a polite good-night. She didn't have to think about it for more than two seconds. Edward was wrong to label her ditzy, but she admitted to being impulsive and uninhibited. She loved doing outrageous things, especially when the target was as appealing as Doug Hunter. If he couldn't take a joke, that was *his* problem.

She dropped her hands to her sides, saying, "You're something else, Doug Hunter, but a girl can't keep up the payments on her talking Cadillac without earning herself a buck or two beforehand. We'll start the car, we'll go to the ATM, and *then* we'll go make love. I'll give you the best time you've ever had, okay?"

"Whatever you say, angel." Doug could hardly keep from laughing. He gave her a lingering kiss, thinking that he was more than willing to play it however she wanted, seeing as how he was about to have the best time of his life.

He put an arm around her waist and led her back up the driveway. She was shivering by the time they reached his car. He unlocked the trunk and took out a lap robe and jumper cables. After draping the blanket around her shoulders, he helped her into the car. It took only about five minutes to get his car into position, attach the cables, and start up the Cadillac.

When the cables were back in his trunk, he moved his car to the opposite side of the driveway and got in beside Vonda in the Cadillac. The name had started to bother him. He doubted it was real and wanted to think of her by whatever her name *was*. As they drove through the front gates, he remarked, "You have an unusual first name. How did your parents come up with it?"

There were times when Cassie loved living dangerously, and this was one of them. Well aware that Edward might have mentioned her existence and even her name, she nonetheless answered, "Actually, I'm not really a Vonda at all. I'm a Catherine."

"And that's what people call you? Catherine?"

She took a deep breath. "They call me Cassie. Even my clients. But Vonda just seemed more appropriate for the girl in the silver lamé shorts."

They talked shop—*her* shop—as they drove toward

the coast and the local branch of Doug's bank, which was only a short distance away from Del Mar Racetrack. He asked more questions about her work than any man she'd ever met, but then, she'd never engaged in this particular occupation before. It wasn't hard to come up with answers, not when she'd literally written the book on the subject, and she knew her answers were good ones. All she had to do was draw from the dozens of authentic case histories that were stored away in her mind.

Doug was astonished by how easily information flowed from Cassie's lips and by how detailed and convincing she managed to make it. Not only was she bright; she had one hell of an imagination. Either that, or she'd been telling the truth all along. He kept trying to trip her up, but all he managed to do was confuse himself. He put the blame on fourteen-hour days and a six-pack of beer, and gave up asking questions.

Chapter Four

$\mathcal{E}$dward Kolby was standing just outside the front courtyard. The coffee had been made and served almost half an hour before, and most of Edward's friends were on their second or third cups by now. Edward, meanwhile, had gone off to look for Doug. It wasn't like Doug to disappear, and it wasn't like Edward to be concerned even if he did, but this was a night for the unusual.

After checking both the house and the guest cottage with no success, Edward had gone the long way back to the front door. His route took him past the garage, where he noticed that Doug's car was missing from its usual spot. Thinking that Doug must have gone for a ride, he reached for the courtyard gate to go back into the house. Then he heard the sound of a car coming up the driveway, turned around to see who it was, and spotted Melanie's leased Cadillac. Cassie was driving, and Doug was in the front along with her. It was a curious turn of events.

Cassie spotted Edward at just about the same moment he spotted her. When he started over to the car, she crossed her fingers and prayed he wouldn't blow her cover. Not only did she have Douglas Hunter eating out of the palm of her hand; she had his three hundred dollars tucked away in her sequined purse.

She never gave Edward a chance to get a word in edgewise, but said as she opened the door, "Well, hi there, lover. What are you wandering around in the driveway for?" Hopping out of the car, she took the lap robe off her shoulders and draped it over Edward's bare back. "Here, you need this more than I do. Why don't you find yourself another shirt? I promise I won't rip it off, honey."

Edward thanked her, wondering what she was doing with Doug when, not half an hour ago, she'd given him the royal brush-off; he was equally baffled to realize she was still posing as Vonda. Doug had gotten out of the car by now and was walking around behind it.

"I thought you left a long time ago," Edward said to Cassie.

He went from puzzled to chagrined when Doug came up behind Cassie and dropped his hands onto her bare shoulders. There was no mistaking the sexual implication of the gesture. Doug and *Cassie* was bad enough, but Doug and *Vonda*? God only knew what she was planning. She had no idea who she was tangling with.

"I had a little trouble with my car," Cassie said. "Doug gave me a jump start and then asked if I'd be interested in spending a little time with him. But you know me, honey. It's strictly cash up front. We've just been to his bank."

Edward knew better than to come between one of the Ford sisters and a good practical joke, so he limited his protest to a flat, "I thought you had another client tonight."

"Now, Edward," Cassie answered quickly, "I know Doug is your friend, but business is business. You and I had a wonderful time together, but by tomorrow you'll have forgotten all about me. Just go on back to your party."

Edward sighed and shook his head. "All right. Whatever you say." He looked at Doug, who was now caressing Cassie's shoulders. "Would you mind getting me that shirt? We'll wait for you in the hall."

Doug had forgotten all about the shirt, and so, he suspected, had Edward. It would have been much more logical for Edward to walk back to the cottage with them to get the shirt, and if he hadn't suggested that, it could only be because he wanted a private word with Cassie. Inside knowledge or not, maybe she was a friend of Melanie's after all. Maybe she read biographies of hookers in her spare time. Maybe she'd even played one somewhere along the line and done some preliminary research.

He decided to give Edward a firm push and watch his reaction. Sliding his arm around Cassie's waist to draw her back against him, he cupped her breast through the sequined top and started to fondle it. "I'll be right back," he murmured, nuzzling her neck. He could feel her heartbeat quicken under his hand as he kissed her. Her ardent physical response to him doubled the excitement of touching her.

Edward didn't say a word. With a tight-lipped frown, he turned on his heel and walked to the gate, holding it open for Cassie to pass through first. One look at his face and Cassie decided not to argue. She giggled and told Doug to behave himself, then wriggled out of his grasp. "I think your friend is going to be as wild in bed as you were," she said to Edward, and sashayed into the courtyard ahead of him.

"Unlike you, I'll be smart enough to take off my shirt the minute we get inside," Doug called after Edward.

Edward paused and looked back over his shoulder, thinking that things had gone far enough. Using the first excuse that came to mind, he said, "If Tawny stops in at the party . . ."

"Tawny?" Doug cut him off with a disbelieving laugh. "Be serious, Edward. They're not even in the same universe."

"Come *on,* Edward," Cassie said, and tugged at his arm. "I'm dying for a drink of water."

Edward went, but he wasn't happy about it. Cassie could tell just how *unhappy* he was by the glowering expression on his face as he marched her up to the door. The minute they were inside the house he looked at her as though she were playing with half a deck that had been short a few cards to begin with. "Are you out of your mind, Cassie? The man thinks you're a hooker! You can't take his money and then let him get you alone!"

Cassie leaned against the wall and crossed her arms in front of her chest. "I hope you don't get this excited when Melanie does something unconventional."

"Unconventional? *Unconventional?*" He ran his hand through his hair. "It isn't unconventional, Cassie, it's insane!"

"Umm. You know, Edward, Horace Miesley has the most stunning collection of modern sculpture in this gallery. My mother-in-law would love to—"

"Never mind the damn sculpture. What about Doug?"

"What about him?" Cassie asked. "Does he beat his lovers up? Give them unspeakable diseases?"

"Of course he doesn't." The lap robe had slipped a bit, and Edward absently pulled it back into place. "Look, Cassie, I could almost understand this if you were dying to sleep with Doug. I mean, a lot of women would like to sleep with him. But since you aren't . . ."

"What makes you think that?" Cassie asked.

"I just assumed . . ." Edward let the sentence trail off and gave Cassie an appraising look. She watched in fascination as the agitated man in front of her turned into the essence of cool self-assurance. "You have no intention of going to bed with him. I've heard enough about your character from Melanie to know that if you decided to have an affair with him, you wouldn't hit him up for—what was the figure? Three hundred bucks?—beforehand. You wouldn't keep playing the happy hooker. You'd tell him who you are and make love openly and honestly."

"Ah, the scientific mind!" Cassie stared up at him, awash in admiration. "You're absolutely right, of course. But this is just too good an opportunity to pass up. I appreciate the fact that you didn't tell Doug who I was, Edward."

"The Ford sense of humor tends to be contagious, Cassie. I even strung Doug along a little after you left. But there's a difference between a harmless joke and a suicidal prank. Whatever you're planning, you'd better forget it. Doug isn't as easygoing as I am. He's got some sharp edges to him, and he doesn't much like it when people promise him something and don't deliver. I saw the way he was looking at you. If you think you can lead him on and then cut out at the last minute with his money . . ."

"I think I've figured out a way to do it."

Edward had been afraid of that. He was also afraid that arguments to the contrary would fall on deaf ears. Trying a different tack, he said, "All right, let's assume that you could. Why would you want to?"

"For one thing, he insulted my sister and he probably deserves it. For another, Edward, he suspects I'm not really a pro, and he's been playing a game of his own. Like I told you before, it's just too good a joke to pass up. And if you say one word between now and the wedding, I will never, ever forgive you." Cassie gave him a big smile. "Besides, I think your best friend has more of a sense of humor than you give him credit for.

He makes me laugh, and he kisses better than anyone I've ever met. By the way, who's Tawny?"

"Tawny Timberlake. She's a good friend of Doug's. . . ."

But Cassie had stopped listening because she was too busy laughing. The Tawny part of it was wonderful enough, but *Timberlake*? The combination was high-society heaven, even better than Buffy Saint-Simon. "You mean a girlfriend?" she asked. "Is it serious?" She could picture Doug with terminal Tawnyitis, a disease characterized by a hangdog look and a collar around the victim's neck.

Edward hesitated just long enough to let her know he was thinking about how honest to be. "He doesn't love her," he finally admitted, "but that doesn't mean he won't ask her to marry him. He thinks he *should* love her because she's so perfect for him. He's looking for somebody cut from the same cloth as Buffy, and Tawny fills the bill. It's the only type of woman he could ever be serious about."

"If logic is the basis of his proposal, then I feel sorry for both of them if she accepts," Cassie said. "Logic is the wrong reason to get married. It should be wild and crazy and wonderful, like with you and Melanie. It should crash over your head like a ton of bricks carried by a tidal wave."

Edward couldn't disagree, since Melanie made him feel exactly the way Cassie had described. "That's beside the point," he said. "We were talking about Doug's sense of humor. No matter how good it is, you can't turn him inside out and expect him to laugh."

"But he wants to play the game as much as I do. He's going into this with his eyes wide open." Cassie looked at her watch, saw that five minutes had gone by, and went on, "Look, Edward, he'll be back anytime now. I promise I won't torture the poor man *too* much. Just before I leave I'll blow my horn three times. Listen for it. Then go to the cottage and, uh, commiserate with him."

Edward thought about asking Cassie what she planned to do, but the truth was, he didn't want to know. The Ford women were a handful and a half, and he had enough trouble keeping up with one of them without taking on the other. Cassie, after all, would be safely back in San Francisco on Sunday, and he'd already made it clear to her that she wasn't Doug's type.

He pictured Doug locked in the bedroom closet or stranded naked in the woods by the cottage and couldn't help but smile. "A part of me would like to be a fly on thé wall," he admitted. "Nobody's gotten the better of Doug Hunter in all the years I've known him. Have a good time, Cassie, but don't make him suffer too much."

Cassie threw her arms around Edward's neck and hugged him, telling him that Melanie had finally found the perfect man. She was about to draw away when Doug opened the door. The embrace was so full of sisterly affection that Doug would have been hard-pressed to miss it. Not for the first time that evening, Cassie brazened it out.

"You're a prince, Edward Kolby. I hope you have a very nice life." She linked her arm through Doug's. "All set, honey?"

Doug tossed the shirt he was carrying to Edward, who pulled it over his head and handed back the blanket. The truth was, Doug was a lot more than all set. The nearest thing he could compare it to was a thoroughbred chomping at the bit before the start of the Kentucky Derby. He couldn't wait to get Cassie alone.

He wasn't sure just why that was so. He'd found her appealing from the first time he'd laid eyes on her, but appealing wasn't the same as irresistible. Up till a few minutes ago, his self-control had been as unshakable as ever. Then he'd walked into his bedroom to get Edward the shirt, taken one look at the bed, and started to fantasize. He'd gone to use the bathroom and lingered to stare at the Roman tub. The swimming pool, the vacant stall in the barn with its floor of fresh hay, the old tree house in the woods—it was like being sixteen again. He pictured Cassie everywhere, naked, eager and totally uninhibited.

He told himself it had something to do with all the stories she'd spun. He didn't have all that much experience with women. He'd married young, remained faithful to his wife, and put far more effort into work than sex during the time since Buffy's death. He'd had a couple of lovers during those three years, but no one had attracted him as strongly as Cassie did. His only doubt was that she didn't really intend to go through with it.

He found himself reaching for her even before they were out of the front courtyard. As he backed her into the shadows cast by the shoulder-high wall, he told himself that a kiss would be enough. It wasn't. Her response was half-kitten, half-tigress, totally overwhelming. She was soft and pliant in his arms, her body curving submissively against his hips, but she pulled his shirt loose from his pants and dug her nails into his bare back at the same time. Sixty seconds of it and he was dizzy with wanting her.

He pulled his mouth away and buried it against her neck. It was a struggle to keep his hands to himself. "At this rate, I'm never going to make it to the bedroom," he mumbled.

She put a hand on each side of his face and gently pulled his head up. "Really, Douglas!" she said with a giggle. "You can't want to do it in the *garden*. Besides, I have better plans for you than that!"

Excitement shot through Doug like a flame-tipped arrow. "Plans? What kind of plans?"

"If I told you it would spoil the fun." And the joke,

Cassie thought. "Put yourself entirely in my hands, Doug Hunter, and I can promise you a night you'll never forget."

Doug let her go, thinking that you only went around once in life. He was used to taking the lead when he made love to a woman, but there would be time for that later—he hoped.

She took a quick couple of steps to the side. "Don't worry, honey, I'm a great believer in truth in advertising. But we'll start in the bedroom, not the garden. Later, when everyone is asleep, maybe I'll take you out to the pool. Or even into the woods."

The tree house, Doug thought, and drifted back fourteen years to a college summer and a girl named Ellen. He had a feeling that Cassie knew things to do in tree houses that neither he nor Ellen had ever even dreamed of. She took his hand, and without a murmur of protest, he allowed her to lead him out of the courtyard.

Cassie didn't figure Doug Hunter for the type who'd make love in a floodlit courtyard when a bunch of his friends were partying not thirty feet away, but she was still highly relieved when he meekly followed along. It would have been better if he hadn't put his arm around her waist and burrowed his hand underneath her sequined top, but you couldn't have everything. The trick was to keep your head and remember what you wanted to do.

It wasn't going to be easy. She had a habit of sizzling like a drop of water on a red-hot griddle whenever Doug kissed her, with the result that her common sense temporarily took a flier. Her earlier responses hadn't been faked. In fact, if she hadn't been so determined to pay him back for his remarks about Melanie, her common sense might have entirely deserted her.

Doug didn't kiss her again as they walked between the house and detached garage to the guest cottage, but his fingers got more and more playful against her bare skin. It took her a while to catch on to the fact that he was deliberately teasing her. He gradually worked his hand up her midriff to the underside of her breast and started to caress her. If the fondling drove her crazy, the way he kept tracing the circumference of the areola with his fingernail was even worse. Her nipple ached to be touched. At first she wondered why a man would bother arousing a woman he'd paid for, and then she remembered that he didn't really think she was a pro. The next fifteen or twenty minutes were going to be almost impossible if he insisted on being so seductive.

He finally removed his hand when they came to the cottage, reaching into his pocket to take out a set of keys. In the car he'd mentioned that he was temporarily living in Miesley's guest cottage while his house on Coronado was being renovated and redecorated. The word "cottage" had led Cassie to picture something small and cozy, but the place looked big enough for a family of four. She walked through a small hall into a living room decorated in a tasteful version of California contemporary: softly cushioned furniture covered in a blue-and-ecru print, wall-to-wall carpeting, inlaid wooden tables, Oriental lamps.

"It's a beautiful room," she said.

Doug closed and locked the front door, then joined her. "My mother did the decorating. She handles the design end of our real estate business, especially the hotels. She's helping me with my house, too, but she's such a perfectionist that it will probably take twice as long before I can move back in than it would if I were supervising things myself."

Wondering where his daughter fit in, Cassie remarked, "It's a lot of room for just one person."

"You're right," he answered. "It is. There are three bedrooms in the house. Which do you want to try first?"

He had a roguish smile on his face straight out of an Errol Flynn adventure movie. Cassie ignored both the smile and the question. "You mentioned somebody named Lisa before. I assumed she was your daughter. Isn't she living here also?"

Doug suspected that Cassie knew rather than assumed who Lisa was, but he didn't make an issue of it. "Yes, she's my daughter, and no, she isn't living here. She prefers to stay in the main house. She claims she likes being next door to her grandmother, but the truth is that she'd got a crush on Horace's houseboy." Since talking about Chris Patterson held no particular charm for Doug, he reached for Cassie and pulled her into his arms. "Nobody will disturb us, angel."

He nuzzled her neck and kissed his way up to her temple. Her response was immediate and passionate, growing hotter when he began to caress her breast. His fingers closed on the nipple he'd teased so effectively outside, and her arms came up to clutch his shoulders. He rubbed the nipple gently at first, and then more roughly, and heard his name escape her lips in a hoarse sigh.

His loins tightened. He'd never known the name "Doug" could be such a powerful aphrodisiac. He was asking himself how he'd ever manage the self-control to play a passive role in this whole charade when his lips brushed her eyelid and encountered a spiky false eyelash.

Under ordinary circumstances he was far too much of a gentleman to comment on a woman's makeup or style of dress, but these were no ordinary circumstances. He enjoyed provoking Cassie. It amused him to picture her dropping all pretense and demanding to be treated like a lady instead of a piece of merchandise.

"Your eyelash just attacked my lips," he said. "You wear three times too much makeup, Cassie. Get into the bathroom and wash your face. And while you're in there, grab my brush and bring it into the bedroom. You have enough spray in your hair to lacquer an entire Las Vegas chorus line."

He caught the briefest flash of annoyance in her eyes before she switched on her dumb-blonde routine and giggled up at him. "Awfully pushy, aren't we, Mr. Hunter?"

"We have a right to be," he retorted. "We paid through the teeth for the privilege."

"So we did," she answered. "Which way do I go?"

The master bedroom was down a short hallway on the left-hand side. Cassie took in little more than the brown-and-blue color scheme of the room and the gleaming brass headboard of the king-size bed as she walked into the adjoining bathroom. She closed the door and looked around. The fact that the bathroom connected directly into the bedroom without a second exit was a possible problem, but there happened to be a large window available. The window ran the full length of the sunken Roman tub, a good six feet up the wall from the tub's bottom. Fortunately, however, there was also a dressing table nearby with a chair pushed underneath.

She turned on the water in the sink and picked up the soap. She didn't mind taking off her makeup—it was more than she'd ever worn in her life, even for television appearances—but she hadn't cared for Doug's arbitrary manner. That was irrational, of course. He was probably only trying to provoke her. He'd succeeded, but she had no intention of letting him know it.

His brush was in a leather shaving bag on the counter next to the sink. Half expecting to find him undressed, she was rather relieved when she walked into the bedroom and saw him lying fully clothed on the bed, with only his shoes removed. She sat down next to him, her hip touching his side, and gave him a cheerful smile.

"Do I pass inspection?" she asked.

"With flying colors." He took the brush out of her hand and dropped it on the bed. Then he straightened up, pulling her around so that his chest was directly behind her back. The next thing Cassie knew, he was working at the double-tied knots that held her top in place.

Letting him take off her clothes wasn't a part of her game plan. "Don't be in such a hurry," she scolded. "They have a saying in the Orient, honey: What's done slowly is done best."

He laughed softly. "You're sure you didn't get that one out of a fortune cookie?"

Cassie had made it up on the spot. "Of course I didn't. I once had a friend from Japan. Her mother was a geisha—they call it 'the willow world' over there—and she knew the most amazing things. My friend was following in her mother's footsteps, and I got her to teach me *everything,* Doug."

She looked over her shoulder, leaning forward until only inches separated her lips from Doug's, and murmured seductively, "They have incredible techniques in the East, secrets that they guard from the outside world. I can touch you in ways that will make you think that you'll drown from the sheer pleasure you feel. I know secrets about certain parts of your body, tricks that will send you into a world you never imagined could exist. I'm willing to show you—but you have to do exactly as I say."

To Doug, all this talk about the mysterious East sounded like a bunch of hogwash. Sex was sex. He might even have said so, except that Cassie's voice had had a smoky eroticism that hit him with the force of a desert sandstorm. "Exactly as you say?" he repeated. "And what would that entail?"

"You have to agree to put yourself completely in my hands." Cassie backed away a little and gave a nonchalant shrug. "You've paid your money, and I'll do whatever you ask. It can be like every other time you've ever had a woman, or it can be so incredibly exciting that you'll sweat and writhe and beg to be put out of your misery. But I won't satisfy you, not right away. I'll take you to the brink and bring you back again and again until, when I finally push you over the edge, you explode like an erupting volcano. Take your pick, Doug. The choice is yours."

Faced with those two alternatives, there wasn't a red-blooded man on earth who wouldn't have wanted to be Mount Saint Helens. Doug Hunter was no exception. He'd never had a woman talk to him the way Cassie had just done, and it turned him on so much that questions seemed superfluous. Or maybe it was her closeness that turned him on. He didn't know and he didn't care. His doubts about whether she really meant to make love to him had just flown out the window.

When he didn't answer right away, she got a hurt look on her face and said, "I don't do this for just anyone, you know. Only the men I like. And the ones I *really* like get more than one ride on the merry-go-round."

"And me?" Doug asked. "Where do I fit in?"

He sounded a lot less smooth and self-assured than he'd been the last time he'd spoken. Reassured by that, Cassie answered, "You're right at the top of my list, honey. I'll tell you what. One volcano, one ride, for as many volcanoes as you can name."

"And do I get to use reference books?"

Cassie giggled and shook her head. "That would be cheating."

"Then here's to Krakatoa," Doug said with a grin. "I can't wait to find out what happens next."

Cassie smiled back and picked up his hairbrush. "You have good ideas yourself on occasion. I love having my hair brushed. When I've had enough I'll let you know. Until then, your job is to devote yourself to giving me pleasure." She handed him the brush and turned around.

He worked out the tangles so gently and patiently that Cassie wondered about his previous experience. Eventually, though, he started to cheat, interrupting the brush strokes to caress her arms and shoulders or to drop lingering kisses on her hair and nape. She would have been blissfully relaxed if she hadn't been so keenly aware of every single violation of the rules. His love-making thrust her into a place where desire mingled with dreaminess, the former gradually gaining sway. She responded with purring little moans of pleasure and never thought of telling him to stop.

Doug, however, could think of little else. The sounds Cassie was making were driving him crazy. He repeatedly reminded himself that *she* was supposed to call the shots, but it didn't escape his notice that she enjoyed being touched and kissed. In the end, her sex-kitten response was more than he could take. A sinuous stretch, an erotic roll of her neck, a throaty moan, and he was pulling her around to face him. The desire he saw in her eyes was his undoing. He tumbled backward onto the bed, taking her along with him, and cupped her chin to bring her mouth to his lips. Her breathless "Doug . . . !" was cut off by a deep, urgent kiss. Volcanoes went straight out of his mind. He wanted her then and there.

Cassie melted against him. She was suddenly functioning on pure animal instinct. The diffuse sense of arousal she'd felt as he brushed her hair grew and sharpened until it was like a fire in the pit of her stomach. She couldn't get enough of Doug's mouth, and when he settled her against his thighs and began a slow, circular thrusting, she couldn't get enough of that, either. She only came to her senses when he hooked his thumbs around the waistband of her shorts and started tugging impatiently. There was no artifice or pretense in her panicky withdrawal. Memories were flooding her mind, memories of what had happened after her husband's death. The lessons she'd learned during those tortured months still had the power to haunt her.

Doug felt like kicking down the nearest wall when

Cassie stiffened and arched away from him. He'd never rushed a woman in his life. On the contrary, he'd always prided himself on his ability to hold back and sense what pace a woman wanted. Breathing hard, he reluctantly removed his hands and mumbled, "I'm sorry if I went too fast."

Cassie barely heard him. She only knew that he'd stopped, that he was giving her the breathing space she needed. In some hazy way she realized that the stakes had risen enormously, but she was too wrapped up in trying to regain her equilibrium to think about that. The important thing was to remember why she was there and to slip back into the role she'd been playing.

She rolled off Doug and onto her side, turning her back to his face. He sighed, recognizing feminine reproach when he saw it. It had been one of Buffy's most effective weapons.

"You don't deserve me," she said, pouting.

Doug was quick to admit it. His marriage had taught him that confession and repentance were the quickest routes to forgiveness. "You're right. I never should have started to kiss you. Give me another chance and I promise I'll do better." He couldn't quite keep the laughter out of his voice. The truth was, Cassie would have made a terrible call girl. She was so passionate she would have burned herself out within a month.

He wiped the smile off his face when she twisted around to look at him, but he wasn't quite fast enough. "What's so funny?" she demanded.

"Nothing. I'm sorry."

Cassie pondered her next move. She hadn't missed the smile, but at least things were back on track. The problem was to make sure they stayed that way. "I have to have total control," she said. "Otherwise I don't enjoy it." She paused. "You want me to enjoy it, don't you, honey?"

"Yes." *Not to mention wanting the writhing and sweating and begging,* Doug thought.

"Where do you keep your liquor?"

"In the cabinet behind the couch. Why?"

Cassie sat up and began to unbutton his shirt. When she was finished, she ordered, "Don't move. I'll be right back."

Doug willingly obeyed, wondering whether she was telling the truth about needing to be in control. In retrospect it made a certain kind of sense. A woman with her obvious sexual experience didn't usually bolt like a frightened virgin just because a man started to undress her. Maybe male dominance panicked her. Maybe she needed to make a game out of sex before she could allow herself to enjoy it. But if that was the case, Doug intended to open up whole new worlds to her before the night was out.

She walked back into the bedroom holding a bottle of amaretto, which she set down on the night table. It didn't take a whole lot of imagination to figure out what she planned to do with it, and having him drink some wasn't one of the possibilities. The anticipation didn't make him writhe or beg, but he felt himself start to sweat.

He allowed her to take his shirt off, as passive as a baby now. Given free rein, Cassie was obviously a very wild lady, and the last thing he wanted was to tame her. She opened the bottle of amaretto and poured some onto her fingers, letting the overflow spill out onto his chest. His heart was beating so hard he could feel it in his throat. All that talk about secret places and erotic tricks was beginning to get to him.

He almost stopped her when she began to rub the amaretto into his nipples, because nipples weren't his idea of an erogenous zone. He only managed to keep his mouth shut because he knew she would get angry with him if he tried to tell her what to do. His only visible reaction was to flinch and go rigid, his only thought not to jerk away.

The fact that he was usually ticklish went straight out

of his mind only moments after she bent her head and took a nipple between her lips. The last things he saw before he closed his eyes and gave himself up to her mouth were the curve of her back and buttocks and the pair of slave bracelets on her arm. The last thing he thought was that now he knew how it felt to be a sultan.

She aroused him with a combination of biting and sucking so wrenchingly erotic that he began to believe her stories about the mysterious East. Her hand moved down to his belly, tormenting him with lightly playful fingers and sharp, unexpected nails. He moaned and started to move restlessly under her mouth, but he knew enough to keep his hands at his sides.

She started on the second nipple, which proved to be even more susceptible than the first. His excitement grew until he ached to express it, and since touching her was apparently forbidden, that left kissing her. He barely recognized the strained, hoarse voice in which he all but begged permission.

Her mouth came down on his, almondy sweet in taste, but the taste was the only sweet thing about her. The kiss was mercilessly teasing one moment and hotly dominating the next. It seemed to challenge the very fabric of his masculinity, until there was no way he could lie there and take it. He wasn't thinking, just reacting, and his reaction took the form of pushing her onto her back and pinning her beneath his body.

She switched off, blazing like the sun one moment, cold as the moon the next. Angry with himself for losing control, Doug rolled onto his back and stared at the ceiling. "I'm sorry, Cassie. I didn't stop to think. Please don't leave."

He was very relieved when she smiled her forgiveness and bent her mouth to his chest again. Her feverishly whispered words were interspersed with arousing tastes and nips. "I can make you feel things you've never felt before. You'll be in agony, it will be so good for you. You'll plead with me to finish you off, but deep inside, you'll be praying I do the opposite. Trust me, Doug. Stop fighting your secret desires and let me show you what the word 'pleasure' can really mean."

Doug was more than ready. He wanted her so much that all he could manage was a husky, "Whatever you say . . . oh, God, Cassie . . ."

"I'm going to leave for a minute. . . ."

"No . . ."

"I'll be right back."

He didn't dare try to stop her. Twenty seconds without her touching him should have cooled him off, but his imagination was working overtime. It was so damn hard to lie there and let her do whatever she wanted, but what choice did he really have? The only alternative was simply to take her, without any enthusiasm on her part. And if he did *that*, he might never find out what he'd missed.

She was carrying her panty hose when she returned. "Slide down a little and put your arms over your head," she said.

He did as he was told, trapped in an erotic fog. It wasn't until she started tying one leg of the panty hose around his wrist that he realized what she planned to do to him. It was automatic to pull his hand away, but he knew he'd let her have her way if she really insisted.

"It turns me on," she said. "I have to know that I can do whatever I want to before I can let myself go. It'll be fantastic for you. Trust me."

He hesitated, but then she kissed him and touched him, and in no time flat he caved in like a dangerously weakened mine shaft. Within thirty seconds, his wrists were tied to the brass bars of the headboard and he was grunting his pleasure as Cassie kissed her way down his chest. He caught at his breath when she unbuckled his belt and pulled it through the loops of his slacks. Her mouth and teeth were incredibly skillful. It was obvious what she planned to do next, and his only reservations concerned how much he'd be able to take.

"I have something special in my purse," she whispered. "I'm going to go get it. When I come back I'll have my clothes off. And then I'll see what I can do about taking off the rest of yours." She gave him a coy look. "Is that all right with you, honey?"

"Nothing you do *isn't* all right with me," he answered in a shaky voice, and silently looked forward to the rest of the night.

Chapter Five

Cassie turned on the water in the bathroom sink, grabbed the cane-backed chair that was pushed under the nearby dressing table, and looped her purse strings around her wrist. When the chair was in place on the floor of the tub, centered beneath the window, Cassie climbed up and stood on tiptoes. The windowsill was just about level with her breasts. She unlocked the window and slid it to the side, then examined the screen. It was the kind that sat loosely in a recessed track, so it was easy for her to remove it and toss it outside. With nothing left to block her way, she was able to lever her stomach onto the sill and look around outside. There was a row of prickly-looking bushes planted against the side of the house, their manicured tops nearly level with the bottom of the window.

She managed to seat herself up on the sill, but not without scraping her thigh on the window track. The ground was about four feet down. Even though she made a swinging wide-arced jump, she couldn't quite clear the hedges and wound up with scratches on her arms and legs.

She landed on her feet but fell to her knees, narrowly missing a sprinkler head. She found herself standing in a grassy area with the cottage to her right, the back of the main house directly behind her but thirty-five or forty feet away, and a gentle slope in front of her. The pitch of the slope got steeper about fifteen feet beyond. There was a full moon out, and once her eyes got more accustomed to the dark, she could see that the slope eventually leveled off into a terraced area containing a corral and some kind of structure, probably a small barn. Miesley seemed to own a substantial chunk of the hillside.

It was a beautiful view, but Cassie didn't have time to stand around and admire it. She was just turning to leave when her attention was caught by the sound of a soft whinny followed by the beating of a horse's hooves. Looking toward the sound, she saw a boyishly slight figure ride off into the night. It was the wrong neighborhood for rustlers and a strange time to go riding, but the person on the horse appeared to be a teenager. Teenagers had a habit of keeping odd hours and doing strange things. Cassie briefly wondered how the rider had gotten access to the property—it seemed to be fenced all around—but then turned her attention back to more pressing matters.

She had two main worries: first, that she would run into somebody on the way to her car, and second, that the car would refuse to start. Both proved groundless. Within half an hour she was walking through the hotel parking lot, her shorts and top covered by the trench-coat she'd left in the trunk. The uniformed doorman at the Miesley Plaza was not the sort of fellow who would have allowed a woman dressed like "Vonda" to enter his establishment.

Most of the people working on Melanie's film were staying in a cheaper place north of La Jolla, but

Melanie herself and about a dozen other VIPs were quartered at the Miesley Plaza. Melanie had learned to demand first-class accommodations after a stay in a roach-infested dive during a previous movie. Cassie's room was on the seventh floor, but instead of going straight to bed she continued up to Melanie's room on twelve. It was past eleven o'clock when she finally knocked on the door, softly, in case Melanie had gone to sleep.

Melanie flung open the door almost at once and looked Cassie up and down as though she expected to see the scars of a night's worth of mayhem carved into her body. Once assured that Cassie wasn't on the verge of collapse or hysteria, she closed the door and launched into a tirade. "Do you know what time it is? Where were you? I was going to wait another fifteen minutes and call the police, I was so worried about you. There's no telling what might have happened to you in that crazy outfit you had on." She paused and frowned. "You *do* still have something on underneath that coat, don't you, Cassie?"

Cassie took off her coat and tossed it over a chair. It was a serious mistake, because the scratches on her arms and legs led to a whole new round of recriminations. Assuring Melanie that she was perfectly all right, Cassie helped herself to a soda from the in-room refrigerator and sat down on the bed.

"I'm sorry you were so worried. I know you have an early call, and I didn't mean to keep you up." She smiled and patted the bed. "Come on, join me. I'll tell you all about what happened."

Melanie sat, her eyes fixed on Cassie's scraped thigh. "You're going to have a wicked-looking bruise by tomorrow," she said. "I wouldn't put on a bathing suit if I were you."

"Umm. Look, Melanie, do you want to know what happened, or do you want to spend the rest of the night clucking about a few scratches?"

"I want to know how you got so beaten up! I've been pacing around the room for the past thirty minutes. Do you know how much time I wasted trying to get Miesley's unlisted phone number? Dammit, Cassie, don't laugh at me. . . ."

"It's hard not to, when I think of some of the crazy stunts *you've* pulled. I thought you'd finally given up worrying when I survived that tour with Acid Reign. I mean, just because I'm a little late and a little bruised, that's no reason—"

"That's *very* late and *very* bruised, and there's *every* reason on earth!" Melanie gave Cassie a reproachful look. "You're my little sister. I worry about you. I'll always worry about you. So what happened?"

Cassie knew it was the nature of older sisters to be protective, just as it was the nature of lionesses to guard their young. Defeated, she again apologized for any concern she might have caused and started at the beginning, when Doug Hunter had first opened the door. Melanie's only reaction was an occasional smile, at least until Cassie passed on the news that Horace Miesley had undoubtedly been the one to hire Lynn.

"I should have thought of him," Melanie said. "He's not what you'd call a nice guy, despite the money he gives to charity and grand gestures like offering to pick up the tab for our wedding reception. But go on—what happened next?"

Cassie picked up where she'd left off and didn't stop until the very end. Melanie's occasional smiles turned into frequent "Dear Lords!" and "You didn'ts!" with some pained groans of horror for emphasis. By the time Cassie finished talking, Melanie had buried her face in her hands and was shaking her head in dismay. "I can't believe you really did that. Not to Douglas Hunter," she moaned. "The man has absolutely no sense of humor."

"Don't worry, Melanie, Edward will untie him in time for the ceremony. I gave him a signal when I left."

Cassie paused to wipe the tears of laughter out of her eyes. "I wish I could have hidden under the bed to see what would happen next! I never dreamed that all that stuff Kineko Sato told me about Oriental erotic techniques would actually work. To tell the truth, I never really thought the whole thing would go as far as it did."

Melanie dropped her hands and gave Cassie a baleful stare. "And what do you suppose Hunter is going to do when he finds out who you are? He doesn't have one iota of Edward's sweetness, Cassie. I wouldn't let him get me alone if I were you."

"I know. I'm starting to regret letting my sense of humor take over so completely. But even *you* admit that he's a perfect gentleman, and perfect gentlemen don't exact revenge." Cassie smiled. "Unlike wacky little sisters. Aren't you pleased that I managed to get the better of him?"

Melanie's sense of humor was too highly developed not to win out over her sense of concern. She tried not to smile, lost the battle, and laughingly picked up a pillow. Cassie ducked the ensuing blow, but not quite quickly enough.

"Now, what was that for?" she asked.

"Your brains are scrambled. I figured a good blow on the head might restore them to their original condition, not that it's that much better." Melanie tossed aside the pillow. "Actually, Cassie, I wish I could have been there. Hunter is such a hopeless prig that it's hard to imagine him writhing in the throes of passion. When it comes to sex, I kind of pictured him making an agreement with his wife to do it once a week, same time, same station, with the blinds down and the lights out."

"I doubt it," Cassie answered. "The truth is, he's terrific in that department."

"As a *lover?*" Melanie cocked her eyebrow skeptically. "Oh. I get it. You're putting me on."

"Nope." Cassie shook her head. "I almost got myself seduced. He can excite me more with a touch on my arm or a kiss on my neck than the average man can by—well, by doing it all. He's got charm to burn, he makes me laugh, and way deep down, there's a lovely touch of innocence there. I didn't expect to find that, not when he's so attractive, but I don't think he's been around all that much. He was too—eager, I guess you'd call it. Much too ready to swallow the line I was giving him. A man who's had dozens and dozens of women would have been much less gullible."

"Doug Hunter?" Melanie said, sounding so astonished that Cassie had to laugh. "Eager and gullible?"

"Doug Hunter," she confirmed. "I'm crazy about him, Melanie."

"Charming? Funny? Exciting? *Innocent?* Good grief, Cassie, are you sure we're talking about the same man here?"

Cassie was sure, but she gave a brief description just in case. "Edward's best friend. Lives on his stepfather's estate in Rancho Santa Fe, at least while his house is being redone. Brown hair, brown eyes and over six feet tall. A fabulous body, a gorgeous face and a voice that could sell icebergs to Eskimos—providing they were female Eskimos."

Melanie wouldn't have denied that Douglas Hunter was physically attractive. She'd even noticed the voice. But he'd been so stuffily correct on the few occasions they'd met, she'd assumed it was the only way he ever acted. Even Edward had implied as much, saying that Hunter was invariably formal and even stiff with all but a handful of his closest friends. Her fiancé had counseled her not to take Doug's behavior personally. She'd tried not to, but distant, sophisticated types like Hunter left her cold. She didn't find them sexy at all.

It took a major readjustment in her thinking to accept the fact that her sister could be attracted to a man she so heartily disliked, but she knew she was too judgmental at times. She'd excused her attitude toward Hunter by telling herself that it was impossible to put any credence in Edward's encomiums about the man's virtues when he was so totally inhuman, but it looked like there was a flesh-and-blood male hidden underneath, after all. Maybe he warmed up in the presence of girls in silver lamé shorts.

"Okay," she finally said, "we're talking about the same man. Maybe we haven't given each other enough of a chance. But if you're that crazy about him, why would you do something guaranteed to make him furious with you?"

"Earlier tonight, Edward told me you'd had him thrown into the ocean the first time you were filming on the ship," Cassie countered. "A practical joke is a practical joke. I really don't see the difference."

"Then you'd better get yourself a pair of glasses," Melanie retorted. "It's one thing to toss a guy into the water in order to loosen up a tense set, and something entirely different to tie him to his headboard and walk out on him—"

"One's cold, the other's hot," Cassie interrupted with a wink.

"Very funny, Cassie. But don't forget, I dove in after Edward, flattered him outrageously, and asked him out to dinner. I knew he was infatuated with me but too shy to make the first move, and an infatuated man will forgive a woman almost anything. You, on the other hand, left Doug Hunter aching with frustration. And if I know Doug Hunter, he's—"

"Don't say it." Cassie held up her hand. "He's a prig, he's a cold fish, he's got no sense of humor, and the only things he really cares about are his balance sheets. Frankly, Melanie, that doesn't sound like the man I met tonight, but maybe it was just the beer in him talking. Maybe he's just as cold and humorless and robotlike as you say. But if he is, I guess I'd better find it out soon before I get in any deeper. Because just for the record, I never had any intention of refusing Doug a return match. I know you can't do what I did tonight to a man and then flatly refuse to sleep with him. It's just—I need a little more time. Assuming he's even interested in me, that is."

Melanie switched gears. Her sister wasn't smiling anymore, and the lightness was gone from her tone. Cassie hadn't lacked for male companionship over the past few years, but this was the first time she'd said anything other than where they'd gone or what they'd done. The relationships had always been superficial. "Do you want to talk about it?" she asked quietly.

Cassie silently sat there, her arms around her knees, and stared at the can of soda in her hands. Her voice was soft yet impassioned when she finally started to talk. "Do you remember the song in *Guys and Dolls* where Sky Masterson and Sarah Brown are telling each other how they'll know when they're in love?" It was a rhetorical question. Melanie had a beautiful voice; she'd played Sarah Brown in summer stock only the year before. Without waiting for an answer, Cassie went on, "I'm like Sky Masterson. I want chemistry. When I first met Doug, I stopped . . . and I stared . . . and I *knew*. I couldn't quite believe it, not after everything you'd told me, but an hour alone with him, a couple of times in his arms, a look behind that smooth facade he tries to keep up, and that was it. I've been by myself for three years now, Melanie, and I'm lonely. For the right man I'd move halfway across the country or halfway around the world. But I can't change the kind of person I am or the way I live my life. I've fought hard to make a career for myself, and I'm not going to give it up, even if you and Jane and a dozen other people hover around me and cluck and worry that I'll get into trouble. It's just—from what I've heard about Doug from you and Edward, I'm not sure he'll approve either of me or what I do. I'm scared. I've waited a long time for lightning to strike again, and now that it has, I've remembered that the lightning isn't always enough. Sometimes it only strikes one of you. Sometimes it strikes both of you, but one of you dies. And sometimes people are afraid of it, so they run as fast as they can and never look back."

"So you kept your distance. You played a game that would keep you safe—at least for the time being. You gave Doug a little test, telling yourself that if he could pass it, you'd allow yourself to hope."

"I guess that was it. But it was mostly unconscious. I really didn't stop to analyze what I was doing."

Melanie didn't know what to say. There was no point in issuing warnings; Cassie had seen the pitfalls and was already running scared. In Melanie's opinion, she had good reason to be.

She edged closer to Cassie on the bed and gave her a gentle hug. The thought of her sister getting hurt all over again brought tears to her eyes. There had been too much pain already.

Cassie didn't have to see Melanie's face to know what she was thinking. In her admittedly biased opinion, they'd broken the mold after they made her older sister. She eased out of Melanie's arms and gave her a watery smile. "You worry too much. I'll be fine. But please don't talk to Edward about any of this. It's just too personal, and if it got back to Doug . . ."

"I won't if you don't want me to, Cassie. But I *am* worried. You have more spirit and joy in you than anyone I know, and twice now—"

"With the obvious exception of yourself," Cassie interrupted.

"Be quiet," Melanie ordered. "I'm making a speech. You glow with vitality, Cassie. Despite everything you've been through, there's more life and sparkle to you than anyone I've ever met. But twice now, I've had to stand by and watch the sparkle fade and almost die, as though—as though you were a wonderful, cheery fire, and somebody had sprayed you with sand to try to put you out. I don't want to see it happen again.''

"Then you have nothing to worry about, Melanie. At this point I barely know the man, so I can hardly get badly hurt.''

"I don't want to see it happen again,'' Melanie repeated.

Edward had gotten everyone out of the house within twenty minutes of the time that Doug and Cassie walked off to the cottage together. Then he'd helped himself to a book from the library and had gone back into the family room to wait. Since there was a large garden and a five-foot wall between him and the driveway, he'd also taken the precaution of opening a front window. He didn't want to miss Cassie's signal.

He was trotting out of the house within seconds of her first blast on the horn. The moment she spotted him running toward her car, she pulled away. It was obvious she had no intention of waiting around to talk to him.

Edward expected to find a very irritated Doug Hunter somewhere in the vicinity of the cottage. He didn't waste any time getting there. The vertical shaft of light shining out the front door told him that somebody had left it open, maybe deliberately. Figuring it was easier to search a small house than a sizable chunk of hillside, he went inside and started to look around. He was just about to call out Doug's name when he heard an angry shout: "Cassie? Dammit, what are you doing in there— trying to flood the place? This isn't funny!"

The first thing that hit Edward was the name "Cassie.'' He was surprised that Doug knew it and wondered how much else he knew. Since the marriage was a sore point to begin with, Edward's only reference to

Cassie had been to remark that "Melanie's sister" would be flying down from San Francisco on Saturday to be matron of honor. He'd never even mentioned her name.

He walked down the hall to the master bedroom and pushed open the door. The scene that greeted him was a feast for the senses: the sight of his best friend, stripped to the waist and beltless, with his wrists bound to the brass headboard by a pair of glittering panty hose; the strong scent of amaretto; the sound of rushing water. It took exactly two seconds for the shock to wear off and for Edward to burst out laughing.

For a moment Doug wondered how Edward had gotten into a locked house, and then he realized that Cassie must have opened the front door when she went into the living room for the amaretto. He realized a couple of other things, too. It was no coincidence that Edward was standing in his bedroom. And Cassie—or Vonda, or whatever her name really was—was no longer in the bathroom.

If anybody else had stood at the foot of the bed, thrown back his head, and laughed so hard that tears started running down his cheeks, Doug would have been furious. And if anybody else had discovered him in this particular situation, he would have been acutely embarrassed. But it was Edward, who'd shared everything from adolescent fantasies to first affairs with him, so the most emotion he could summon up was a healthy irritation.

"When you get yourself under control, would you mind turning off the water?" he asked. "And then getting a pair of scissors and cutting these damned stockings off my wrists?" He looked down at his chest and grimaced. "And wet a facecloth for me while you're in the bathroom, Edward. This stuff isn't only sticky; it itches."

"Anything for a friend in need." Edward strolled off to the bathroom, returning a few seconds later with a dripping facecloth. He dropped it on Doug's chest, ignoring the loud curse he earned for his troubles.

"I said wet it, not soak it," Doug grumbled as rivulets of water trailed off his chest and onto the covers. "Damn you, you're enjoying this."

"Me?" Edward took a closer look at Doug's wrists. Cassie had done a very efficient job of tying him up. "I couldn't possibly derive any amusement from my closest friend's misfortune. But you know, I'm not sure there's enough room to get the blade of a scissors underneath that panty hose. I may have to call in the fire department."

"Very funny." Doug could see the headline now: "Prominent Developer Rolled by Hooker and Left Tied to Bed." "I suppose she got out through the bathroom window," he muttered.

"You suppose right. It was wide open, with the screen knocked out and a chair underneath. I closed the window for you and moved the chair back where it belongs, but you'll have to put the screen back in yourself. It must be somewhere in the bushes." Edward took pity on Doug and sponged off his chest. Then, taking the facecloth along with him, he went off to the kitchen in search of some scissors.

Doug *still* felt sticky. It didn't help his mood when Edward started whistling, because the song was "Don't Fence Me In." He yelled that he could do without the concert, and Edward stopped, but he was still grinning when he walked back into the room.

He picked up Doug's amaretto-stained shirt with his thumb and forefinger and waved it gingerly back and forth in obvious imitation of Doug's earlier display of his own shirt. "Lost your shirt as well as your head, I see."

"I can do without the bad jokes, too," Doug said. Twenty years of friendship and he'd never known how sarcastic the man could be. "Who the hell was she, Edward?"

"Vonda? A lady of rare beauty and even rarer talent. These knots are a work of art." Edward dropped the shirt in Doug's lap and slid the scissors under Cassie's panty hose. "Obviously she liked me a lot better than she liked you, but don't let it bother you, Doug. You can't win 'em all."

Doug decided to keep his mouth shut, at least until his wrists were free. He no longer trusted Edward's sense of humor. The skin underneath the panty hose stung because the more he'd tugged and twisted in an effort to get loose, the more the nylon had cut into his flesh. It was a relief when Edward finally finished.

Doug wanted some answers, but he wanted the amaretto off his chest even more. He went into the bathroom and washed himself off, grabbing a bottle of lotion on his way out. Edward had moved away from the bed by then and was sitting in a chair.

Doug leaned against the doorjamb and stood there rubbing lotion into his wrists. "She told me her real name was Cassie."

"Nice name," Edward observed.

"If Cassie is a call girl," Doug went on, "then I'm the queen of Sheba. You didn't take her to bed any more than I did, Edward."

"Whatever you say, Doug." Edward was caught between a rock and a hard place. Cassie wanted silence, Doug wanted answers. If he hadn't been so amused, he might even have worried. "If she isn't a call girl, what is she?" he asked. "I mean, if it looks like one and it acts like one . . ."

"Then it's probably a friend of your future wife's," Doug finished. "God knows, she was enough of a screwball. The only thing I can't figure out is Horace's reaction. When she first walked in I could have sworn he was expecting her, but he lost interest too fast. What happened to his finely tuned taste for malice?"

"Beats me. Listen, Doug, I'd like to stick around and talk it over, but I promised Melanie I'd stop by tonight." It was an out-and-out lie. Melanie had a 7:00 A.M. call and planned to turn in early.

"To give her a firsthand report?" Doug asked.

"She wanted to hear about the party. With you as host, she figured it would be a regular orgy."

Doug knew when he was being needled. He also knew he wasn't going to get another word out of Edward Kolby without forcing the issue, and the whole business wasn't important enough to him to bother. He took out a clean shirt, telling Edward he would walk him to his car.

His mind was working double time as he buttoned the shirt. Whoever Cassie was, Edward hadn't been expecting her. He'd been too off-balance at first, too embarrassed. But then, out of nowhere, he'd done a hundred-and-eighty-degree turn. That meant that not only had he figured out who she was; he was absolutely sure of it. So Cassie had to be somebody Melanie had described in detail. It made Doug wonder just who'd been the ultimate target of tonight's little caper: Edward, somebody else at the party, or himself.

They were walking out of the bedroom when he remembered the car. He felt like a fool for having overlooked the obvious, but then, dark-colored Cadillacs were hardly a rarity in his particular world, and his mind had been elsewhere at the time. Melanie had a dark-colored Cadillac, so there was no longer any doubt that Cassie was her friend. Doug stopped walking. Melanie also had blonde hair, blue eyes, and a slender but nicely curved body, just like Cassie. Edward was reaching for the doorknob when Doug put a hand on his shoulder to stop him. Melanie Ford also had a younger sister.

When Edward turned around to look at him, Doug said nonchalantly, "I thought Melanie's sister wasn't getting in till tomorrow morning."

The remark had its intended effect. Taken by surprise, Edward reddened and dropped his hand. By the time he reached for the door again, both of them knew it was too late.

"So tell me about it," Doug said.

Edward gave a sheepish shrug. "She, uh, she got in early, Doug."

"Obviously."

Edward walked back into the living room and sat down. Stalling, he asked for a cold drink, and Doug went off to the kitchen. By the time Doug came back with some sodas, Edward had decided that there was no point refusing to talk, not when Doug had worked things out on his own already. He pointed to the sodas, teasing, "Had your fill of beer?"

Doug tossed him a can and sat down. "You could say that."

"Are you blaming the beer for the state you were in when I arrived?" Edward asked as he opened the can.

"Beer had nothing to do with it—well, almost nothing. She had me so turned on I couldn't have told you what day it was, what city I was in, or who the Padres played tonight." It was an exaggeration, but not much of one. "To be honest, I would have gone along with anything short of leather whips. So?"

Edward talked. He told Doug about Lynn, the actress-turned-call-girl, and about Cassie's decision to pinch-hit. He speculated that Horace must have initially assumed that "Vonda" had come because Lynn couldn't make it, and lost interest as soon as he realized that the joke wasn't going to go as planned. And he explained about the conversation that he and Cassie had had in the hall. "She asked me not to tell you who she was, but I didn't know what she planned to do. I mean, if I'd known she was going to tie you up in knots—" Edward grinned "—both literally and figuratively, come to think of it . . ."

"You would have done precisely nothing." Doug failed to see the humor in the situation. Edward's explanation had been sketchy, but he could fill in all the necessary blanks. "What you're saying is that Melanie doesn't like me and neither does her sister. They think I'm a heel for daring to suggest that you and Melanie should know each other a little better before you get married. Since Cassie was coming here anyway, they decided she should have a little extra fun at my expense."

"Well, yes and no." Edward paused, trying to remember Cassie's exact words. "Cassie and Melanie are very close, but I think Cassie understands your point of view about the marriage. Like me, she just doesn't happen to agree with it. Still, the person who hired Lynn was their primary target, not you. My guess is that you were a spur-of-the-moment addition. Cassie likes to be outrageous. She enjoys practical jokes. She told me you'd insulted Melanie and that you were playing some kind of game with her, but she also mentioned how well you kiss—a fascinating piece of information, by the way—and the fact that you can make her laugh. All in all, you should be flattered, Doug."

"To be turned on, tied up, and walked out on?" Doug shook his head. He generally tried to steer clear of people like Cassie and had never played a practical joke in his life. On the contrary, he believed in being polite to strangers, honest in business, and loyal to one's friends and family. In his opinion, conducting one's life with a little grace and dignity didn't automatically make one priggish or stiff.

That being the case, he was surprised to realize that he suddenly didn't care *what* the lady had done. So she liked the way he kissed. So she thought he had a good sense of humor. He wanted to know more about her.

Taking a drink of soda, he remarked, "She had quite a line, Edward. She claimed she had a Japanese friend who'd taught her everything there is to know about driving a guy crazy in bed. I didn't really believe it—until she got out the amaretto and started to prove it. Where in hell did she learn that stuff?"

Edward laughed. "I don't know, but I hope she teaches it to Melanie. Seriously, though, if I had to guess, I'd say it has something to do with the book she just finished. It's a study of San Francisco's top-of-the-line call girls. If you're interested in seeing it, I'll get you Melanie's copy of the manuscript."

"She's a writer?"

"Right. She uses the name Catherine Ford, or sometimes just C. R. Ford, for Catherine Ruth. Melanie calls her the female George Plimpton because she researches some of her articles by actually doing things, like umpiring minor-league baseball games or working on a freighter or touring with a rock band. . . ."

"Or being a call girl?" Doug asked pointedly.

"No way. Not Cassie."

Doug was about to ask Edward what made him so sure, but then he remembered why Cassie was in San Diego: to be Melanie's *matron* of honor. "Her husband would object," he said.

"Not unless you believe in contact with the great beyond, Doug. He died three years ago."

Weary of extracting information from Edward bit by tedious bit, Doug said, "Why don't you just tell me whatever you know about the lady. I'm intrigued. I admit it. Okay?"

Edward and Doug had always been straight with each other, but not to the point of violating anybody else's privacy. "I can give you the broad outlines," Edward said, "but anything more would have to come from Cassie herself. It's just too personal."

"Understood." Doug's curiosity shot up another few notches. "I don't expect the story of her life, just a little background."

Edward settled back on the couch and crossed his legs. "I don't have a problem with giving you the family history, Doug, as long as you keep in mind the fact that Cassie is a very nice person and my future sister-in-law. She's obviously very attracted to you. I don't want to see her hurt."

Doug paid very little attention to this speech. Edward was inclined to be protective of the women in his life, even of Melanie Ford, who surely didn't need it. In any event, Doug wasn't out to hurt anyone. He was always completely honest when it came to love affairs, letting a woman know where he stood long before he ever suggested going to bed. "I'll keep it in mind," he agreed. "Go on."

Apparently satisfied, Edward told Doug that Louis Ford had taken off when Melanie was six and Cassie four. Then he continued, "Nobody knows why or where he went—he just walked out of the house one morning and never came back. Melanie and Cassie grew up in Susanville with their mother, Jessica, who was a schoolteacher and amateur actress. Eleven years later a lawyer called them from Cheyenne, Wyoming, to say that Louis had died. There was a small estate, a couple of thousand dollars, but Jessica was sick with cancer at the time and the money went for medical bills. She died a year later. Melanie had just turned eighteen and was finishing up high school, but Cassie was only a junior. Jessica had no close relatives, so she'd named her college roommate as Cassie's guardian. Her name is Jane Valkenberg. She's married to Warren Valkenberg."

"The San Francisco attorney?" Doug recognized the name because it was in the papers so often.

"Right. The Valkenbergs had one child, a son named John, who was a college student in Denver at the time. He and Cassie had met every now and then, but when he came home that summer and each of them took a look at how the other had turned out, it was love at first sight. They were married the following summer, after Cassie finished high school, with the Valkenbergs' blessing and financial support. She wasn't even eighteen at the time. Their daughter was born exactly nine and a half months later. They named her Jessica, after Cassie and Melanie's mother. She's the same age as Lisa."

"And Cassie's husband? How did he die?"

"In a mining accident. He was taking some geological samples in an area being strip-mined when a narrow section of roadway directly above him started to cave in. There was a Cat up there, and when the road started to give, the driver lost control of the Cat and went right off the side onto John. Neither of the two men stood a chance. Valkenberg sued on behalf of Cassie and Jessica and negotiated a multimillion-dollar out-of-court settlement. Cassie had finished college by then and had published about half a dozen articles. Obviously she has no financial need to work, but she enjoys it and she's good at it. I've read her book and it's excellent."

Doug had a hard time thinking of Cassie Valkenberg as filthy rich, well connected, and a serious writer. She was more the wacky-dilettante type, who lived from hand to mouth and would do anything for a clever story . . . or a clever practical joke. "And since then? I've run across a lot of guys who wouldn't mind getting serious about a beautiful widow with a few million in the bank."

"That's one of the areas you'll have to ask Cassie about, Doug. I don't think she'd want me to talk about anything so personal."

Doug interpreted that as meaning that the lady's past included a few lovers. He would have kept his distance from a professional-widow type, but Cassie Valkenberg hardly fit *that* description. "Is that all I'm going to get out of you?" he asked Edward.

"About Cassie, yes. I've already said more than I should have."

Doug accepted Edward's statement without a murmur of protest. He was beginning to regret inviting Tawny to the wedding. Because before the weekend was over, he intended to get Cassie back into bed. And this time he wasn't going to be the one who wound up half-naked and tied to the headboard.

Chapter Six

Cassie knew prewedding jitters when she saw them, and Edward Kolby had a classic case. She ordered him a margarita that he finished during lunch, but it really didn't help. More often than not, he allowed the conversation to flow around him without taking part in it. He seemed to be a hundred miles away.

She would have liked to get him alone to offer some reassurance, but the Valkenbergs and Jessica were sitting at the table and would be spending the rest of the afternoon with them. Cassie and Edward had met them late that morning at the airport, then taken them out to eat at a Mexican restaurant in Old Town.

Technically speaking, of course, Warren and Jane Valkenberg had no claim on Edward Kolby, because Melanie had never actually been their legal ward. But the legalities had little to do with the reality of the situation. For all intents and purposes, Melanie was just as much of a daughter to the Valkenbergs as Cassie was, and they looked Edward over just as any set of concerned parents would have done, especially when their daughter had already made two mistakes. Cassie wasn't sure whether being inspected made Edward even more nervous than the thought of his wedding did, but she figured she'd been lucky to escape this kind of meeting in her own life. There was a lot to be said for marrying the son of the guardians you adored.

They were just finishing their coffee when Jessica started talking about going shopping, a relatively new interest of hers. Cassie had noticed a large plaza about a block away, its surrounding streets closed to traffic. Dozens of craftspeople sold jewelry, pottery and clothing there, and it was obvious that Jessica couldn't wait to explore it. Wanting to be tactful, Cassie shot her mother-in-law a meaningful look and said to Jessica, "Give us five more minutes, honey. I ate so much I can hardly move."

Jane picked up on the cue immediately, but being Jane, she didn't waste her breath on subtlety. "Grandpa and I will take you," she said to Jessica, and took her by the hand. "You'll get a lot more loot out of us than you would out of your mother, especially when all she can think about is talking to your uncle Edward." She looked at Cassie and Edward. "Meet us in about forty-five minutes in front of the Visitors' Center. And in the meantime, Cassie, buy the poor man another margarita and try to settle him down."

Reddening slightly, Edward asked, "Do I really look that nervous?"

"It's all right, Edward," Jane said. "Bridegrooms are supposed to be nervous. But you and Melanie are going to be very happy together. You're exactly what she needs, and as for Melanie, there's nothing she won't do for the people she loves. Just ask Cassie about it."

The waitress came over to see if they wanted anything else to eat just as the Valkenbergs were leading Jessica away from the table. Edward asked for more coffee rather than another drink, telling Cassie, "I have to admit that I'm relieved lunch is over with. For some reason, I kept waiting for Valkenberg to cross-examine me. He was too damn quiet for my peace of mind."

"He always is. He's only fierce in a courtroom," Cassie answered as the waitress went off for the coffeepot. "Jane is the one you have to watch out for, but you made a big hit with her so you can relax now. But what about the marriage? Are you having second thoughts?"

"Maybe about the big wedding, but never about Melanie. You know how much I love her." He paused. "To be honest, I've been thinking about last night. I never should have let you out of my sight. I can't believe what you did to Doug. Talk about living dangerously. . . ."

"I thought I'd *never* get you alone to ask about it," Cassie said with a smile. She was glad to know that there was nothing more serious on Edward's mind. "Are you afraid that when the mayor comes to the part about anyone knowing a good reason why the marriage shouldn't take place, Doug will jump between you and Melanie, wave his arms back and forth, and say, 'Yes, insanity runs in the bride's family?' "

"Not exactly. Maybe I should have said that I've been thinking about *you*. First of all, you're going to have to do without the pleasure of seeing Doug reel with shock tonight. He figured out who you were and bluffed me into admitting it."

Cassie dismissed this piece of information with a casual wave of her hand, then held out her empty coffee cup for the waitress to fill up. The truth was, she'd expected Edward to tell Doug who she was. Men stuck together. "Not only is he successful, rich and sexy, but he's smart, too. Talk about having it all!"

"You're not annoyed with me?"

"Of course not. Why would I be annoyed?"

"Let's put it this way. I once tried to talk Melanie out of taking part in a publicity stunt and nearly got my head snapped off for my troubles. I've learned that it's dangerous to come between the Ford sisters and their sense of humor."

Cassie took a sip of her coffee. "Melanie's the one with the temper, not me," she said blithely. "You're completely forgiven, Edward. So tell me, is Doug ready to kill me?"

"Maybe he was at first, when I stood at the foot of his bed and couldn't stop laughing, but not anymore." Edward explained that Doug's annoyance had quickly given way to curiosity and that he himself had satisfied some of that curiosity by sketching out the basics of Cassie's life. He concluded with a sober warning: "Doug has a passion for finishing what he starts, Cassie. You'd better be prepared for it."

Pretending to be scandalized, Cassie gasped, "In the middle of a formal wedding reception, Edward?"

"Not unless he's roaring drunk. But don't forget, he does a fair amount of traveling. You might find him kicking down your door someday."

Cassie winked and in her best "Vonda" voice drawled, "Well, I certainly hope so, honey."

Edward didn't answer right away. Cassie had expected a laugh or at least a smile, but all she got was a distracted frown. Finally, in a voice meant to tease, he accused her of having another prank up her sleeve, but Cassie wasn't fooled by his casual tone. The man was worried that she was going to get hurt. It was written all over his face.

She was careful to keep her answer light. "I wish I did, but I'm fresh out of good ideas. Actually, I've been thinking that I might like to know Doug better."

Edward's frown got a little deeper. "Are you telling me you're serious about him?"

"No, not at this point, but I think I could be. Why?"

Edward stared across the table at her, so grim by now that Cassie flushed in reaction. "I should have spelled it out more clearly last night. Doug isn't quite rational when it comes to women. His response to Melanie is only one example of it. His childhood was like a sail on quicksand, so when he married, he chose somebody who was everything his mother wasn't: conventional, proper, socially acceptable, conservative, safe. . . . Are you getting the general drift, Cassie?"

Edward wasn't telling her anything she hadn't already suspected, so it made no difference in her attitude. She'd always been something of a professional optimist. It was the only way she'd been able to survive a series of traumatic tragedies. "People change," she remarked. "What you want at twenty and what you want at thirty or thirty-five are often very different."

Edward shook his head. "Not for Doug. He and Buffy had a very happy marriage. He was devastated when she died."

"Melanie told me about it." Buffy Hunter had been murdered during an early morning horseback ride, the victim of a parole violator whom she'd caught breaking into the grounds of a nearby estate. "It was a horrible, senseless thing, Edward. I know that, and I of all people can understand a little of what Doug must have felt. But you have to move on. You can't recreate the past."

"I don't think Doug would agree with you. If he marries again, it will be to somebody exactly like Buffy."

"You mean no outside job, the perfect wife and mother, active in all the right causes . . ."

"No. I mean exactly what I said before: conventional, proper and conservative." Edward sighed and picked up his coffee. Cassie could see how concerned he was and thought to herself that Melanie was lucky to have someone so sweet; but he was a little *too* sweet, at least as far as *she* was concerned. She didn't want to be protected.

"Doug isn't a male chauvinist," he went on. "Buffy started law school when Lisa was five, with his complete support. She was two months short of graduation when she died, and she'd already lined up a job with a prestigious old-line firm. Some of her clients might have made headlines, but Buffy never would have. There would have been no Warren Valkenberg-style flamboyance, I can guarantee it." He drank down some coffee. "Or look at Tawny Timberlake. She's taking a one-year medical residency, but then she's going to switch to dermatology and eventually join her father's practice. Dr. Foster Timberlake treats the most elite warts, pimples and suspicious growths in San Diego County. Tawny cares about being a good doctor, but she also wants regular hours, good money, no emergencies and plenty of time for her horses and charities. She's literally the girl next door, the one Doug has known most of his life, and that makes her predictable and safe. Now tell me what you have in common with women like that."

"Brains?" Cassie suggested.

"All right, what else?"

"Well, I helped raise money for the opera last year. And my in-laws are certainly socially acceptable." Cassie wouldn't have been half as successful a journalist as she was if she'd given up at the first sign of an obstacle. But persistence wasn't the same as recklessness. She understood Edward's warning.

Falling back on humor, she continued, "I suppose I could always learn to ride a horse if it's really part of the job description, but graduate school is absolutely out."

Edward didn't even crack a smile. "Stop making jokes and take a good look at yourself, Cassie. That book tour you're doing—Melanie says that your publisher is arranging an all-out media assault. I can see it now—you and three call girls on the Phil Donahue show, lobbying for legalized prostitution. A hot topic, an interesting idea, and you're off and running, even if it means going on tour with a drug-crazed rock band. You don't keep a low profile. You throw yourself into things with a passion. Doug finds you interesting, even intriguing, and I'd lay odds that he'd love to have an affair with you, but you aren't his idea of wife material. Unless your only interest is a session in bed every now and then, you'd better forget him."

Cassie listened and understood, and her first thought was what women have been thinking for hundreds of years: *I can bend a little. I can change for him, if he needs me to.* It didn't take long for the reaction to set in. She wasn't about to confine herself to writing about the local ladies' chamber-music society. She liked to travel. It was a challenge to seek out the bizarre, the shocking, the amusing, the obscure. She would have jumped at the chance to go on the Donahue show with a couple of her San Francisco sources.

"Doug can't be as straight as all that," she finally answered. "He went along with my Vonda routine, he enjoyed making a game of it, and he's still interested in me. . . ."

"I said he was straight, not fossilized. He isn't morally opposed to having a good time. But wanting an affair and proposing marriage are two different things." Edward grimaced. "Remember, he spent the first fourteen years of his life with Valerie Hunter in her heyday. He loves his mother, but she inflicted a lot of scars."

Cassie knew almost nothing about it. She'd still been in grade school when Valerie Hunter had retired to marry Horace Miesley. "Was Valerie really that notorious?"

"In show-business circles, yes. You may even get the inside story someday if she ever finds a collaborator she can work with. She's gone through three of them already."

It sounded like a fascinating project, so much so that Cassie would have happily offered herself up as victim number four. She wasn't about to tell Edward that, though. It was obvious he'd listened to too many of

Melanie's stories about Cassie's tragic past, probably complete with sand and sputtering fires.

It wasn't hard to picture him going to Doug, having one of those man-to-man talks that seemed to be part of their relationship, and convincing him that Cassie was much too fragile to survive an affair. She sensed that Doug was a very decent man—it was one of the things that had attracted her to him—and decent men didn't deliberately hurt people.

With the best of intentions, both Melanie and Edward were trying to live Cassie's life for her, and she wasn't about to let them do it. If there were risks involved, *she* would decide whether or not to take them. As much as she disliked lying, it seemed like the only alternative.

"Poor Doug," she said, and pushed away her coffee cup. "Scratched off my list without ever finding out he was right up there at the top of it. Are you ready to leave?"

Edward was more than ready. It hadn't been a comfortable conversation for him. He couldn't shake the feeling that he'd stuck his nose where it didn't belong, but he loved Melanie too much to do otherwise. He didn't want to think about how she would feel if Doug hurt her beloved sister.

He settled the bill and walked Cassie over to the plaza. Jessica and her grandparents were at a jewelry stall, examining gold necklaces. After looking through the rest of the stalls and stopping into a couple of restored buildings, they drove up to La Jolla, where Edward showed them around the Scripps Institution.

Originally a small, privately financed research station with only a single ship and a handful of scientists, Scripps was now a graduate school of the University of California at San Diego. Its once-modest physical plant had sprawled to include numerous buildings on both sides of La Jolla Shores Drive. Along with the buildings it also had half a dozen research vessels, twelve hundred students and staff members, and an international reputation. Cassie could see that Edward loved his work almost as much as he loved Melanie, and she considered that a very good thing. It was all well and good to say that marriage and a family should come first, but she'd learned that they weren't always enough.

After a drive around the campus, Edward took them to the institution's small aquarium, which was open to the general public. The building also contained a bookstore and a small museum. On the way into the aquarium they passed a box for donations, and it reminded Cassie of the three hundred dollars she had in her purse. Leaving Jessica and her in-laws to study the fish, she took Edward by the arm and led him to the checkout counter. The clerk, who seemed to be a student, was taking some money from a girl about Jessica's age. She'd picked out a picture book from the bookstore and some rings made out of shells.

As soon as the clerk had given the girl her change, Cassie said, "I'd like to make a donation."

He pointed to the box. "You can put it in there, ma'am."

Cassie took out her wallet and removed the fifteen twenty-dollar bills. Fanning them out like a deck of cards, she said, "I have three hundred dollars here. Can you give me a receipt?"

The clerk, momentarily at a loss for words, stared at the money. Edward, meanwhile, had started to smile. "Why don't you let me take care of that?" he said, and reached for the money.

Laughing, Cassie yanked the bills behind her back before he could get his hands on them. "Not so fast. This money represents the wages of sin, Dr. Kolby, and I have to be sure it will go to a worthy cause. Promise me you won't return it to Doug."

Edward assured her that the possibility had never even crossed his mind. "Doug is a faithful contributor to Scripps, Cassie. He'll be delighted to learn he's tossed a few more bucks into the pot.''

Cassie affected great disappointment as she handed the money over. "What a shame to pick a cause he approves of! I should have donated it to COYOTE." COYOTE was a prostitutes' rights organization based in San Francisco. The word, an acronym, stood for "Call Off Your Old, Tired Ethics."

Judging by the way Edward smiled and shook his head, he'd obviously heard of the group. He folded the stack of bills in half and shoved it into his back pocket, saying that Scripps was the better cause. Cassie didn't argue. Instead, pointing into the bookstore, she gave him a vampish look and invited him to meet her between the shelves and show her his publications.

Being a bridesmaid was old hat to Cassie Valkenberg. After all, she'd done it twice before for her sister alone. But never, she thought as she dressed for the ceremony, with more enthusiasm and pleasure.

Melanie's wedding was being held at the Miesley Plaza, in a charming garden that overlooked San Diego Bay. The ceremony was scheduled for six-thirty, when there would still be plenty of sunlight for pictures. The reception, which was private, was being held in a second-floor ballroom. And if Melanie hadn't been so stubborn, it wouldn't have cost her a penny.

Horace Miesley had offered to foot the bill as a gift to the groom, who was, of course, an old and dear friend of the family, but Melanie had flatly refused. The man rubbed her the wrong way and that was that. She'd brushed aside Edward's concern that offending Miesley could cost Scripps money by saying that the man wouldn't dare risk the negative publicity, and she was right. Miesley could be a cheap, cantankerous son of a bitch in private, but in public he was Mr. San Diego. His company was responsible for a whole array of stunning, innovative projects; he'd given millions to

charity over the years; and he'd brought the city a
victory in the World Series. Politicians and cultural
leaders quaked in their boots at the thought of uttering
a single negative word about him, at least in public, and
Miesley, in turn, relished his image as a philanthropist.
The last person he would have taken on was a nationally known actress whom reporters loved to quote. In the
end he'd suggested donating the money he would have
spent on the wedding to Scripps, and everyone had
wound up happy.

Unlike those Hollywood brides who showed up for
second, third or even fourth weddings in ankle-length
gowns of virginal white, Melanie Ford went by the book
when it came to getting remarried. Her ivory-colored
silk dinner suit was so conservative that one never
would have guessed it came from California's glitziest
show-biz designer. Cassie was wearing a dress by the
same man. It was a sleeveless sheath with a matching
fitted jacket to wear during the ceremony. The ice blue
shade of the dress and the sleek French knot in her hair
made her look as cool and perfect as a Hitchcock
heroine.

The rehearsal was scheduled for forty-five minutes
before the ceremony. None of the guests had arrived
yet when Cassie and Melanie walked outside, but there
were several dozen curious onlookers watching from
beyond the roped-off lawn and garden. A number of
hotel security men were standing guard in front of the
crowd. Folding chairs had been placed in neat rows on
the lawn, creating a rather narrow aisle that led to a
canopied area directly in front of the garden. San Diego
Bay was beyond. Doug and Edward were huddled
under the canopy with the mayor, while a florist
positioned baskets of flowers along the aisle. The string
quartet Edward had hired was setting up its music
stands to the right of the canopy.

Melanie smiled and waved to the applauding crowd
as she walked down the patio steps toward the lawn. A

pair of teenaged girls called out the name of her soap-opera character and tried to dash around the security men to get an autograph, but they were quickly stopped. The commotion attracted the attention of the huddled men. Edward smiled, the mayor waved, and Doug simply stared.

Although Edward and Melanie had spoken several times on the phone, they hadn't actually seen each other since Tuesday. In a scene straight out of the most schmaltzy sort of Hollywood love story, they broke into a run simultaneously, flinging themselves into each other's arms when they met. Edward gave Melanie a careful kiss, trying not to mess up her hair and makeup, but Melanie couldn't have cared less about those things.

Taking Edward's face in her hands, she said, "I missed you like crazy. Can't you do any better?"

Edward mumbled something about an audience, gave her a helpless look, and started to kiss her in earnest. The crowd went wild, clapping and yelling its encouragement. The two lovers finally came up for air just as Cassie and Doug caught up with them, approaching from opposite directions.

Melanie put her arm around Edward's waist and looked from the matron of honor to the best man, her smile getting wider and wider. "I believe you two have met," she drawled.

Cassie would have made a joke about being old and intimate friends, but Doug's expression stopped her cold. He wasn't outwardly hostile or disapproving, just stiffly correct. The polite smile, the military bearing, the fact that he was standing just a little too far away, as though he wasn't really part of the group—if Edward hadn't told her otherwise, she would have assumed he was smarting from Friday night but was too well-mannered to show it.

He took the hand Cassie had tentatively started to extend and coolly shook it, dropping it almost at once.

"Mrs. Valkenberg," he murmured, giving her a nod of recognition. Then he turned to Melanie, who got a respectful peck on the cheek. "You look beautiful, Melanie, as always. How did it go on the set today?"

Cassie had asked that same question earlier, receiving an answer that was sidesplittingly detailed. The action had revolved around Melanie's underwater encounter with a mechanical sea creature that had continually refused to do what it was supposed to, necessitating take after waterlogged take. Somehow Melanie had kept her sense of humor until the shot was in the can, but she swore she'd wound up as wrinkled as a prune.

Knowing Melanie, Cassie expected at least a shortened version of this tale, but all her sister said was, "We had a technical problem or two, but we're almost back on schedule."

"Edward mentioned that you have some complicated special effects in the movie," Doug remarked.

"That's true. We do. And they don't always work the way they're supposed to."

"I see." Doug looked at his watch. "Let's go ahead and begin. I'll make sure the musicians are ready." He turned around and started back toward the canopy.

"What's with *him?*" Cassie hissed at Edward as soon as Doug was out of earshot.

Melanie looked puzzled. "What do you mean, Cassie? He's always like that. So polite that you just know you've bored him senseless."

"Not with me, he isn't. Is he angry with me, Edward? Should I go over and apologize?"

"Of course not. There's no problem." Edward paused to look up toward the patio. His brother Tom had just arrived along with his wife and family. He motioned them over and continued, "I thought you understood that you can't judge Doug by what happened last night. He's usually a lot more reserved." He smiled at Melanie. "Reserved, darling, not bored senseless, so stop taking it so personally."

"One standard of behavior for call girls and another for everyone else?" Cassie asked archly.

"Could be. My brother just got a better look at you, Cassie. If he doesn't recover soon, I may be short one usher. Come on over—I'll introduce you."

Edward wiped the smile off his face and limited himself to a straight exchange of names, but Tom Kolby knew he'd been had. He didn't seem to mind, but laughed and asked Cassie if she was an actress like her sister. They stood and made small talk for another minute or so, until Edward had reached the canopy and the quartet had started to play.

The rehearsal was over within ten minutes. The mayor, mindful of the growing crowd of spectators, ran through the ceremony as quickly as he could so that Melanie could get back inside. Afterward he went over to shake some hands. He was up for reelection in November and never missed a chance to campaign.

As the bridal party walked back up the aisle, Doug put a hand on Edward's shoulder and said, "I can't let you go between now and the reception without a glass of champagne and something to eat. Why don't the four of us wait upstairs?"

"Upstairs" meant the revolving restaurant on the top floor, but they only escaped the garden after Melanie had signed about a dozen autographs. Cassie realized that Doug's suggestion had been something other than spontaneous when the maître d' hurried over to them. "We're all ready for you, Mr. Hunter," he said, and led them to a windowside table. It was already set for four, with champagne glasses and salad plates, and there was a bottle of wine chilling in the ice bucket that was standing nearby. Edward and Melanie sat down next to each other, holding hands, with Doug and Cassie across from them.

A waitress appeared almost at once with a platter of imported cheeses and fresh fruits. Cassie was a little surprised when the woman pulled the wine out of the ice bucket, because the label was in English rather than French. Dom Pérignon was the conventional choice for occasions like this, and Doug Hunter was nothing if not conventional.

When the waitress was finished pouring, Edward took the bottle out of her hand to study the label. "Horace was right about the graphics," he said to Doug. "The print design he wanted *is* better with the woodcut. But I thought this wasn't coming on the market till fall."

"Horace had a couple of dozen cases shipped down for the wedding. I thought I'd give you a chance to taste it before we serve it." He explained to Cassie and Melanie that the wine was the result of a joint venture between a Napa Valley winery owned by Horace Miesley and a well-known French vintner who'd decided to expand into California. Then, raising his glass, he said, "To Edward and Melanie. May you have a long and happy marriage."

Cassie smiled at Melanie. "May I add 'fruitful' to that, Doug?" Her sister was already talking about having a child. It was something she'd wanted for years.

Cassie didn't miss Doug's quickly squelched surprise, or the silent question he immediately directed to Edward, or the way Edward forced back a smile and subtly shook his head. The whole exchange was so utterly and ridiculously civilized that Cassie burst out laughing. "Have you forgotten your basic biology?" she asked Doug.

"I'm sorry," he answered. "That was unforgivable. . . ."

"It was funny, not unforgivable." Cassie only hoped a little champagne would loosen the man up. "Melanie and Edward have only known each other for six weeks, and it took her at least half that long to storm his defenses and hopelessly compromise him. Even if she *were* pregnant, she would hardly have had time to find it out."

Melanie pretended to be outraged. "Compromise him? I did no such thing, Catherine. I merely encouraged him a little. Now you, on the other hand . . . well, all I can say is, I think your actions were perfectly shocking!" She gave Doug a sympathetic look and teased, "Poor Douglas! Do you have nylon burns on your wrists?"

"They were gone by this morning. The only permanent damage was to my ego." It was a smooth answer, and not without a certain dry charm, but Doug's manner was as reserved as ever. "To get back to the matter at hand . . ." He raised his glass a little higher. "Edward, Melanie—here's to you and your family. Your future family, that is." He gave Cassie a polite smile. "Was there anything else you wanted to add, Mrs. Valkenberg, or have we covered the bases adequately now?"

"If I don't get something to drink soon, I'm going to die of thirst!" Cassie laughed and clinked her glass against Melanie's. "Here's to love and marriage and babies. Cheers, everyone!"

If the toast was a taste test, the champagne passed with flying colors. They talked about wine for a while, and then Doug asked Edward how his future relatives were enjoying San Diego. When Edward mentioned that they were staying until Sunday night, Doug proceeded to suggest half a dozen places that Jessica might like to visit.

Every few minutes he checked his watch, as though the time was of far more importance than the company. Finally, when everyone had had a glass of champagne and something to eat, he announced it was time to go downstairs. Cassie had found it an awkward twenty-five minutes and was glad it was over. To make matters worse, every now and then they'd been interrupted by one of Melanie's fans, and each time it happened Doug got even stiffer and the atmosphere got more stilted. Cassie was tense and restless by the time they left the table.

She and Melanie got off the elevator on the twelfth floor, while the men continued downstairs. As they made their way to Melanie's room to freshen up, Cassie grumbled, "I've had my fill of hearing about San Diego tourist attractions. And if Doug calls me Mrs. Valkenberg one more time . . . I swear to God, Melanie, I'm tempted to lure the man into an empty hallway and make violent love to him, just to see if he'll pant, 'I can't take any more of this! Let's get out of here, Mrs. Valkenberg!' He was so stuffy and uptight I felt like pouring my champagne over his head."

"I suppose I have that effect on him. I think he says and does the right thing because anything less would hurt Edward's feelings, but his heart really isn't in it. He doesn't respond to joking and teasing. Maybe now you can understand why I was so surprised about last night. I can't picture Doug losing control of himself— not in bed, not in a business setting, not anywhere."

Cassie didn't argue the point. She was beginning to think that Doug's behavior the night before had been an anomaly caused by too much beer and a bachelor-party atmosphere. The next hour or so gave her no reason to change her mind. Everything went off beautifully, largely because Doug made sure that it did. When Melanie decided she wanted the string quartet on the patio during the cocktails and hors d'oeuvres, Doug got them moved. When photographers from the media began to get on Edward's nerves, Doug got rid of them. When people were needed for family pictures, he found them and got them over to the garden, and when a group of teenaged hotel guests circumvented the security men and descended onto the patio to collect autographs from Melanie and her Hollywood cronies, he negotiated a one-to-a-customer settlement and sent them on their way. Melanie noticed and was grateful, but Cassie had the feeling her sister would have traded it all for a smile with some genuine warmth behind it.

Regardless of Doug's reserve, Cassie had no reason to think he was unreasonable. She told herself that he simply lacked the facts about Melanie and that she could change his mind if she could only get him alone. She decided to wait till he was a little less busy, and then set about the business of enjoying herself.

She was one of those people who almost always have a good time at parties, perhaps because she started with the premise that almost everyone had something to offer. An excellent listener, she had a knack for drawing the best out of people. More than one acquaintance had been amazed when, months later, Cassie had phoned for information based on a passing conversation. Her memory was like a filing cabinet.

Early in the cocktail hour she walked up to Tom Kolby and, with an insider's wink, asked him for reintroductions to everyone she'd met the night before. She had a picnic watching their reactions, which ranged from acute embarrassment to good-natured laughter. The one who surprised her most, however, was Horace Miesley.

If he minded Cassie's little act of sabotage, it certainly didn't show. He took her off to a quiet corner of the patio and delivered a rueful speech about how his "little joke" had backfired and how he hoped that Cassie's "delightful sister" hadn't taken it seriously, because Edward Kolby was "almost like a son" to him and Valerie. Cassie didn't believe a word he said—she couldn't forget the cat-who-swallowed-the-canary look on his face when "Vonda" had first strolled in—but she had to admit he was convincing.

He was also charming. He asked her about the hotel—what she liked, what should be improved—and then drew her out about her work. He had the knack of looking at you as though nothing could be more important than what you were saying, and since he was extremely handsome in a distinguished-older-man kind of way, it was flattering.

Cassie was intrigued. Power was always more interesting when it was wielded by complicated people. Men like Miesley, who were so totally different in reality from the way they appeared on the surface, made wonderful biographical subjects. If Valerie Hunter decided to tell the truth about Miesley and her marriage to him, her book would make compelling reading.

The predinner cocktail hour had gone on exactly long enough when Doug started shepherding people upstairs to the ballroom. Cassie was seated at a table with her in-laws and a group of their closest friends, people she'd first met within weeks of her mother's death. One of the women teasingly told Jane Valkenberg that she always loved coming to Melanie's weddings because she had such a good time at them, prompting Cassie to smile and reply that this would definitely be the last of them. "Edward is Mr. Right," she insisted. "You'll see, Mary."

"And what about you, Cassie? Don't you think it's about time you put aside the past—" Turning beet red, the woman cut herself off. "I'm terribly sorry, Jane. I've had too much champagne."

"Don't be silly. Warren and I couldn't agree more. John is gone now, and nothing can bring him back. We want Cassie to be happy. And don't forget, we'll always have Jessica." Jane looked around the ballroom. "Speaking of Jessie . . ."

Cassie pointed across the room. "She's over there at table four. She and Lisa Hunter made friends during the cocktail hour and disappeared with a bunch of Edward's nieces and nephews. Lisa seems to be the local Eloise. Everybody at the hotel knows she's the boss's daughter, so they do their best to spoil her rotten. Jessica is reaping the benefits. Do you think it's possible to overdose on Shirley Temples?"

Jane laughed and said something about sugar shock but was interrupted by a burst of applause. A small orchestra had replaced the quartet, and it swung into the theme from *Flashdance* as Edward and Melanie walked in. They were surrounded by a group of friends, including Doug Hunter and a striking redhead who was clutching his arm and laughing up at him. Watching her, the first adjective that popped into Cassie's mind was "doll-like." Even in spike heels, the top of her head was only about an inch above Doug's shoulder. Her build was reed thin, but nobody would have mistaken her for a boy. Her green silk dress was too feminine, her hair was too long and sultry, and her face was nothing short of stunning. She reminded Cassie of an antebellum plantation belle, the type who sat and sipped lemonade on the veranda while suitors fluttered around like lovesick butterflies. Appearances were obviously deceiving, though, because you didn't make it through medical school without brains, stamina and determination. Cassie wondered why Doug *wasn't* in love with her. She seemed to have everything.

Chapter Seven

$\mathscr{I}$t was very bad form to think about one woman while dancing with another. Doug Hunter knew that. It was even worse form to listen to what she was saying with only half an ear, all the while hoping that her beeper would go off. Doug was hard-pressed to sound empathetic when Tawny apologized for the third time for the last-minute switch in schedule that had left her on duty all weekend and fretted that the resident pinch-hitting for her that evening really didn't know the patients well enough. The fact was, Doug had plans for the next twenty-four hours, and they didn't happen to include Tawny Timberlake.

When he noticed Horace dancing with his mother, he steered Tawny in their general direction and engineered a change in partners. He wanted to talk to Valerie privately, and besides, Tawny was one of the few people he knew to whom Horace was unfailingly charming. Doug was at a loss to explain this, except that Horace was something of a hypochondriac who saw cancer in every mole. Because of that, he made regular visits to Dr. Foster Timberlake, who'd never found a single thing wrong with him aside from the angina that was a perennial problem. Horace was always reasonably courteous to people he needed, and Tawny was of course Foster's future partner.

Doug didn't waste time on small talk once he'd palmed Tawny off on Horace, but danced his mother to a less congested part of the floor and asked, "Have you met the bride's sister?"

"The cool, elegant blonde who moonlights as a call girl?" Seeing Doug's surprise, Valerie went on, "Horace told me all about it. Hoist with his own petard, but he was really quite amused about it, dear. I thought, Good for Edward! He's finally gotten the better of the bastard! In any event, he introduced me to Cassie out on the patio, but we didn't get a chance to do very much more than shake hands."

"She's a journalist," Doug said.

Valerie knew her son well enough to realize that an observation like that was neither casual nor coincidental. "Is she really?" she murmured.

"Yes. And a good one, from what I hear. She's your kind of woman, Mother: unconventional and uninhibited. Maybe you should unshelve your autobiography . . ."

"Why, Douglas! What a perfectly amazing about-face!" Valerie stopped dancing and gave him a coy smile. "And when did you stop hating the whole idea of the book?"

Doug hadn't, and he figured his mother knew it. But he also figured that no collaborator in the world would ever satisfy her, including Cassie Valkenberg. Since there was no danger that she would ever summon up the discipline to sit down and write the damn thing herself, there was no possibility of its ever seeing the literary light of day.

He didn't say that, but remarked with a sigh, "I've

resigned myself to the fact that you'll do whatever you please, Mother. You always have. So why not work with someone who looks at life the same way you do? I thought you might want to ask Cassie to lunch tomorrow to talk the project over with her."

Valerie turned to the side and stared into the middle distance. Waving her arm like a magician about to conjure up a rabbit, she said, "Ah! A light begins to dawn! You want me to act as your procurer."

"Offer somebody a little friendly advice and what do you get in return? Nothing but slander." Doug took his mother's arm and started back to her table. "In other words, you're much too perceptive. Let's just say I have a score to settle with the lady and I'm trying to be creative about it."

Valerie patted his cheek. "How marvelous, dear. I always knew that somehow, someplace, sometime, a little of your mother's vitality would fight its way through that overly decorous hide of yours, and surface. Any lady who can make you act a little less like a dried-up English butler and a little more like a charming young rake has my undying admiration."

Valerie Hunter had been making comments of that sort for as long as Doug could remember. He didn't really mind them, except that Lisa was beginning to parrot her grandmother's lines. He didn't want to think about what his daughter would be like in a couple of years, when she attained that teenaged state of wisdom and enlightenment where parents become embarrassing, boring and utter fools.

"I trust you'll keep your undying admiration to yourself," he said, and helped Valerie into her seat. She answered that she wouldn't think of doing otherwise.

Doug spent the next half an hour doing what he'd done all evening: making sure things went smoothly. It wasn't so much that he considered it his duty as best man—although he did—as that he could never attend a function at one of the company's hotels without automatically checking on everything, from the amount of starch in the napkins to the cleanliness of the floors. The notes he made, both good and bad, would wind up in memos to the appropriate people.

In between eating and dancing he kept an eye on Cassie Valkenberg. That wasn't hard to do, since she seldom left the floor. She was a very good dancer, with a style that owed more to Michael Jackson than Arthur Murray and that contrasted sharply with her prim hairstyle and proper little dress. Since the orchestra was playing songs from the last few years' worth of Top 40 hits, she had plenty of opportunity to attract attention. Far from being embarrassed by that, she appeared to thoroughly enjoy it.

As the main course was being served, the orchestra swung into a stately waltz, and the leader called on the bride and groom to take the floor. Doug had been to enough of these affairs to know what came next: the best man danced with the matron of honor. He was already halfway to Cassie's table when their presence was requested on the dance floor. He held out his hand and murmured a polite, "Mrs. Valkenberg?" mostly because he'd realized that calling her by her last name drove her crazy. It amused him that anyone would react so negatively to a little polite formality.

She hadn't been in his arms for more than two seconds before she complained, "Do you have to keep calling me that?"

"I wasn't invited to call you anything else," he answered. It was hard not to smile. He was holding her at dancing-school distance, which was only proper given the circumstances, but *that* seemed to annoy her, too.

"After last night, I didn't think you would need an invitation," she said.

"A gentleman always waits for an invitation."

She gave an exasperated sigh. "Well, in that case, Doug, why don't you call me Cassie?"

"I'd be honored to," he agreed.

"And why don't you hold me a little closer?" She laughed. "I promise you, I don't have any infectious diseases."

When he drew her closer and swept her into the lilting rhythm of the waltz, she nestled into his arms and started humming along with the music, her body soft and pliant. He would have loved to take her to the nearest bedroom, but two things stopped him. First, you didn't duck out in the middle of your best friend's wedding. And second, he was here with another woman. Besides, the idea of waiting was erotic rather than frustrating. He had the feeling that between now and tomorrow, he would contemplate a dozen different ways of seducing her.

Cassie wasn't contemplating anything, least of all her own seduction. She was simply relaxing in Doug's arms, enjoying his warmth and strength, and allowing the music to carry her to an enchanted place, far away from anguish about sex and commitments and relationships. In fact, she was so bewitched by the feel and scent of Doug Hunter that she kept right on drifting even after the music stopped. It was an effort to fight her way back through the champagne-induced haze and remember that she had something she wanted to say.

When Doug put a hand against the small of her back to coax her over to her table, she dug in her heels and announced, "I need to talk to you. Let's take a walk."

"I really shouldn't leave," he answered. "I've been keeping an eye on things. . . ."

"Just five minutes, Doug. It's important."

Doug agreed, trying to forget that the key to the company suite was on the key chain in his trouser pocket. This was hardly the time or place. He suggested a very public spot, the ground-floor bar. It wasn't far, he told Cassie, just down the escalator to the ground floor and across the lobby to the west side of the building.

Cassie was a trifle unsteady on her feet as she followed Doug out of the ballroom, but not so tipsy that she didn't realize it would be a mistake to let him get her alone. After all, she'd been warned about the man. She wanted things to happen between them, but only after she got to know him. She told him the bar would be fine.

He ordered a couple of Irish coffees and then sat there without saying a word, waiting for her to begin. She liked that. Men who were pushy and impatient got on her nerves.

"My sister is very different from what you think," she said once the drinks had come. "It's true that she's an actress and maybe even a little wacky at times, and it's true that she's been married twice before, but all of those things are superficial. If you don't unbend a little and give her a chance to show you what she's really like, either you'll risk causing friction between Edward and Melanie, or Melanie will instinctively protect herself by trying to put some distance between you and Edward. I can't believe you'd want either of those things to happen."

Although Doug didn't enjoy being lectured, he recognized and admired Cassie's motives. Family loyalty was a fine thing. "I've never been anything but friendly and respectful to your sister," he pointed out. "Naturally I hope that Edward and Melanie will be happy together." He didn't add that he figured the "together" part of it would last about three months maximum.

"Is that what you call it? Friendly and respectful?" Cassie rolled her eyes. "You're so polite you're practically embalmed. I now know what the term 'frozen smile' really means. Honestly, Doug, I wouldn't have dared tie you up if you'd been like this last night."

Doug stiffened. He didn't know which was worse,

being attacked for behavior that was completely proper or being reminded of what a sucker he'd been the night before. "I can only repeat," he said, "that I've never treated your sister with anything less than respect. And as far as last night goes, you'll have to excuse me if I don't consider being teased half to death one of the high points of my life. I have no desire to repeat the experience."

"Now you're angry with me," Cassie said mournfully. "I'm sorry, Doug." She knew she should have been more tactful and blamed it on too much champagne.

"You don't have to apologize. I meet a lot of eccentric people in my work, Cassie. I try to keep a sense of humor about dealing with them."

"And that's how you see me? As eccentric?"

"Impulsive might have been a better choice of words." Doug sipped his Irish coffee, telling himself it was stupid to argue. It wasn't going to resolve the fundamental differences between him and Cassie, and it might even keep them from enjoying each other in the future. "Let's just forget about last night," he went on. "You were out to play a practical joke, and you succeeded brilliantly. I walked into it with my own agenda and my eyes wide open, so maybe I even deserved it. Basically, Cassie, you and I are two very different people with two very different personal styles. But the fact that I'm more formal than you are doesn't make me either embalmed or closed-minded, any more than your impulsiveness makes *you* a dumb blonde. I assume you want to talk to me about your sister. I'd be happy to listen to whatever you have to say."

Cassie stared at the table. The crisply rational man across from her wasn't even anyone she liked. Yet last night . . . Where had all the passion gone? What had happened to the wit and charm and warmth? He'd been ten times more human on the dance floor.

Confused and unsettled, she decided to stick to the topic at hand. "I know Edward told you that our mother died when Melanie was eighteen and I was sixteen, and that our father had taken off years before, but you can't possibly understand how hard those things were on Melanie." She paused, looking for some reaction, but none was evident. Taking a deep breath, she plunged ahead. "I don't remember my father at all, but Melanie does. She adored him when she was little, but suddenly he was gone. She kept waiting for him to come back, and when he didn't, she decided it must be her fault. It left permanent scars. When my mother got sick, most of the burden fell on Melanie's shoulders, because she was older and because she and my mother got together and decided to protect me from how bad things really were. Melanie really believed she could save Mom, and when she couldn't, it was like being abandoned all over again. Afterward I went down to San Francisco to live with Jane and Warren, but Melanie was old enough to be on her own, at college. It was such a huge place, and she felt lonely and a little lost, so it's not surprising that she was flattered when one of her professors fell in love with her. He was a lovely man, in his late forties, and anyone who's taken basic psychology would understand why she convinced herself that she loved him back and agreed to marry him. But admiration and gratitude aren't enough to base a marriage on, and within a year both of them realized it."

Cassie took a sip of her drink and went on. "The second marriage was different—a passionate love affair with a brilliant actor who couldn't stay away from liquor. Melanie lived with him for four years, sobering him up, keeping him going, telling herself that if she gave him enough love he would be able to stop drinking. That was crazy, of course—nobody can cure an alcoholic—but Melanie is a very loyal person." Cassie's eyes had filled with tears. She knew firsthand just how strong that loyalty was. She glanced at Doug and then looked away, wondering how he could sit

there so impassively. Was that how he'd lived his life?
At a distance from people and emotions? "In my book,
Edward is damn lucky," she said hoarsely. "Melanie is
a terrific person. Maybe I'll tell you all about it—
someday."

Doug had as much curiosity as the next man, but
considered it an unforgivable invasion of privacy to
shoot questions at someone who was on the verge of
breaking down. There were good reasons for his attitude toward Melanie Ford—his own childhood, his
special relationship with Edward, his personal prefer-
ences in women—but it never occurred to him to bare
his soul to Cassie Valkenberg. If he'd learned one
lesson in his thirty-three years, it was that strangers
took admissions of weakness and flung them back in
your face. There were only two people he'd ever really
trusted, and one of them was dead now.

Sitting there and thinking it over, he began to see
that Melanie had taken his formal manner and very
logical reservations and had interpreted them as out-
and-out hostility. Maybe that wasn't so surprising, since
she moved in a world where people kissed and hugged
and fawned over each other even when they hated each
other's guts—and even when they planned to stab each
other in the back at the first opportunity.

"I don't have anything against your sister personally," he said. "I just have doubts that she and Edward
are right for each other. I thought it was a good idea for
them to wait, to know each other better before they got
married. Edward asked for my honest opinion, and I
gave it to him. Believe me, Cassie, nobody wants me to
be wrong more than I do."

Cassie heard something new in his tone—a sympa-
thy, a gentleness, a wish to be understood. "You really
mean that, don't you," she said.

"Of course I mean it. Edward is the closest thing to a
brother I've got. I was very happily married for over
ten years, Cassie. He used to tell me he envied me. He

wants a home, a wife who puts him first, and a family. Those things are hard to come by nowadays, especially in a two-career marriage."

Cassie had to admit that Melanie Ford seemed like the wrong woman to give Edward what he needed, but that was only on the surface. "Melanie is going to surprise you," she said. "She wants the same things out of life that Edward does."

"Until the next hot role comes along." Doug knew it wasn't a particularly diplomatic observation to make, but he made it anyway. If Cassie wanted to talk—really *talk*—he could be as blunt as the next man. "Your sister hasn't had the easiest time of it. I understand that and I can sympathize with it. But you don't get a starring role in a major film without ambition, hard work, and push. You're a parent yourself, Cassie. What happens to the kids when Edward is in the middle of the Pacific studying ocean currents and Melanie goes off to the South American jungle to shoot a new version of *Tarzan*?"

It didn't take a genius to figure out where *that* one came from. "Not the same thing that happened to Douglas Hunter," Cassie answered. For the first time all day there was some old-fashioned, heated emotion coming from Doug, and it made a world of difference in Cassie's attitude. Explaining about Melanie would mean explaining about herself, and she hadn't been willing to risk that—until Doug had opened up a little.

"My mother died in April," she said. "Melanie was supposed to go to Juilliard that fall, on a scholarship. It was a dream come true for her. All she'd ever wanted out of life was to sing, to perform. But all of a sudden I was alone, going off to live with people I liked but really didn't know, in a city so big it frightened me just to think about it. I felt as though my whole world had crashed down around me. So, without telling me, Melanie informed Juilliard that she wouldn't be coming and registered at a Bay Area junior college instead. She presented it to me as a fait accompli, because she knew I never would have agreed if she'd asked me in advance. In the end Warren Valkenberg used a little pull and got her into Berkeley. The Valkenbergs have been terrific to both of us, as close to parents as we could have hoped for. But it works two ways. There's a reason they're down here with their friends, standing on the receiving line and treating Melanie as a daughter, and it has nothing to do with legalities because she never was their ward like I was. It has to do with mutual love and respect. Melanie has earned that from them by being the kind of person she is."

Cassie paused. Doug was leaning forward slightly, listening intently. "After two years at Berkeley and one lousy marriage, Melanie finally made it to Juilliard. Once she graduated she hustled her tail off to make a career for herself. She did a successful television commercial, got into the chorus of a Broadway musical, and did some straight acting off-Broadway, practically for free. In the meantime, I'd married John and moved to Denver. I started college a few months after Jessica was born. In my junior year I got pregnant again, but I had one of those miscarriages where everything goes wrong—hemorrhaging, transfusions, the works. When I didn't get any stronger after a couple of weeks in bed, John started to worry. He took me to San Francisco to stay with his parents and see a specialist they knew. Melanie left the play she was appearing in as soon as they could replace her and came to San Francisco to cheer me up. That was how she met her second husband. He was acting with American Conservatory Theatre at the time."

Cassie shook her head, a wry smile on her face. "You have no idea how glad I am that Melanie's meeting Edward had nothing to do with me. Every time she charges to my rescue and meets some man, he turns out to be Mr. Wrong. It even happened when she took me to Europe after John died, but she had sense enough not to marry him. *That* one was an Italian count with tons of money, charm to burn, and a string of torrid love affairs behind him. Melanie kept telling him she was a non-Catholic with two marriages behind her, and he kept proposing. We finally escaped to Spain. By the way, at the time Melanie took me to Europe she was under consideration for the starring role in a Broadway revival of *Oklahoma!* Naturally she didn't mention what she might be giving up."

Doug got the message loud and clear. When it came to choosing between family and career, Melanie Ford would always choose the former—at least when it came to her younger sister. For a moment he wondered why Edward hadn't told him any of that, and then he realized that he hadn't been particularly approachable lately. Part of it was his immediate disapproval of Melanie Ford, but it was also the pressure of his work. He'd been so wrapped up in his own problems that he hadn't made time to listen, and now he regretted it.

His thoughts jumped back to Cassie. He was curious about why Melanie had felt it necessary to bow out of a possible starring role on Broadway to take her sister to Europe. He didn't ask, though, because Cassie's life was none of his business. He knew how *he* would have reacted if some stranger had started prying for information about his reaction to *Buffy's* death.

"I appreciate your talking to me," he said. "If I've come across as judgmental or even antagonistic, I hope Melanie will forgive me. In my experience, instant love and approval are pretty meaningless commodities. I prefer to take my time getting to know people."

In other words, Cassie thought, it wasn't easy being Valerie Hunter's bastard. She herself tended to like and trust people until they gave her a reason not to. Doug held back, only giving his approval when he was convinced that somebody had earned it.

They finished their Irish coffees and went back upstairs. Their dinners had been sitting around so long by then that they were stone cold. A waiter spotted Doug just moments after he'd reached his table and offered to bring him a fresh meal, but he wasn't hungry. He told the waiter not to bother and sent him over to Cassie.

Then he apologized to Tawny for leaving her alone for so long. He knew she hadn't minded—she wasn't the clinging-vine type—but that was beside the point. Smiling, she admitted she'd been brooding over an elderly patient and had spent the entire time Doug had been gone talking over the case with a fellow doctor who happened to be sitting at their table. Doug thought she looked almost relieved when her beeper went off and she had to call the hospital. She went off to use the phone, returning a few minutes later with the news that she'd decided to go back to work. Doug walked her down to her car and kissed her good-bye, thinking about Melanie Ford. He didn't know what to do about the lady.

He wasn't prepared to say she'd be the perfect partner for Edward, but she was looking better all the time. The last thing he wanted was for Edward to feel uncomfortable about scheduling an occasional social evening with the two of them in the same room. Although far too honest to hand her a line, Doug finally decided that it would be possible to make his peace with her without bestowing his unconditional approval at the same time.

The orchestra was playing a romantic ballad when he walked back into the ballroom. Edward was dancing with Jane Valkenberg, while Melanie was sitting and talking to one of her Hollywood friends. Doug put a hand on her shoulder and, when she looked up at him, gave her a devastating smile. Then he asked her to dance.

It wasn't hard to tell what she was thinking. She wanted to keep talking to her friend but was afraid she'd offend Doug if she refused to dance with him.

The smile had obviously confused her. She glanced back at her friend, excused herself, and got up. "I'd love to," she said to Doug, managing to sound as though she really meant it.

Doug led her to the center of the floor and took her in his arms, holding her a little closer than she'd expected. She wasn't exactly stiff as a board, but she was very far from relaxed. "I want to thank you for everything you've done to make this such a special day for us," she said. "Everything is perfect. There's nothing like having the boss around to keep an eye on things, is there?"

It was the kind of polite little speech Doug would probably have made if he could have crawled inside Melanie's skin. He didn't know whether to be amused or sheepish. "Is that really the way I sound?" he asked.

"You?" She drew away a little and looked at him. "I didn't mean to comment—why are you smiling? Is there something funny about what I just said?"

It wasn't funny at all, only revealing. Melanie was always the picture of sunny self-confidence in Doug's presence, so much so that he'd never seen her off-balance or unsure of herself before. Pulling her closer, he murmured, "Relax, Mrs. Kolby. My bark is worse than my bite."

She settled into his arms, still noticeably uneasy. "I'm very glad to hear that, Doug."

"I can imagine you would be. But tell me if the same is true of your sister. She's been raking me over the coals about you, and I wondered if I should invest in a bodyguard."

"Cassie? I don't believe it!" Some of the tenseness left Melanie's body. "She's not the coal-raking type at all."

"Ah, but you don't know her like *I* know her," Doug said with a sigh. "I had the feeling that if I didn't mend a few fences I'd find myself in even worse trouble than last night. My real weaknesses are black stockings and

Kahlúa. If Cassie ever finds out about that, I figure I've had it."

Melanie laughed, genuinely amused now. "I'll file that information away, just in case I ever need a favor from you, Douglas." Then, settling closer against him, her hair touching his cheek, she added softly, "I don't know what Cassie's been telling you, but if it's convinced you that I'm not some sort of Hollywood ogress, I'm grateful. I love Edward. I intend to make him happy."

Doug didn't want to get into what he thought Melanie was or wasn't, or would or wouldn't do, so he answered that he was sorry if he'd given her the impression that he disliked her. "In a single evening," he admitted, "I've been accused of acting as stiff as an English butler—that one was from my mother—and of having a frozen smile and behaving like I'm embalmed. The last two were courtesy of your sister. The truth is that it takes me a while to get to know people, Melanie. Give me a little time and you might even get to like me."

Five minutes later Melanie was in the ladies' room, repeating the conversation to Cassie. "So I said I intended to give him years and years and years, and he laughed and answered that nothing could please him more. After a few moments I started singing along with the music, sort of unconsciously, and he told me I had a beautiful voice. He wanted to know if I planned to sing tonight, and I said no, but I have the feeling he's going to tease me into it. Of course, I'd love every minute of it, and I think he knows it. Edward walked over with Jane when the music stopped, and Doug kissed my hand, handed me over to my husband, and strolled away with Jane." Melanie gave a mischievous grin. "I *still* can't picture him tied up and panting, but I'll admit he can be charming when he wants to be. Even funny. Maybe he's human after all."

"I told you he was."

"Umm. So you did. But how on earth did you loosen him up, Cassie?"

"It wasn't hard. I just told him about your marriages, and about what a wonderful sister you are. He seemed to be very interested."

"In you, I think, not in me, but I suppose that's understandable. Still, if he flatters me a little more there's no telling how much I'll end up liking him." Melanie freshened her lipstick and breezed out of the ladies' room.

Cassie stayed behind to repair her own makeup and check on her hair. The French knot was a little the worse for wear. Rather than try to fix it, she took out the pins and brushed it loose. She could hear Melanie singing the title song from *Fame* as she walked through the hallway, and felt a little sorry for the orchestra's regular vocalist. The woman had a lovely voice but wasn't half the entertainer Melanie was. There was a burst of applause when Melanie finished singing, followed by shouts for an encore.

Cassie was about to go back into the ballroom when somebody called out her name from the direction of the powder room. She turned to see Valerie Hunter striding down the hall, looking just as fresh and beautiful as she had out on the patio.

Doug's mother had to be in her late fifties by now but looked more like forty-five. Cassie wondered if she'd had a face-lift, how she kept in such perfect shape, and whether she flew to L.A. to get her hair done. She wore it in a soft sideswept style, and it couldn't possibly have been so free of gray no matter how natural it looked. She had green eyes and blonde hair where Doug's eyes and hair were brown, but despite the difference in coloring there was a noticeable resemblance between the two of them.

She took Cassie by the arm, saying, "Let me steal you away for a couple of minutes. I'm just dying to talk to you."

It was more of a command than a request and, as such, called for obedience rather than verbal acknowledgment. Valerie Hunter reminded Cassie of a tall, stately ship as she sailed across the lobby to a group of empty chairs. She wondered whether Valerie's regal self-assurance stemmed from her position as the wife of a multimillionaire, or whether it had always been there, even before she'd turned her back on society's mores and borne an out-of-wedlock child.

They sat down next to each other, Valerie frowning at the ashtray on the table in front of them. She raised her hand, and a uniformed hotel employee hurried over, looking worried. "Young man," Valerie said, "I can scarcely believe what I'm seeing here. A dirty ashtray in the lobby of the Miesley Plaza! Take it away at once. And see that somebody waters that plant. It's drooping."

"Yes, Mrs. Miesley." The man grabbed the ashtray and, pulling a handkerchief out of his pocket, wiped some stray ashes off the table. "May I get you something to drink?" he asked.

"Just see that you get the *plant* something to drink," Valerie snapped, and turned her attention back to Cassie. Summarily dismissed, the man hurried away with the ashtray.

"I expect my hotels to be perfect," Valerie said, and added with a complacent smile, "All the staff members are terrified of me. Every last one of them."

"You mean you'd fire somebody over a dirty ashtray?" Cassie asked.

"Not the first time, no. Perhaps the second. But I didn't dragoon you away from the wedding to discuss my personnel problems, Cassie. Horace tells me you're a journalist—and a good one, rumor has it. I'm looking for a collaborator to work on my autobiography with me. I can't write worth a damn and I don't have the discipline to talk my life into a tape recorder, so that leaves me no choice but to pay somebody to pull the

WIN The Silhouette Diamond Collection

Treasure the romance of diamonds.
Imagine yourself the proud owner of
$50,000 worth of exquisite diamond jewelry.

GLAMOROUS
DIAMOND
PENDANT

PRECIOUS
DIAMOND
EARRINGS

EXOTIC
DIAMOND
RING

CAPTIVATING
DIAMOND
BRACELET

*Silhouette
Diamond
Sweepstakes*

facts out of me and put them down on paper. I've been through three collaborators already, and every one of them stank."

"I see," Cassie answered, and asked Valerie for names. She recognized two out of the three, and by no stretch of the imagination did either one "stink." Both were well-respected journalists with impressive lists of credits.

She didn't hesitate to point this out to Valerie, adding, "If they didn't satisfy you, I doubt I would do any better."

"Maybe it was me, then. I've been told I'm difficult to work with." Valerie paused to watch an employee scurry over with a watering can and tend to the wilted plant. "I'm having a group of friends over to lunch tomorrow. I want you to join us. We can talk about it then."

Cassie changed her mind about Valerie Hunter. She wasn't a tall, stately ship—she was a battle tank. But nothing, not even a tank, mowed down Cassie Valkenberg. "Miss Hunter . . ."

"Call me Valerie, dear."

"Valerie, then. I'm going on a book tour for two weeks, starting a week from Monday. After that I'm free, but I've never done this kind of project before, and I'm not sure I'm right for it."

"Don't worry, Cassie. I'll be the judge of that."

Valerie got up to leave, but Cassie pulled her back down with a firm, "I'm afraid you don't understand, Valerie. It's not *you* I'm concerned about pleasing, it's me. I hear you've had an interesting life. You're married to a complicated, fascinating man. Obviously you have the makings of a very strong book in all that, but I don't see any point in collaborating with you on it unless you're willing to tell the truth, both to me and to your audience. To be blunt, I'm not interested in helping you write a self-serving Hollywood puff piece."

Cassie expected annoyance, or maybe even a set-down, but what she got was a delighted burst of laughter. "My God, I'd have to kill him first. Horace, that is." She gave another laugh. "Come to think of it, maybe that's not such a bad idea. I can see we'll have a lot to talk about. That's twelve-thirty, dear, and bring along your daughter and in-laws if you want to. My granddaughter will be there, too, of course. We're very informal—lunch by the pool, a swim and a little sunbathing, horseback riding if you're in the mood . . . we'll make an afternoon of it. Do you remember how to get to the house?"

When Cassie said that she did, Valerie got back up again, and this time Cassie followed in her wake—or tracks. Adrenaline was suddenly surging through her system. There was nothing like the prospect of a hot story to set her blood on fire and bring a smile to her face.

Chapter Eight

$\mathscr{T}$echnically speaking, Cassie Valkenberg was a millionairess. The settlement after John's death had made her one, but she didn't think like one and she didn't live like one. True, she owned a nice little house in one of the nation's most expensive cities, San Francisco, and true, she was able to send her daughter to an excellent private school; but she didn't own furs or jewelry or fancy cars and she didn't dash off for weekends at La Costa when her weight went up a few pounds too many and she only rubbed elbows with San Francisco society when her in-laws invited her to dinner. The most important thing in her life was her daughter. The second most important thing was her career. She spent most of her time researching and writing her articles and books, earning a pretty fair living in the process. Her investments paid for the extras, the things that the average free-lance journalist could never have afforded.

She liked her life just fine, but a couple of hours at

the Miesleys' place made her realize that luxury had a lot to recommend it. The Miesleys were filthy rich and, unlike the Valkenbergs, made no apologies for it. They had a full-time gardener, a daily maid, and Chris Patterson, who did whatever Horace told him to do. They had four cars, two horses, and a priceless collection of sculpture. They even had a live-in cook. Her name was Juanita Perez, and she could turn out everything from California health-food to classic French cuisine. She didn't speak much English, and Valerie was forever tracking down Spanish-language versions of recipes and cookbooks, but she cooked like an angel. Lunch had been served on the patio under a cloudless sky. The outside temperature was neither too hot nor too cold, just like the water in the swimming pool. If a guest got bored eating or sunbathing, he could always go riding, play a game of pool, borrow a book from the family library, or go for a walk in the woods. To Cassie, collaborating with Valerie Hunter on her book was looking more and more like a paid vacation.

Lisa Hunter and Cassie's daughter, Jessica, who'd become fast friends within half an hour of meeting each other, had eaten lunch, taken a swim, and then gone off riding. Horace Miesley had retired to the family room to watch the San Diego Padres, who were losing yet another game. Doug was in there with him, along with Chris, Warren Valkenberg, and most of the other male guests.

Among them was a middle-aged man with the air of a besieged cavalry commander. His name was Sam McGuire, he'd once played professional baseball and was still in darn good shape, and he had the misfortune to be the general manager of the Padres. It would have been an understatement to say that Horace Miesley was disenchanted with him at the moment.

Before the start of the game, McGuire had walked Cassie down to the corral to show her the horses, telling her a little about himself in the process. His tenure with the team had started when McDonald's millionaire Ray Kroc was still alive. Kroc's widow, of course, had eventually sold out to Miesley, and according to McGuire, things had never been the same since.

"If Miesley is so tough to work for, why not take another job?" Cassie asked.

He shrugged. "I like it down here. I like the people I work with. Miesley's been the owner for three years now, and sooner or later the novelty is going to wear off. When it does he'll leave me alone to do what I want."

Cassie asked him his favorite part of the game, and he said it was discovering and developing young talent. His dream was to own a team of his own someday, even a minor-league team, but he doubted he'd ever have the money. "Unless I win a lottery or hit it big in Vegas," he added with a laugh. Cassie had liked him immediately. He was street-smart and down-to-earth.

She was still waiting for an opportunity to talk with Valerie Hunter about the book, but the lack of a private conversation hadn't stopped her from getting a fairly clear picture of the woman. Valerie and Miesley were more like business partners than a loving husband and wife. She had a finger in all of his pies, but her primary bailiwick was the hotel chain. She supervised everything from the choice of building sites to interior design to advertising, and even appeared in the company's commercials. She was a charming hostess and an entertaining conversationalist, but Cassie detected very little warmth in her. There was only one person who received her unconditional love and approval, and that was her granddaughter, Lisa. In her own way, Valerie was just as reserved as Doug was, but not when she talked to Lisa.

After a swim in the pool, Cassie lay down on a lounge chair and closed her eyes. Between too much celebrating at the wedding and too much food at lunch, her normally high energy-level had taken a dive. A

Vivaldi concerto was being piped into the courtyard from the stereo in the living room, and it didn't take long for the music to lull her to sleep.

She awoke with a start when somebody sat down beside her and stroked her arm. She opened her eyes to find Chris Patterson waving a plastic bottle of number fifteen sunscreen under her nose.

He grinned at her. "You can't charge three hundred bucks an hour if you're too sunburned to lie down, Cassie."

"I guess you're right," Cassie said with a yawn. She straightened up and smoothed back her hair with her hand. Chris had gone from confused to embarrassed when the woman he thought of as Vonda had arrived earlier that afternoon with a family in tow, but in the end he'd had a sense of humor about the whole business. A bit of a Don Juan, he'd told Cassie to give him a call if she ever got lonely, and promised not to charge her a dime for his services. "Thanks for keeping an eye on me," she added. "I didn't mean to fall asleep."

"Thank Doug, not me," Chris said. "He just looked at his watch and then told me to get you some sunscreen."

Cassie peered into the family room, but there was too much glare off the window to see much of anything. She pressed her thigh with her thumb and quickly took it away, testing to see how burned she was. The skin went from white to red. The lotion she'd been using had a protection factor of six, but that obviously wasn't strong enough when you spent most of your time indoors.

She took the bottle out of Chris's hand and opened it up. "Then thanks for bringing it outside. I guess you want to get back to the ball game."

He shook his head. "Not really. We're losing again. Miesley's cursing the team, cursing the taste of that crummy beer he's always drinking, and cursing Sam for every trade he ever made. He won't admit that the good ones were mostly Sam's idea and the bad ones were mostly his. But what the hell, he's the boss, he can do whatever he wants."

Cassie could hear frustration as well as dislike in Chris's voice. "It must be tough to watch the team on television when you'd rather be out there contributing. By pitching, I mean."

"Yeah, well, those are the breaks. I wrecked my arm trying to stay in the starting rotation, you know? The man wants results, and if you can't give 'em to him, you find yourself on the next bus to the boondocks."

"Miesley, you mean."

Chris looked around, checked out the umbrellaed table where Valerie was playing bridge with her friends, and then turned back to Cassie. Lowering his voice, he said bitterly, "Yeah, Miesley."

He didn't simply dislike the man, he hated him. Cassie wondered why he'd ever gone to work for Miesley. She squeezed out some lotion and started to smooth it over her shoulders, then bluntly asked him.

He shrugged. "Okay pay, easy hours, a great place to live, and fifty grand in the old man's will if I'm still on the payroll when he kicks off. It's a living, you know?" Suddenly more cheerful, he added with a grin, "Besides, the rest of 'em are okay and the food is first-cabin. I'll see you around, Cassie."

Valerie walked over about twenty minutes later, saying that she was sitting out of the bridge game for a while so that somebody else could play. "It will give us some time to talk," she added. "I've spent the morning checking up on you, Cassie, and I've decided that you and I are a match made in heaven."

Cassie assumed she'd made a few phone calls. People like Valerie Hunter always seemed to know the right people. "Who did you talk to?" she asked.

"Nobody. I have no interest in other people's opinions. I simply sat down at my computer, plugged into one of the data bases we subscribe to, and got myself a list of your articles. Then I printed out three of them. And I've decided that anyone who can cope with those maniacs who call themselves 'Acid Reign' can certainly cope with me. Tell me about this book tour you're going to do."

Cassie did so, although she didn't know much more than the names of the cities and a couple of the programs she was scheduled to appear on. Afterward they talked about how to be effective on TV and radio—Valerie gave her some expert advice—and about *A Hundred And One Nights*. While Cassie didn't delude herself into believing that Valerie's autobiography would have more than passing historical or literary interest, she *did* believe it would be fascinating to work on and had potential as a best-seller. Valerie claimed she intended to be candid in what she wrote and cooperative about getting the book done as quickly as possible. In the end she announced that her agent would contact Cassie's agent about a contract.

Cassie swam a few more laps in the pool and then, having had more than enough sun for one day, grabbed a towel and went inside. It was only the third time all summer that she'd worn a bikini, and her midriff was noticeably pink.

She'd left her clothes in one of the bedrooms. Vacant at the moment, it looked out over the central patio but had no outside access. The easiest way to reach it was through a door from the patio into a narrow hall that bisected the bedroom wing of the house. Cassie took a left when she came to the main hallway and went directly into the connecting bathroom. A look in the mirror told her her sunburn was quite mild, the kind that only hurt if you made the water in the shower too hot. There was some moisturizing lotion on the counter, and it felt cool and very soothing on her skin. After toweling her hair dry and combing out the tangles, she opened the door into the adjoining bedroom.

What she saw there stopped her dead in her tracks. Doug Hunter was lounging on the double bed, his hands clasped together behind his neck. Cassie had once wondered whether the word "casual" was even in his vocabulary, and she'd gotten her answer a few hours before. He'd been wearing white gym shorts, tennis shoes and a college T-shirt when she arrived. Now he was barefoot, and his clothes were actually a little wrinkled.

She'd never seen him look sexier. The shorts accentuated the muscles in his thighs, and the shirt did the same for his chest and upper arms. Sprawled out on the bed that way, he reminded Cassie of a lion sunning itself: outwardly harmless, but capable of springing into action at a moment's notice.

She stood there staring at him, momentarily at a loss for words. She hadn't heard him come in and wondered what he was doing there. Waiting for her? Simply resting? He picked up the can of beer on the night table and held it out to her. "Thirsty?" he drawled.

She gave him a weak smile. Both of them knew she'd enjoyed a little too much of Miesley's champagne at the wedding. She'd had a bit of a hangover that morning but felt fine now and intended to stay that way. She shook her head and walked over to the chair where she'd left her clothes. It was in the far corner of the room, on the other side of the bed from the bathroom.

Doug stood up, taking the beer along with him. "I hope you weren't planning to put those on," he said, and brought the can to his lips. It was obviously nearly empty, because he had to tip his head way back to drink. When he was finished he put the can back on the night table and smiled at her. A little off-balance, she picked up her clothes and held them protectively in front of her chest.

She knew that smile. She'd seen it once or twice before, on Friday night. The confusing thing was that she hadn't seen it since then, and certainly not that day.

Doug had been friendly enough, but the moments of emotional intimacy they'd shared during the wedding might never have happened. He'd eaten his lunch and gone off to watch the Padres, paying no more attention to Cassie than to anyone else at the house.

That being the case, she couldn't quite believe he was looking at her like the Big Bad Wolf must have looked at Little Red Riding Hood just before he took the first bite. "I've had a little too much sun," she said. "Even with number fifteen sunscreen you still have to be careful. . . ."

"So don't go back outside. Don't you know that some of life's most pleasurable activities can be pursued under artificial light? Or even in the dark?"

"Is that so!" Cassie no longer had any doubts about what he was doing in the bedroom. But as much as she adored the twinkle in his eye, she wasn't about to stick around to play the leading lady in the seduction scene he'd planned.

She edged toward the door, the one that led into the hall. On some level she realized that Doug wasn't running to stop her—that he was in fact moving away from her, toward the center of the room—but it simply didn't register. "Well, maybe we can talk about your favorite indoor activities some other time," she said, "but right now I've really got to be going."

Laughing, she dashed for the door, dropped her clothes, and reached for the knob. She was baffled when it wouldn't turn, because she hadn't had a problem when she used the room before lunch. She tried to force it, but it didn't give an inch. She took a closer look. She remembered seeing a push-button lock, but the doorknob in her hand had nothing but a keyhole. And it was evidently locked from the hall side. She stood there feeling exceedingly foolish for a couple of moments before finally turning around. As she'd expected, Doug was holding a key between his thumb and forefinger.

"Looking for this?" he asked.

"What tales that bed must have to tell!" Cassie eyed the bathroom door, assessing her chances of running a successful misdirection play. "Imagine, a bedroom where you lock people *in* rather than *out!*"

"I changed the knob while you were swimming. Did I mention I was once a Boy Scout? I've always believed in being prepared. The only thing I forgot was the rope. To use on you, not me, angel, but I'm sure we'll manage to improvise."

Cassie didn't have to ask him what the rope would have been for. It was a four-poster bed. She feinted to the right, and he took a step to match her, but the rest of the maneuver didn't work at all. When she tried to slip around him to his left, he simply backed himself up and blocked the open doorway with his body.

Cassie looked around the room, searching for a way out where none existed. There was a large picture window above the bed, but it was covered by a set of shutters. At the moment the slats were open, so people on the patio could see into the room if they looked hard enough. Audience or not, though, there wasn't a ghost of a chance of getting out that window if Doug decided to stop her. She wouldn't have even tried it. Her legs were scraped enough already.

Doug noticed the way she was studying the window and laughed. "We'll have to close those shutters," he said. "I don't give public performances."

"Just private ones?" Cassie shot back. "For an audience of one?"

"Not even private ones. I don't perform at all, Cassie; I make love. I'm much more interested in giving a woman pleasure than in impressing her with what a stud I am." Doug took a few steps forward; Cassie automatically retreated. "On the other hand, I *did* hear something about your opinion of my talents in that department. Let's see now. You said I was good at kissing. . . ."

Blushing, Cassie moaned, "Edward didn't really tell you that!"

"Don't be too hard on him. He was only trying to calm me down. He wanted me to understand that your motives weren't persecution and revenge; it was just that you couldn't keep your hands off me. But it's okay, angel. I forgive you. We all have our human weaknesses."

Cassie didn't know which was more astonishing: the rakish smile on Doug's face, his teasing tone of voice, or the slow but steady way he was stalking her. She'd never seen a man look less like an embalmed English butler in her life.

She darted around the bed, putting it between her and Doug, and held her hands straight out in front of her as though they could somehow ward him off. "Now, Doug, you have to be reasonable about this. . . ."

"The hell I do! Stop using the bed for protection, Cassie. There are better things to do with it."

"But Doug, you, uh, you can't . . ."

"Yes, Cassie? Was there something you wanted to say?"

"No. I mean, no, I won't sleep with you, not no, I don't have anything to say. I *do* have something to say." Doug took a quick couple of steps around the perimeter of the bed. "I can't talk to you when you—when you *hunt* me that way. Will you please keep still?"

But Doug paid no attention to her. Another couple of steps brought him within striking distance, giving Cassie no choice but to hop up on the bed. She took a flying leap off the opposite side and ran toward the bathroom but was grabbed by the bottom of her bikini well before she reached the doorway. Doug didn't let go of the bathing suit until he'd slipped his forearm under her chin and brought his hand to rest on her shoulder.

Cassie's heart was already pounding wildly from her efforts to get away from him, and his closeness made it even worse. She could feel the heat of his chest as it pressed against her back, and then, a few moments later, the touch of his lips on her hair. The next thing she knew, he was stroking her bare stomach with his free hand, sensuously and persuasively. Her breathing quickened.

"I've been meaning to talk to you," he said, "about this neurotic need of yours to be in control. What we need here is a little aversion therapy—making you confront the thing you're most afraid of. To be precise, the dominant male." He bent his head and started to nibble her earlobe. "It should only take a couple of hours in bed to cure you."

"I'm afraid it's too late for *me,*" Cassie answered, "but there are probably thousands of women out there who would, uh, love to avail themselves of your services, if only they knew about them. Maybe you should advertise, Doug."

"I'd need a testimonial first." Doug traced the outline of her ear with his tongue, arousing her so much that she closed her eyes and swallowed hard. "What are my chances of getting one from *you,* angel?"

"Nonexistent," Cassie said. Doug's hand crept up her stomach to her breast. "I'm a hopeless case."

His laugh said he didn't believe her. "We'll have to see about that. Come on, turn around and let me kiss you. We'll have a good time together."

Cassie was drop-dead crazy about Doug Hunter but had pictured their relationship evolving along different, more temperate lines. In three or four weeks she'd be back in San Diego to work on his mother's autobiography. There would be time to get to know each other, time to draw closer, time for him to see her as something other than a casual fling. When he started to turn her in his arms, she took the only course of action open to her: she bit him on the hand.

It wasn't particularly vicious as bites go, but it startled him into loosening his grip. She ducked away and ran to the other side of the room, but this time she got herself some tangible protection. The chair she picked up was Louis the something or other and had been tucked under an escritoire. It didn't look especially sturdy, but Cassie figured that was a plus. It had probably cost a fortune, and Doug wouldn't dare risk breaking it.

He started after her but backed away fast when she poked the legs of the chair at his middle. "Watch where you aim that thing," he said with a grin. "I won't be much use as a sex therapist if you spear me—"

"I don't *need* a sex therapist," Cassie interrupted. "I'm not going to sleep with you. I barely know you."

His smile crumbled into a look of grievous disappointment. "I'm cut to the quick. I would have said we were intimately acquainted."

"That was Vonda," Cassie answered.

"Hmm. Disintegration of the central personality in addition to all of her other problems. The lady definitely needs my help." Ignoring her for a moment, he walked to the window and leaned over the bed to close the slats of the shutters.

It was the opening Cassie needed. She broke toward the bathroom, planning to slam and lock the door and escape through the opposite door into the hall. This time she made it into the room, but the final result was the same. Before she could close the door, Doug was forcing it back open, and before she could escape into the hallway, Doug was grabbing her around the waist. He tossed her over his shoulder like a sack of dirty laundry and carried her back to the bedroom.

She wriggled and kicked and demanded her freedom, but she was laughing at the same time, so Doug had to be excused for failing to take her seriously. It was a very fine line to tread, to say no to a man and still keep him hotly interested. She knew darn well he wasn't smitten enough to keep pursuing her if she made it too tough for him to catch her, and she knew equally well that he'd drop her like a hot potato if he suspected how involved she was.

When he dumped her onto the bed, she rolled to the side and started to get up. She never had a chance. One moment he was pushing her onto her back and the next he was sprawled out on top of her. A large male hand closed around her wrists and forced them over her head, and a second male hand clasped her chin so she couldn't bury her face in the pillow to evade his mouth.

She looked into his eyes, saw a gleam that said he wasn't going to take no for an answer, and shifted her gaze to his shoulder. "In deference to your neuroses," he said, "we'll take this one small step at a time. All you have to do is tell me when you want me to kiss you. And don't worry if it takes a little time. I'm a very patient man."

"Patient?" Cassie repeated. Doug started to nuzzle her neck, setting a fire that went straight to the pit of her stomach. Her voice unsteady, she went on, "You're not patient at all, Doug Hunter. This is—it's rape, that's what it is, and . . ."

"Seduction," he corrected hoarsely. "I'm seducing you, not raping you." He kissed his way up her neck to her mouth and took her bottom lip between his teeth. The nip he gave her sent a lightning bolt of pleasure through her.

"Anyone could walk in. . . ." she gasped.

"Sad but true." He brushed his lips back and forth across her mouth, barely touching her, making her long for more. "We won't be able to work on more than the first step or two of your cure in here. But like I said, I'm in no particular hurry. We don't have to leave till you're ready."

True to his word, he coaxed and teased as though he had all the time in the world to squeeze a response out of her. It was hard to fight what she'd wanted all along, especially when she'd just been assured that some harmless necking was as far as it could go. Doug settled himself against her and wedged a leg between her thighs to part them, his teeth still toying with her lips. Cassie finally gave in and closed her eyes. What he was doing made her ache to be kissed, but she didn't say a single word. A silent tug-of-war was going on, each of them wanting the other to be the first to cry uncle.

When Doug started a slow, circular rocking, Cassie couldn't stop herself from thrusting back. He traced the outline of her lips with his tongue, and she caught at her breath and fought for air. The excitement was almost suffocating. Her heart racing, she tried to pull her hands free because she wanted to touch him, but he wouldn't let them go.

He drew back slightly so that his mouth was barely touching her lips. "I'm going to make you feel things you've never felt before," he said seductively. "You'll be so excited you'll beg me to finish you off, but deep inside, you'll be praying I do the opposite. Trust me, Cassie. Stop fighting your deepest desires and let me show you what the word 'pleasure' can really mean."

She recognized the speech, just as she recognized the fact that it was one more way of teasing her into surrender. The problem was, she was fresh out of pert comebacks by now. Nobody had ever smashed through her defenses this way.

It was one thing to come on like a sexual pentathlete when she was playing the role of Vonda and had a mental script and a dozen case histories to fall back on, and another when she was just plain Cassie, confused and a little shell-shocked by feelings she'd never experienced before. She opened her eyes and stared into Doug's. "You already have. We have to stop now. . . ."

"In a minute." His mouth opened over her own, impatient now, and his tongue probed at the line between her lips. Overwhelmed, Cassie finally gave him the response he wanted. All the frustration of holding back for so long exploded into the kiss they shared.

For Cassie, it was a shattering experience. Doug refused to release her wrists, but after the first few moments she was too aroused to fight him. If it was begging he wanted, he had the satisfaction of getting it. At least that was how it felt to Cassie, because every time he teased her by lightening the kiss, she arched feverishly against him and moaned his name. A bathing suit and a pair of gym shorts weren't much in the way of insulation, and she could feel the increasing urgency of his response.

His movements were jerky and his breathing uneven when he finally rolled off of her and onto the bed. "Let's get the hell out of here," he muttered. "I want some privacy."

Cassie felt herself panic. Things had gone so far so fast that she could barely think straight. She couldn't say no—not after doing this to him *again*—but she couldn't say yes, either. She didn't know what to do. "I have to talk to you," she answered. "I just can't . . ."

"In the cottage." He got off the bed and held out his hand. "Come on, let's go."

She shook her head. "No. I can't go there with you. Let's just—let's just take a walk first. Please."

She was sure Doug was furious with her. He stared so hard, his expression grim, that she blushed. But he didn't refuse to do as she'd asked.

They went out through the bathroom, Cassie grabbing a towel on the way. She didn't know it, but Doug was more confused than angry, at least now that the first surge of arousal had eased. Unlike Cassie, he knew exactly what he wanted, but wasn't sure if he'd get it. She'd been saying no from the moment she found him in the bedroom, but her actions and many of her words had indicated the direct opposite. A woman who joked and teased and pretended to run away was sending you a very clear message. She wanted to be caught and made love to. When the same woman put her body and soul into a kiss and murmured protests whenever you tried to break things off, the message was that much stronger. Suddenly, though, she'd changed her mind, and he was at a loss to understand why.

He led her out the side door and around the garage into the woods, which was what he'd intended from the start. Neither of them spoke. He could see that she was struggling with something and was glad not to have to talk just yet. In the brief time he'd known her, Cassie Valkenberg had succeeded in arousing more sexual frustration in him than he'd endured in the previous thirty-three years. He had no intention of putting up with an instant replay of Friday night, but if something was really troubling her he wanted to know what it was.

Cassie walked along beside him, trying to decide what she could possibly say. It wasn't so much a question of lying as of how much of the truth to tell. It was ironic, really, because she could breeze through interviews with strangers on the most intimate aspects of their lives without batting a single eyelash. But let those same subjects come up in relation to herself, especially with a sophisticated man like Doug, and it was hopeless. She was immediately embarrassed and defensive.

They stopped in front of a large elm with a rope ladder hanging parallel to the trunk. Cassie followed it with her eyes and saw that it led to a tree house. The house sat on a large branch, with four stiltlike legs coming down to the ground to provide support. It consisted of a deck surrounded by a railing, and a walled-in room.

"Let's go sit on the deck," Doug said. "There should be a couple of lawn chairs up there."

The house had been freshly stained, making it hard

to tell how old it was. "Did you build this for Lisa?" Cassie asked.

"My mother gave it to me as a sixteenth-birthday present." Doug held the ladder steady so Cassie could climb up. Once he'd joined her on the deck he added wryly, "This place has a lot of good memories for me, Cassie. Maybe I should tear it down before Lisa reaches puberty."

"Are you going to be *that* kind of father?" Cassie asked.

"Maybe. Ask me in two or three years."

The lawn chairs were folded up and stacked in a corner. Now that she was on the deck, Cassie could see that the little room had windows and a door, but the shades were down and the door was shut. She wondered what was on the other side of it. An empty space? Air mattresses and sleeping bags? Portable cots?

She looked out over the railing at the view. They were near the top of the hill, and she could see through the trees to the valleys and peaks beyond. It was a marvelous setting and would have been very peaceful if she hadn't been so nervous.

Doug unfolded the chairs and set them side by side. Both of them sat down. After thirty seconds went by, Doug realized Cassie wasn't going to say anything. What he wanted first of all was a simple yes or no, but the situation seemed to be a lot more complicated for Cassie Valkenberg than it was for him. He finally settled on, "You said you wanted to talk. What about?"

"I thought I should explain . . ." Cassie looked into her lap. "It's just—I get pregnant at the drop of a hat, Doug. I can't afford to take chances."

Her explanation seemed to amuse him. "And *that's* why you went into a panic? Because you left your diaphragm—or whatever—in San Francisco?"

Actually, there wasn't a diaphragm or anything else in San Francisco. Cassie hadn't needed one in years. "I should have thought of it," she said. "I know I owe you an apology—well, a lot more than an apology, I guess—but . . ."

"Just hold it a minute. You don't owe me anything, least of all sexual satisfaction. Back in the house, I got the impression that you wanted to make love as much as I did."

"I did, but . . ."

"But you were worried about getting pregnant." He reached over and ran a teasing finger down her cheek. "We won't do anything that can get you pregnant, Cassie. Were you worried I'd have a problem with that?"

Cassie felt like sinking between the slats of the deck. Doug obviously had high expectations, and after his run-in with "Vonda" it was little wonder. But the intimacies he was talking about were simply impossible. They'd never been a part of her marriage, and she was bound to disappoint him.

She figured she had two choices, and neither was at all palatable. If she said no he'd be angry, and if she said yes she'd embarrass herself. Either way, it seemed more than likely that he wouldn't want to have anything more to do with her.

Faced with an impossible choice, she elected to hold onto her self-respect. "I think it would be better if I went back to my hotel now," she said. "But I thought—maybe when I come back to San Diego to work on your mother's book, we could go out to dinner. Would that be okay?"

Doug sat there cursing his bluntness. He was sure that he and Cassie wanted exactly the same thing. The difference was that women never came right out and said so. They needed the hearts and flowers first.

He told Cassie that dinner would be fine, thinking he would have to schedule it right away, before his mother tired of her latest collaborator. He was surprised to realize that he hoped Cassie lasted longer than the rest of them had. He was so attracted to her he was willing to put up with almost anything to get her into bed.

That being the case, he found himself wondering why in hell he was letting her go. She had a beautiful body that the bikini did nothing to conceal, and as they got up to leave, it was all he could do to keep from touching her. It didn't take him long to decide that if she wanted romance and seduction, he would give her romance and seduction. It was pointless to wait through three weeks and a dinner date before starting an affair that was nothing short of inevitable. A little privacy, a little patience, and he figured he could get whatever he wanted from her.

He touched her arm and smiled reassuringly. "Come see the site of my misspent youth, Cassie. When you come back to San Diego you'll probably have a tough time getting Jessica to sleep anyplace else. Lisa loves to stay out here with her friends."

Relieved that Doug was taking her refusal so well, Cassie pushed open the door to the tree house and walked inside. Then she couldn't help laughing, because the place was almost as fancy as the main house, complete with rug, curtains, bunk beds, an antique chest of drawers, and framed prints on the walls. The furniture took up most of the floor space, leaving only a dozen square feet to maneuver around in.

She turned and almost tripped over Doug, who had closed the door and come up behind her. "I should have known you weren't the type to rough it. All you're missing in here is electricity."

"Edward and I spent a lot of nights out here. We'd take a lantern, a cooler full of food, and a deck of cards, invite a few friends, and play poker half the night out on the deck."

"No women?" Cassie asked.

He winked at her. "Do I look like the type of guy who would lure an unsuspecting woman into a place like this?"

It was exactly what he looked like. In the first place, he was blocking the door, and in the second place, the bottom bed was freshly made up. Cassie pointed to it, saying, "Were you expecting a houseguest?"

"Only for the next hour or so. Are you going to make me chase you around the room again? Because if you are, it's only sporting to point out that there's really no place to run to."

Cassie backed up and promptly bumped into the dresser. "We agreed on dinner in three weeks," she reminded Doug.

"I haven't forgotten." He pulled off his shirt and tossed it on the floor. Then, walking to within six inches of her, he went on, "I think I'll take you to Mexico. I know a terrific place down there."

"I'd like that, but . . ."

"But nothing. You don't want to wait three weeks any more than I do." Without another word, he closed the gap between them and took her in his arms. He didn't coax or tease this time, but lifted her lips to his mouth and gave her a hard, searching kiss.

He was right about not wanting to wait, and she knew it the moment he kissed her. It was as though she were one of Pavlov's dogs, conditioned to respond automatically. The stimuli were the feel and scent and taste of him, and the response was unbridled desire. Each time Doug touched her it took less and less time for her heart to go haywire, her legs to turn to jelly, and a raw hunger to swamp her common sense.

He drew her to the bed without even breaking the kiss. Cassie felt his hands at the back of her neck, underneath her hair, but didn't take much notice of them. She wanted to please him, and the low grunt he gave when she ran her hands up his chest and playfully nipped at his lips told her she was succeeding. His hands left her neck to close around her back, and in between kisses and nips of his own, he murmured that he couldn't have waited, that three weeks would have been a lifetime, that he'd never wanted a woman the way he wanted her.

No man had ever aroused Cassie the way Doug could, but what really swept her away was the overwhelming force of his response to her. It made her feel beautiful, even irresistible. It gave her a confidence she'd never felt before. And it encouraged her to try all the things she'd heard or read about but had been too inhibited to do.

He had untied the double-knotted bow behind her neck but hadn't given it the final little pull that would have undone the strings completely. His hands roamed over her breasts and then firmly pushed until she tumbled backwards onto the bed. The next moment he was stretched out beside her, pulling her close against his body, kissing her with deep thrusts of his tongue. He caressed her until her nipples were taut between his fingers and her breasts ached for the touch of his hand against her bare flesh. In the end, she was the one who yanked at the now-unwelcome bow and shoved down the interfering top.

She opened her eyes when Doug broke the kiss and saw that he was smiling at her, not seductively or complacently, but very tenderly. Then, without a word, he sat up, pulled the top down to her waist, and turned it around to unfasten the clasp at the back.

Still staring into her eyes, he trailed the top back and forth across her breasts again and again, playing with her, and finally tossed it aside. She felt herself start to tremble when his palm replaced the scrap of cloth and began to work its magic. And when she was finally back in his arms, this time underneath him, his bare chest felt even more erotic than his hand had.

She'd reached the point of no return faster than she'd ever dreamed possible. When he started the sensuous thrusting she remembered so well from before, she moaned his name and matched his rhythm. She scarcely understood what was happening to her. At its best, lovemaking with John had been warm and full of emotion. She'd never paid much attention to her own satisfaction, feeling that if it happened, it happened, and if it didn't, at least John was content and loving afterward. Never once had there been this raw, searing need that turned her inside out with longing.

Doug lifted his mouth, and she moaned his name, wanting the kiss to go on forever. He eased himself off her, and she clutched at his hips to bring him back. But then his mouth was on her breast, sucking and biting, and his hand was stroking the inside of her thigh, skittering across her flesh. She gave herself up to the moment, craving the thrill of having her fate in her lover's hands. The helpless passion she felt was the most exciting thing she'd ever experienced.

His hand went higher, and she arched her body to meet it, but he didn't touch her where she ached to be touched. Her frustration grew till it was almost unendurable. Finally she realized that it wasn't male ignorance or clumsiness that denied her the ultimate satisfaction, but a deliberate act. All she could manage was a hoarse, "Please . . . oh, God, Doug, don't tease me this way . . ."

"It's okay. I was just waiting . . ." His gentle murmur faded into silence. He slid down the bottom of her suit and moved his lips to her belly. She felt a moment of utter panic and tried to jerk away, but then he was teasing the spot he'd avoided earlier, giving her such pleasure that her protests died unspoken. There was nothing she wouldn't have let him do.

Every time she thought she couldn't take another moment of stimulation without exploding into a million pieces, he moved away to explore elsewhere. In the end she was writhing feverishly, begging him not to stop, and digging her nails fiercely into his back. There was nothing but her own overpowering need, and, at last, a shattering release. Her pleasure was so intense and prolonged that she was scarcely aware of the declaration she moaned, over and over again: "I love you . . . oh, Doug . . . I love you . . ."

Doug was very pleased with himself for taking Cassie so high—until he heard those unexpected words. Taken alone, he would have brushed them aside. It wasn't unheard of for a woman to cry "I love you" in the heat of passion, even when she wouldn't have dreamt of saying such a thing in her more rational moments. What troubled him was that brief but unmistakable withdrawal as his mouth traveled down Cassie's belly. He hadn't expected any inhibitions. He'd credited her with a lot of sexual experience, maybe far too much. He even wondered if her husband had been her sole previous lover. Because if he had been, it was very possible that she'd meant those breathless "I love you's." And as much as he'd wanted to sleep with her, he wasn't remotely serious about her. He didn't want to hurt her. The conversation he'd had with Edward drifted through his mind, and he felt guilty about how little attention he'd paid to it.

He couldn't keep the anxiety off his face. Cassie saw it, knew the reason without having to ask, and plummeted to earth with a painful thud. She reddened and put her arms in front of her chest, suddenly embarrassed about having him see her naked.

In the end, she tried to handle it as she'd handled so many other difficult situations: with humor. Picking up a pillow to cover herself, she said, "I have the feeling I've just committed the most awful *faux pas*. One should never say 'I love you' the first time in bed."

Far from smiling, Doug got even grimmer. "Cassie, I'm beginning to feel like someone who's walked into a play in the middle of the second act. Do you make a habit of saying that kind of thing?"

"It's one of my worst faults." Wanting to avoid any further discussion, Cassie slid her hand onto Doug's stomach and started exploring. He trapped it just before it dipped under his shorts, and put it back at her side. "Don't stop me," she said. "You made me feel wonderful, and I want to do the same for you." She grinned at him. "Trust me, and I'll show you . . ."

"What the word 'pleasure' really means," Doug finished, and shook his head. Cassie caught a fleeting smile before he went on, "I don't doubt it for a minute, Cassie, but I have to know what's going on here. Have you slept with anyone since your husband died?"

"That's none of your business. . . ."

"It's very much my business, and you're going to give me an answer. You'll be living here. We'll be sleeping fifty yards away from each other. We'll see each other all the time. Before this goes any further I need to know if 'I love you' means 'I haven't been with a man in a long time, and you made me feel terrific,' or 'I'm serious about you, and I want something more than an affair.'"

Cassie couldn't meet his eyes. She knew she couldn't squirm her way out without answering, and she didn't want to lie. But the consequences frightened her. "I guess it meant both," she said quietly. "But my feelings aren't your responsibility, Doug."

"The hell they're not! You think I want to say good-bye to you when you finish my mother's book and know that all I've done between now and then is make you miserable?"

"I know you don't want to do that. You're not that type of person." It was part of the reason she loved him.

"Then let's get out of here," he said.

Cassie recognized self-sacrifice when she saw it. Doug was playing the part of the perfect gentleman, putting her feelings above his own no matter how much frustration he felt. She ran her fingers down his arm, saying, "Edward once told me you have a passion for finishing what you start. So do I. We can talk about the future later."

"There *is* no future," he insisted.

Cassie tossed aside the pillow and snuggled up behind him. "All right, then, there is no future. So let's talk about the present."

"I can't let you do this . . ."

"Sure you can." She started to nuzzle his neck, slipping her hand under his shorts at the same time. Despite all the noble speeches, he couldn't control how much he wanted her. "I'd feel selfish and upset if you didn't," she said, and then lied baldly, "It's no big deal. It would hardly be the first time."

Doug knew he should stop her, but it was all but impossible to be honorable when a beautiful woman with no clothes on rubbed herself against your body and touched you in a way that drove you crazy. He took her statement to mean that she'd been with other men, maybe even a lot of other men, and told himself that it wasn't so terrible to take what she was offering. "If you're sure . . ." he muttered.

"Of course I'm sure." And she was, because she loved Doug Hunter and longed to give him the kind of pleasure he'd given her. The heat of his response soon melted her shyness, and her imagination and desire to please took over from there, more than making up for her previous lack of experience. She was making Doug feel wonderful, and that was all that mattered.

It was only afterward that her doubts returned. Doug was sprawled on his back, totally spent, staring at the underside of the top bunk, and his face wore a brooding look that made her nervous all over again.

"I shouldn't have let you do that," he said. "It felt too good. It's only going to make it harder to stay away from you when you come back to San Diego, but that's what I'm going to do. I've hurt you enough already."

Cassie felt herself pale. Ever since Friday night she'd been telling herself that the things she was most afraid of might never have to happen. If only everyone was

wrong about Doug . . . If only he got to know her
first . . . If only he wanted her too much to help
himself . . . If only . . .

It hadn't worked out that way. He didn't want to hurt
her, so he was ending the relationship before it even
began. She just couldn't accept that, not after what
they'd shared.

She took a good, hard look at the situation and
realized that she'd run out of options. Things couldn't
possibly have been worse. And that being the case, she
had nothing left to lose. So maybe if she laid her past on
the line and explained exactly how she felt, it might
make a difference. Maybe he would change his mind, at
least about continuing to see her.

"After John died, I went on with my life as though
nothing had changed," she said softly. "I told myself I
had a child to think about and a career to succeed at.
Within a month I'd moved back to San Francisco to be
closer to Jane and Warren and started writing again.
About eight months after that I decided it was time to
start dating again. I'd had more invitations than I could
count—the rich young widow and all that—and I told
myself I had to get out and meet people. I went through
men like other women go through shampoo, but I could
never let any of them get close to me, either physically
or emotionally. I'd just drop one and go on to the next.
It was a desperate search for love, intimacy, happiness
—I don't know what else—and once I got started I
couldn't seem to stop. My work went to pieces and my
daughter wound up feeling resentful and confused.
Jane and Warren were there to give her what I couldn't,
thank God, but I've never forgiven myself for the pain I
caused her. After three months or so Jane called
Melanie in New York and told her I was on the verge of
a breakdown. So Melanie took me to Europe, and after
a couple of weeks away and a lot of nights of talking, I
began to see that I'd never accepted John's death, that
I'd never let myself grieve, and that, until I did all those

things, I would always feel empty inside. That was almost two years ago. I've done what I needed to do, but I didn't realize I was ready for a new relationship until I met you. You make me feel things I'd forgotten could exist. I'm a big girl now, Doug, and I'll take what I can get. I loved John dearly, but frankly . . ." Cassie took a deep breath, struggling to get the words out. "Frankly, sex was never—it was, uh, a problem area for us. Even when it was okay, it was nothing like what happened today. I know you like me and I know you're attracted to me, and if a couple of months is all you want to give, well, I guess I can live with that."

Doug had been watching Cassie carefully, and he didn't like what he saw. She was so tense she was trembling, and every now and then a quiet note of despair had crept into her voice. He felt like the prize heel of all time. He didn't believe in love at first sight to begin with, but even if he had, he didn't consider himself the type of man to inspire it. The nearest he could figure it, Cassie was confusing great sex with true love.

In the end, he couldn't bring himself to say no to her, not now, not yet. It was easier to temporize, to say they would talk it over when she got back to San Diego. He took her into his arms and held her, and the trembling stopped.

Chapter Nine

𝒞assie left San Francisco for New York on a cool, foggy Sunday in late June. Her book had hit the stores early the week before. Despite a full-page photo on the back cover and an ad in that morning's paper, not one person recognized her face, although a few would have recognized her byline and many had read her articles. When she rolled into Los Angeles fifteen days later for her final appearance of the tour, *A Hundred and One Nights* was number four on the *New York Times* best-seller list. On the plane back to San Francisco a flight attendant asked Cassie for her autograph. People nudged each other when she walked down the aisle to the rest room, or craned their necks for a better look at her.

She was that uniquely American phenomenon, famous—as Andy Warhol had once put it—for fifteen minutes. Or maybe it would be fifteen days, or even fifteen weeks. She'd done Donahue and the network morning news shows and had appeared on local radio and television stations in so many major markets that she'd lost track of what day it was or what city she was in. Sometimes she'd appeared with women of the type she'd written about, and every now and then they'd thrown an antagonist up against her, the type who thought that her book was garbage and that she'd surely go to hell for sympathizing with the scum of the earth. She hadn't minded the controversy. It made good television. It sold books.

It was beside the point that she'd tried to give the reader an objective, balanced, factual look at the women she'd interviewed and the lives they led. The subject matter lent itself to sensationalizing. Some of the women had clients who were nationally known politicians or businessmen, and it became a popular game to speculate on the identities that Cassie had so carefully concealed. And then there were those revealing looks at what really went on behind closed doors. Given Cassie's previous articles, it was inevitable that the speculation would eventually extend to *her* and to how thorough her research had been.

She was careful to project a serious image, but all the prim hairstyles and conservative suits in the world couldn't disguise her sparkle and wit. She loved the camera and it loved her back. Meanwhile, down in San Diego, Cassie's growing celebrity wasn't lost on Valerie Hunter. Valerie issued a press release announcing their collaboration before Cassie had seen so much as a preliminary contract. In reality the two agents were haggling over the fine print. Back in New York, the publisher who had paid Valerie a six-figure advance a whole year before allowed himself to hope he would finally get a book out of the woman.

Cassie stayed in San Francisco just long enough to pick up Jessica from the Valkenbergs, do the laundry, and pack a pair of suitcases. Then she drove to the family cabin at Lake Tahoe. She and Jessica went boating, waterskiing and hiking, saw a couple of shows, and played the slot machines in one of the casinos until a guard came along and chased Jessica away. By the time Cassie got back to San Francisco five days later, she had finally started to unwind. She found the contracts waiting for her, along with a tapeful of messages on her answering machine.

Listening to the tape told Cassie that she'd reached the pinnacle of American notoriety: *Spotlight* magazine wanted to do a story on her. One of their reporters had spoken to her famous father-in-law, her famous sister, and her famous collaborator. All three had left messages for her, as had the reporter himself, who'd continued to call once a day. She called him back and told him she'd be happy to cooperate as long as she wasn't asked to pose in a skintight dress or to walk down the street in hot pink short shorts.

She arrived back in San Diego precisely a month after she'd left. Edward was waiting for her at the airport, along with a reporter and photographer from the local newspaper. *A Hundred and One Nights* had edged out a diet book and a book on how to make a fortune in the commodities market to take over the top spot on the best-seller list, so Cassie was hotter than ever. The photographer shouted, "Over here, Cassie! Give me a smile!" but Cassie held up her hand and turned away. She didn't want Jessica's picture in the paper.

The photographer didn't really care about the daughter; it was the mother he'd been told to shoot. Leaving Jessica with Edward, Cassie gave him his pictures and answered five minutes' worth of questions from the reporter. Later, waiting in the baggage-claim area with Edward and Jessica, she said, "It's a zoo out there, Edward. I'm beginning to like the idea of Miesley's locked gates and unlisted phone number."

"Melanie and I were hoping you might change your mind and stay with us," he answered.

"I appreciate the offer, but four's a crowd, especially

when two of them are newlyweds. Besides, Jessie will have Lisa to keep her company. They're going to camp together. It's in my contract."

Cassie had called Melanie twice while she was away, so she knew that the movie was two days behind schedule and the marriage was sheer bliss. She asked Edward how he was holding up in the face of Melanie's long working hours.

"I've never been happier," he said. "I love waking up in the morning and finding Melanie next to me, especially on Sundays, when she doesn't have to leave. I've been working hard myself, so I manage to fill up the time. Right now I'm in the middle of putting together a proposal to study certain aspects of ocean-floor thermal vents. My major problem is the funding."

Cassie gave him a smile. "That should be easy enough. Just ask Miesley for the money. Promise him you'll name your submarine after him."

"The way things are going, I wouldn't ask Miesley for the price of a cup of coffee. He doesn't talk these days; he snarls. Doug took as much abuse as he could and then went off to Acapulco with Tawny for some R and R."

Cassie fought down a wave of nausea. Nothing had been settled on that Sunday afternoon over four weeks ago. No promises or commitments had been made. Doug had insisted that there was no point talking till Cassie came back to San Diego, and Cassie, sensing it would have been a mistake to push too hard, had reluctantly agreed.

She no longer knew what she felt. A month was a long time to be separated from somebody you'd only known for forty-eight hours, especially when you'd been as busy as Cassie had. Sometimes she told herself it was nothing more than a strong but transient physical attraction, and other times she missed him so keenly that she longed to call him up. But she'd never done so.

One thing, however, was clear to her: she hated the

idea of his vacationing with Tawny Timberlake. Hiding her feelings behind a nonchalant facade, she asked Edward if Doug had come back yet.

"He's due in tomorrow." Cassie reached for a large suitcase, but Edward pulled it off the carousel before she could get to it. "Unfortunately, the Padres won only half their games while he was away, so Miesley is going to be as sour as ever. Between the team and the problems with that downtown construction project, he's been foaming at the mouth ever since you left. The local sports reporters are having a field day watching him and Sam McGuire tear each other to pieces. Miesley fired the field manager two weeks ago, and everyone figures Sam is next."

"For Sam's sake, I almost hope they're right," Cassie said. "He's too nice a man to have to put up with Miesley's abuse. But why is Miesley harassing Doug about the downtown complex? Isn't it Doug's responsibility?"

"Practically speaking, yes, but Miesley is still the corporation's chairman. He considers Miesley Center to be the architectural jewel in the company's crown. Doug finally blew up when Miesley started negotiating with the city on his own. Six weeks of work went up in flames. Tawny was down at her parents' place in Acapulco at the time, and Doug really likes it down there. He figured a couple of days away from Miesley might stop him from killing the bastard."

Cassie told herself it was better than a planned vacation and changed the subject to Melanie's movie. Once the three remaining bags had come through, Edward drove to a seafood restaurant on Harbor Island for lunch. The gates to Miesley's Rancho Santa Fe mansion were closed when they arrived, but Edward waved at a nearby tree and they soon slid open.

Cassie followed the direction of his wave and spotted a camera perched in the tree's branches. She hadn't noticed it before. "Why the elaborate security measures?" she asked as they drove up the driveway. Miesley loved publicity, so it couldn't be some sort of mania for privacy.

"Horace claims it's to protect his sculpture collection from burglars and Lisa from kidnappers," Edward said, "but I'd give you good odds that he's more worried about himself than about both those things put together. The man has more than his share of enemies."

Cassie filed that fact away. The more she heard about Miesley, the more interested she got. She believed that Valerie's twenty-year relationship with the man was potentially the most riveting part of the autobiography —if she could be persuaded to tell the truth.

Chris Patterson met them by the courtyard gate and carried the two heaviest pieces of luggage into the house. Cassie had been given the bedroom next to Valerie's office, while Jessica was sharing a room with Lisa at the opposite end of the hall. Later, looking around the house, Cassie would be struck by the layout of the master suite. It consisted of two bedrooms separated by a parlor and twin bathrooms, affording total privacy to both husband and wife. Both bedrooms had back exits, so one could even go outside without anybody else knowing about it.

Cassie spent the rest of the afternoon with Jessica, walking around the property, visiting the horses, and swimming. Valerie showed up at five-fifteen with Lisa in tow and immediately pulled a lounge chair over to Cassie's to talk. Cassie quickly saw that her first hurdle as Valerie's collaborator would be to pin the woman down to some sort of work schedule. She claimed to be up to her ears in commitments. It took a threat to pack up and go home, but Valerie finally agreed to set aside two hours a day, either first thing in the morning or after dinner. For the time being that was fine with Cassie, who intended to start the project by reading everything she could get her hands on concerning Valerie Hunter and the people whose paths she'd crossed. It was only sensible to track down any independent sources she could in order to check on Valerie's version of the facts.

Cassie and Jessica had dinner with Edward and Melanie that night, Cassie driving the sports car Valerie had leased for her. The car was in her contract, right along with Jessica's camp and unlimited use of Valerie's computer hookups. The list of perks earned Cassie some good-natured teasing from her older sister, who claimed that Cassie had finally gone Hollywood. "A little national attention and you're demanding the moon and the stars," she said. "I thought *I* was the famous one in this family."

"That's what you get for leaving your soap opera for so long. Off the air for two months and they forget all about you." Cassie paused, a thoughtful expression replacing her smile. "Actually, Melanie, the whole tour had a dreamlike quality to it. I loved it, but half the time I was exhausted. In retrospect I feel very disconnected from the person who autographed all those books and appeared on all those TV and radio shows. It was a real ego trip, of course, but all in all I'd rather be Cassie Valkenberg than Catherine R. Ford."

Edward claimed he didn't believe a word of it. "I have you on tape, Cassie. Four different national spots. Come on, admit that you like to mix it up a little. Put you in the middle of a battle with a camera running and you come alive. Now that you've hit it big you're not going to want to go back to writing anonymous little articles."

"And what's wrong with that?" Melanie demanded, crossing over to the television set. "Cassie deserves to be recognized. She's a born saleswoman with a first-rate product to offer." She switched on the VCR. "Just watch the tape, honey. I want you to see how good you were."

What Cassie saw was a woman who exuded confi-

dence and who combined the instincts of a piranha with
the manners of a lady. She only hoped that neither of
those assets would desert her when it came to dealing
with Valerie Hunter and Horace Miesley, because it
looked as though she was going to need them.

Like Edward and Melanie, Doug Hunter had taped
all of Cassie's network television spots. He'd tried to
tell himself it was for his mother, but he knew damn
well that it wasn't. He was curious about how Cassie
would do. And maybe he just wanted to see her face.

The interviews had appalled him, but they had also
fascinated him. Never in a million years would Doug
have traded his privacy for a slot on the best-seller list.
He didn't even like doing local interviews to help get
projects off the ground, but they were a business
necessity. If anyone had dared to ask him the kinds of
personal questions that Cassie seemed to field with such
style and dash, he would have been tempted to punch
the interviewer in the nose.

At the same time he recognized good television when
he saw it. Whenever he watched one of Cassie's
appearances, the same thoughts ran through his mind:
he'd forgotten how lovely she was, how animated and
clever. She had tremendous charisma, especially when
she smiled or teased, and she sounded so knowledge-
able that he might have bought her book even if he
hadn't had a personal reason for doing so.

He took it down to Acapulco with him and spent
hours each day on the beach reading it. It was enough
to make him regret that he'd ever gotten Cassie together with his mother. The book was too good. Cassie was
too good. There were only two types of people who
could get along with Valerie Hunter: the placaters, who
did whatever she wanted, and the self-confident ones,
who firmly stood their ground even when she tried to
run roughshod over them. Cassie was obviously in the

second group. Doug was beginning to realize that it was quite likely the book would actually be written, and he didn't much care for that.

On the plane back to San Diego he found himself thinking that a brief relationship with Cassie Valkenberg would be the perfect affair. She was beautiful, passionate and intelligent. She'd done a lot of interesting things in her life and had met a lot of interesting people. Give him an empty evening or two, and he couldn't think of anyone he'd rather fill them with.

The perfect lover, however, was not the same thing as the perfect wife. Perfect wives didn't splash themselves all over the airwaves, hustling themselves and their books to a prurient audience. They didn't play at all sorts of bizarre occupations just for the sake of a story. If they had to attract attention, they attracted the right kind of attention, the kind Buffy had attracted: academic honors such as election to law review, awards for volunteer service, employers who stood in line to hire them.

The bottom line couldn't have been clearer: it read, "Stay away."

Cassie was working in Valerie's office when Doug got home. The printer was clacking away, and she didn't hear him walk into the room until it stopped. She looked over her shoulder to find him standing just behind her, reading the final page.

The vacation had left him with an even deeper suntan, but he didn't look particularly relaxed. Although Cassie knew with the first glance that the physical attraction between them hadn't diminished, she couldn't tell if anything deeper remained.

He bent down and brushed his lips over her cheek, but somehow the gesture was cool rather than warm. It reminded Cassie of the way he'd kissed Melanie just before the wedding rehearsal.

"Welcome back to San Diego," he said. "Congratulations are obviously in order. We'll have to break out the champagne."

His tone was cordial but distant; it warned her to stay away. Picturing him in Tawny's bed, Cassie asked, "How was Acapulco?"

"It was fine. I read your book. It's very good, Cassie."

"Thank you." She couldn't think of anything else to say. He was making it crystal clear that he had no intention of picking up where they'd left off.

He nodded at the printout. "Background research for the book?"

"It's a section of Scott Clayton's autobiography." The book had been published twenty years before. Clayton, who'd starred with Valerie in two pictures before drinking himself to death, had written extensively about his relationship with her. "He claims he was your mother's lover at the time you were conceived," Cassie added. "He implies that he's your real father."

"I've seen it," Doug answered.

"And?" Cassie prodded.

Doug hesitated, then answered reluctantly, "Clayton was a close friend of my mother's and a closet homosexual. There was never any affair, but my mother was willing to acknowledge one for the sake of his image. I wish he *had* been my father. He was a sweet man, but also a tortured one."

Cassie took the phone out of the computer modem and hung it up, then carefully tore off the printout. She'd never been one to believe everything she read, and that seemed like a prudent policy when you were dealing with Hollywood biographies. "I guess that's enough work for one day," she said, and stood up. "I hope you'll be able to sit down with me and tell me what you know. I have the feeling that your mother and her pals have different versions of the truth depending on who asks the questions."

Doug said he would think it over, but Cassie was sure that was a polite way of saying no. He wasn't happy about the project, and while he wouldn't interfere, he wasn't about to cooperate, either.

Once she'd straightened up the desk they went next door to the family room. The bar was open, and there was a bucket of ice sitting on top of it. Cassie walked over to pour herself a soft drink, almost knocking over the glass when Tawny Timberlake strolled in with a bowl of lime wedges. She was just as stunning as Cassie remembered.

They hadn't met at the wedding, so Doug introduced them. Cassie asked Tawny a polite question about her work, and then, listening to her answer, realized that she might have liked her if she hadn't been Doug's lover. She was articulate, friendly, and dedicated to her patients. Doug mixed her a gin and tonic and handed it over as he joined her on the couch. The conversation continued, with Cassie listening more than talking.

She had a good antenna for picking up what lay beneath the surface, but the signals she got confused her. There was affection and even intimacy, but none of the silent messages that lovers typically exchange. They neither touched each other nor acted like they wanted to. Either their affair was singularly tepid or Cassie was simply seeing what she badly wanted to see.

The other members of the household gradually filed in. Lisa, who'd been out riding with Jessica, gave her father a welcome-home hug and then followed Jessie down to the shower. Horace Miesley appeared with Chris trailing after him. He sent the younger man into the kitchen for a beer and then sat down in the family room catty-corner to Tawny. It didn't escape Cassie's notice that Miesley and Doug never even exchanged hellos; instead, Miesley immediately started up a conversation with Tawny about Acapulco restaurants.

Chris came back with a can of Dudweiler beer and then, hearing the front door open, returned to the hall.

He walked in a few minutes later with Valerie Hunter and, without being asked, went to the bar and fixed her a scotch on the rocks. Valerie, at least, said hello to Doug, but then proceeded to dump a whole series of problems in his lap. He listened for fifteen straight minutes and then cut her off, mumbling something about chilling some champagne.

Tawny wound up staying for dinner, which consisted of marinated barbecued chicken and three different salads. The cook was a benevolent sorceress, conjuring up a meal after magic meal. She was also in the habit of buzzing Cassie on the intercom at regular intervals while Cassie was working in Valerie's office, and offering irresistible delicacies. Cassie was already worried about her weight.

Horace Miesley had carried his half-empty can of beer in to dinner with him, but everyone else was drinking champagne. A little earlier, Doug had made a gracious toast to current and future best-sellers while his mother sat there and laughed. Like Cassie, she knew how unenthusiastic he really was.

The sight of everyone enjoying the champagne was too much for Horace to take. Pushing his can of beer across the table to Chris, he said, "I'll have a glass after all. Put that in the refrigerator. I'll finish it later."

Tawny snatched up the can before Chris could touch it. "You shouldn't finish it at all, Horace. One and a half cans are enough, and you can do without the champagne. You already have intestinal side effects from the Inderal, and the alcohol won't help any."

"A second-year resident and she thinks she knows everything," Horace grumbled. "Go on, Chris, put it away." Horace looked at Tawny. "If you would get me those pills I want . . ."

"I've already told you, you'll have to deal with Dan Goldman on that. He's your doctor, not me."

"It takes him two years to get around to trying anything new. He's too damn conservative."

"Maybe so," Tawny said, "but you shouldn't believe all the hype you read about Cardioprim being the miracle drug of the eighties. Like anything else, there could be risks—"

"It's *my* blasted heart," Horace interrupted irritably. "I'm the one with the chest pains!"

Valerie gave him an impatient look. "If you're unhappy with Dan then change doctors, Horace."

"I don't want to change doctors. I'm used to Goldman."

"You're impossible, Horace." Unlike Valerie, Tawny was amused rather than aggravated. "I'll talk to Dan if you want me to, but I can't make any promises."

Chris was standing and waiting, his eyes on the can of beer. Holding it out to him, Tawny went on, "Pour it down the sink, Chris. It's bad enough he insists on drinking at all, but drinking *this* stuff . . ." She shook her head. "It's a wonder he hasn't developed food poisoning."

As Chris walked off with the beer, Valerie called out after him, "Bring me my matches and cigarettes, would you, darling? They should be in my purse, in the family room." Chris mumbled something about smoking being bad for Valerie's health, but he didn't refuse to do as she'd asked.

Smiling, Cassie said to Doug, "And who nags you about *your* bad habits, Mr. Hunter?"

The answer came from Lisa. "Daddy doesn't *have* any bad habits." She looked at Jessica and giggled. "Jessie says maybe you could teach him some. She says you've got lots of them."

Cassie gave Jessica a stern look, but it was strictly for show. "Oh, really? And what would those be?"

"You yell when you get angry. You forget to give me my allowance half the time, and then you don't have any cash. And you drank too much at Aunt Melanie's wedding."

"That's quite a catalog of sins," Doug said with a

wink at his daughter. "A woman like Jessie's mother could really corrupt a man."

"All truly creative people embrace life with a passion," Valerie informed her son. "Their emotions are close to the surface. That's why Cassie and I get on so famously. We're going to write a marvelous book together. We'll go on TV and we'll shock the nation—" She cut herself off and sidled a sly look at Cassie. "Did I mention that Doug taped every single one of your network spots? You've terrified him, Cassie. It's bad enough that the book will actually get written, but the thought of the two of us running about the country publicizing it—well, it's simply too much for him, especially now that he's seen you in action." She held out her hand to Chris, who'd returned with her cigarettes. "Thank you, darling. If you would fetch me that ashtray from the sideboard . . ."

"Shock the nation, hell!" Horace muttered. Then, glaring at Valerie, he bellowed, "Nobody's publishing a damn word until I see it and okay it first!" He turned to Tawny, suddenly the picture of civilized charm. "Tell me what you think about Acapulco, my dear. Isn't it a better hotel site than Mexico City?"

Tawny laughed and said she wouldn't touch the question with a ten-foot pole. From the conversation that followed, Cassie gathered that there was a running argument between Doug and Horace about whether to enter the resort-hotel market. All the Miesley hotels to date had been commercially oriented. Horace wanted to change that; Doug didn't.

Summer evenings in the Miesley household were spent in only one way: watching a baseball game, either in person or on television. The Padres, as it happened, were at home that night. Everyone went to the ballpark except Valerie and Cassie, both of whom stayed home to work. Valerie wasn't too pleased to be reminded that she still owed Cassie two hours, but she gave in soon enough once Cassie put her foot down.

"It's just that I've got the advertising agency breathing down my neck," she said as they sat down in her office. "I promised to make a decision on the new campaign, but I'm just so busy these days. . . ."

By now Cassie had decided that Valerie wanted her to play the heavy. She could picture the woman on TV, murmuring charmingly, "Well, you know, I never intended to say so much in the book, but Miss Ford simply *pulled* it out of me. I never stood a chance."

Cassie made sympathetic noises about Valerie's schedule and then got down to business. "I'd like to get the ground rules clear in advance. First of all, I'll need total honesty. Second, I'll need the freedom to speak bluntly when it's called for. And third—"

"I'm all for bluntness, dear," Valerie interrupted. She crossed her legs and settled back in her chair, smiling like one of those soap-opera femmes fatales who relishes all the mischief she causes. "For example, you're dying to sleep with my son. There's nothing wrong with that, mind you, he could use somebody like you in his life, but don't let him pour on the charm and persuade you to give up the book. Because he'll try it, you know."

Cassie didn't waste her time commenting on Valerie's so-called advice. Let her change the subject, let her control the conversation, and you were finished. "The only real obstacle to the completion of this book will be you, Valerie. *I'm* totally committed to the project. Which brings me to point number three. I'll need the cooperation of your friends. I want you to call them up and make it clear that you want them to be open and frank with me."

"Consider it done, my dear." Valerie gave a dramatic sigh. "There *is* Horace, however. I'm afraid his enthusiasm, like Doug's, is something less than boundless. There are so many skeletons in his closet, you know."

"Then maybe we should talk about that." If there

was one question Cassie wanted answered quickly, it was how far Valerie would go in writing about her husband and marriage. "It's no secret that Horace has enemies. It's no secret that he manipulates people, although I have to say I've never heard it suggested that he's done anything blatantly illegal. To be frank, Valerie, he doesn't seem like the most pleasant of men, which makes me wonder why you've stayed married to him all these years."

"We understand each other." Valerie lit a cigarette, drawing in the smoke with quick, intense breaths. Cassie switched on her tape recorder, and while Valerie noticed, she didn't object. "Sex and money. That's what it was in the beginning. I was getting older. They were starting to offer me character parts. It was ridiculous—I wasn't even forty yet and looked ten years younger—but you know how Hollywood used to be. Still is, I suppose. Horace was good in bed, very good in bed, and he could offer me an interesting life. The marriage filled both our needs. Horace got the publicity and attention my status as a star could bring him, and I got the opportunity to run a business any damn way I pleased, to be in charge for a change. The sex was over years ago, but the rest of it hasn't changed. Horace may be unpleasant, but he knows where I draw the line and he's never once stepped over it. We understand exactly what to expect from each other and exactly how much the other will tolerate. I consider my marriage to be very successful."

At that point, Cassie should have asked if Horace would "tolerate" an honest autobiography. It was the logical point to raise. Instead, allowing emotion to get the better of her, she asked about things like love and tenderness and caring. Hadn't Valerie missed them? Weren't they essential to any successful marriage?

Valerie responded with predictable disdain. Cassie had the feeling that her impulsiveness had cost her some of the respect she'd managed to earn. "Love?

Caring? I ran away from an abusive stepfather when I was seventeen years old. People used to tell me I was beautiful, that I should be in the movies. Cattle's Fork, Montana, was a thousand miles away from Hollywood, but I made it. God knows how, but I'd even managed to hold on to my virginity. It didn't last long. I was all but raped by the first man who was willing to see me. He was a producer three times my age, but I'll give him this much, he came through on his promise and signed me to a studio contract. I was used—I *permitted* myself to be used—by a lot of men after that. God knows what I was looking for—a benevolent father, a knight in shining armor, whatever. And Doug's father was probably the worst of them. I can forgive him for pretending he loved me, but not for lying about being sterile. When I became pregnant he said it was impossible, that the father had to be somebody else. And then he had the gall to offer to marry me anyway. Of course, the studio head had told him he'd never work again if he didn't. They didn't expect me to put my foot down. I wasn't going to give my child that man's name. The rest, as they say, is history."

Valerie stubbed out her cigarette and immediately lit another. "I decided to live my life on *my* terms. I refused to play the grieving ex-lover when he went and got himself killed, and I refused to apologize for having an illegitimate child. They tarred me and feathered me and sent me into exile, but eventually it blew over. At first I was infamous, unhirable, but long before I met Horace I'd been *rehabilitated*." Valerie rolled the word off her tongue, giving it a mocking lilt. "Their publicity machine turned me from a scarlet slut into a courageous madonna. All in all I have no complaints. My life has been tough at times, but anything would have been better than wasting away in a two-bit backwater like Cattle's Fork, Montana."

Cassie took her time about responding. While it was possible that Valerie had revealed some stark, fundamental truth about herself, it was equally possible that her "confession" was nothing but a con job. Nobody had ever accused her of being a lousy actress.

In the end Cassie came back to the question she should have asked at once: "Just how honest are you willing to be about Horace, Valerie?"

Valerie looked her straight in the eye. "If I laid it all out, it wouldn't be Horace who would wind up looking like a fool. It would be the cowards and lackeys who've kowtowed to him all these years. Still, it could tarnish his public image as a visionary and philanthropist, and he wouldn't like that at all. I will be absolutely candid with you, Cassie, but I will also be extremely careful about what I permit to appear in print. Our conversations *must* be treated as confidential and off the record. I intend to depict Horace as a man who saw what had to be done and did it, with tough methods if necessary. I'll tell the truth—some of the truth—but not until I've sanded off the rough edges. Agreed?"

It was as much as Cassie could hope for. Valerie Hunter, after all, still had to live with the man. She still had to live in the community. "Agreed," she said, and then, curious, went on, "But what if you were free to be completely honest, Valerie. Would you do it?"

"You mean if Horace should drop dead of a heart attack?" Valerie had an ironic smile on her face, as though the prospect had occasionally crossed her mind. "I'd write a book that would explode across this town like a thousand firecrackers. Then I'd move the business to another city, marry my lover, and buy him the wedding present of his dreams."

"Your lover?" Cassie repeated. "Who would that be? And what present would you buy him?"

"Another time," Valerie said, and gave a sinuous stretch. "Another time and a different book."

Chapter Ten

Cassie discovered a lot about Valerie Hunter over the next couple of weeks, but not the identity of her lover. It didn't matter, though, because whoever he was, he wasn't going to wind up in print. Neither would any of the others Valerie had taken during her marriage to Horace Miesley—and there had been others, Cassie was sure of it. Every now and then Valerie would delicately allude to one of them, but the hints were for private consumption only. Publicly Valerie and Horace were a team.

Cassie tried to be philosophical about the whole business. It was, after all, Valerie's book. When it came to the first thirty-five or forty years of her life, Valerie had agreed not to pull any punches. It was only sensible to focus on that part of her life she was willing to be candid about and save the rest for volume two. With its tales of the crasser, more sordid side of Hollywood and its inventory of famous lovers, volume one was sure to be a smash.

Cassie discovered something else during those same few weeks: Doug Hunter was a master at erecting invisible but unbreachable walls. He could warn you to keep your distance without uttering a single specific word. It was all in the polite tone of voice and reserved manner. Whole days went by when Cassie never even saw the man. He would pick up the girls from camp, take them out to dinner or a movie, then drop them off at the house and return to the office for the rest of the night. When the first weekend came around, he took Lisa to Palm Springs to visit his late wife's parents.

Cassie let things ride. She was busy with her work and smart enough to know that a man like Doug Hunter couldn't be led around by the nose. The first order of business was to melt a little of his reserve, and then perhaps they could talk.

She acted the way she always had: vivacious, friendly, unaffected. After that first weekend, Doug stopped going back to the office every night, so they saw a little more of each other. Cassie found a great deal to admire in him. He had a lovely relationship with his daughter and was gracious enough to include Jessica in their activities. He was tolerant of his mother, which wasn't always easy given how self-centered and demanding she was. And he stood up to Horace Miesley, remaining polite but firm in the face of the man's unceasing provocation. He was, Cassie decided, one of the most stable and mature people she'd ever met.

It wasn't easy to play this kind of waiting game because after a single week she was as smitten with him as ever. Fortunately, she was an active person who enjoyed physical exercise, and she was able to use it as an outlet for her frustration. She would swim laps for thirty or forty minutes every afternoon and take long, quiet walks at night. She found it soothing to walk through the woods, surrounded by nocturnal whispers, to sit on the tree-house deck and stare through the waving branches of the trees, to visit the corral and pet the horses, to explore the farthest reaches of the property. There was, she learned, a gate beyond the

corral in the most distant part of the fence that encir-
cled Miesley's land. The gate was secured by a padlock,
but one night she found it open and a strange horse
standing in the corral. She knew by then that the
Timberlake property adjoined the Miesley estate on
that particular section of hillside. She sat down in the
shadows to wait and wasn't surprised when, half an
hour later, Tawny came running down to the corral and
trotted away on the horse. It brought back memories of
the night that Cassie had slipped out of Doug's window
and of the slight figure she'd seen riding off in the
moonlight. It had obviously been Tawny, but on neither
occasion had she been with Doug. The first time Cassie
had been with him herself, and the second, he'd been
at a city council meeting in San Diego.

Her late-night walks often took her past the guest
cottage, but she never gave in to the temptation to
knock on the door. Sometimes, though, she would
pause by an open window and listen to the classical
music that Doug liked to play. They had similar tastes.

Once, a few nights after seeing Tawny, Cassie walked
by Doug's house and heard a torrent of angry words
instead of the usual restful music. Maybe she shouldn't
have eavesdropped, but it was hard to pass up a speech
like, "I could crush you! I could move in and take over
again, and nobody would say a word. I could paint you
as an administrative and financial disaster and make it
stick, Douglas! Nobody would touch you again, not in
this town! And you'd damn well better remember it!"

Miesley was the one making the threats, but Doug
didn't answer him in kind. In a cool tone with only the
slightest emotional edge to it, he said, "I assure you
that it will never be necessary to force me out, Horace.
Anytime you want my resignation, all you have to do is
ask for it—in writing, of course."

Sounding enraged, Miesley bellowed, "Don't you get
smart with me, Douglas! I whipped your ass when you
were a snot-nosed adolescent, and I can do the same

thing now. I taught you every damn thing you know, and don't you dare forget it!"

"I've never forgotten it for a moment," was the calm response. "But one of the things you taught me was that one man has to be in charge. That man is me, Horace, and I have to run the company as I see fit. Times have changed. You can't get away with riding roughshod over people anymore—"

"Get away with? *Get away with?!* Hell, no wonder you never get anywhere. You don't have the guts for it. I treat you like a son, I hand you what I built up from nothing on a silver platter, and what do I get? A craven weakling! A soft-bellied, bleeding-heart philanthropist! I want that deal nailed down on my terms, Douglas, and I want my name on those buildings. If I don't get what I want, I'm taking this company away from you. And don't you think I can't do it, just like I took away your mother, just like I took away your mistress, just like I could have taken away your skinny bitch of a wife if I'd ever really wanted her. A month, dammit, do you hear me? A month! That's how long you have!"

The next thing Cassie heard was the sound of the front door slamming violently shut. Horace passed within fifteen feet of her, but she was hidden by the shadows of the house and he didn't see her. About fifteen seconds later the sound of a Mozart symphony came drifting out the window.

Doug Hunter had been raised in a world where people routinely violated each other's deepest and most sensitive feelings, until the body and soul grew so protectively callused that the feelings became unreachable. It might have made him into another Valerie Hunter or Horace Miesley, ready to trample on anyone who got in the way of what he wanted, but it hadn't. He'd been kicked in the teeth time and again as a child and didn't want to do it to anybody else.

For the first time in his life, though, his strongest

principles and his strongest desires were sharply at
odds. He wanted Cassie Valkenberg more with each
passing day but hated the thought of hurting her. He
was smart enough to read her very clearly: she was still
as interested as ever but wasn't going to push him. She
was giving him time to get to know her, time to see her
in a different light.

The strategy worked. He started to believe that he
and not she controlled the situation. His guard slowly
dropped. He didn't change his mind about getting
romantically involved with her but came to believe a
casual friendship might be possible.

By the second Saturday of her stay, he'd relaxed to
the point of accepting her invitation to accompany her
and the girls to the zoo. He'd gotten fond of Cassie's
daughter, Jessica, who got along extremely well with
Lisa and had inherited her mother's teasing charm. The
four of them walked their legs off, ate too much junk
food, and in general had a terrific time. They returned
at about five and immediately headed for the hot tub to
soak away their aches and pains.

On Sunday he decided to ask Cassie and Jessica if
they wanted to go to Coronado with him and Lisa to see
how his house was coming along. For all that his mother
drove him crazy at times, she had been generous
enough to offer to supervise the workmen. The bulk of
the job—removing parts of several walls, putting in a
new kitchen and bathrooms, renovating the entire
second story—was done now, with interior finishing
and decorating still left to accomplish. Doug hoped to
move back into the house by the start of the school
year.

By the following Wednesday, when Edward and
Melanie invited him and Cassie to join them for dinner
at the house, accepting was no longer unthinkable. As
it happened, Doug had had an unusually productive
day and wasn't about to spoil his good mood by

dwelling on whether he was asking for trouble. He left the office early, found Cassie working at the computer, and persuaded her to knock off for the day and head down to La Jolla as soon as they both had changed. As usual, she asked him how his day had gone, and as usual, he answered, "Fine," but for the first time since she'd come to San Diego he found himself wanting to elaborate.

At first it baffled him that he was willing—no, eager—to discuss important business affairs with any outsider other than Edward Kolby. It wasn't until he'd changed his clothes and helped Cassie into his car that he understood what was going on in his own head. He'd heard enough over the dinner table to realize that by the time Cassie was through, there was no aspect of his mother's life—including the business end of it, and including his own childhood—that she wouldn't be intimately familiar with. Thorough and determined, Cassie was more than a match for his mother's propensity to shade the truth.

The astonishing thing was that he felt so calm at the knowledge. He'd never liked the idea of the book in the first place, and the thought of a book that was actually honest should have had him climbing the walls.

That it didn't was a tribute to *A Hundred and One Nights.* Cassie had taken a controversial, even offensive topic and handled it with skill, objectivity and good taste. If Doug was put off by the way she'd hustled it onto the best-seller list, he also recognized the fact that she was a very fine journalist. The bottom line was that he trusted her not to sensationalize the story of his mother's life.

So he spoke of his problems with the central city project and told her how Horace had complicated things with a heavy-handed brand of interference that had undermined and almost destroyed a whole series of sensitive negotiations. He confided that the two of them had had bitter arguments marked by malicious threats on Horace's part. He even admitted that the man's criticism could hurt him at times.

Listening to him, Cassie realized that Doug was giving her a gift far more precious than physical pleasure, and she valued it accordingly. Encouraged by his openness, she told him about her habit of taking walks in the evening and admitted that less than a week before, she'd overheard part of a violent quarrel between him and Horace. She was afraid that he might be angry that she'd stayed around to listen, but he claimed to be relieved. He told her he was glad that somebody else in the world had a gut-level understanding of what he'd had to put up with all these months. Sharing his frustration, he said, made it easier to handle.

If Doug had taken the most direct route to Edward's house, they would have arrived by that point in the conversation, but he hadn't. He'd crossed under the freeway to the coast road, going past the Scripps Institution and into La Jolla, and then continued south for a couple of miles before turning inland and heading back up to Edward's. Obviously he wanted to prolong their private time together, and Cassie couldn't have been more delighted. They'd grown closer over the past few days, but she'd never dared hope that his defenses would drop so quickly.

Feeling the confidence that comes from shared intimacies, she risked asking about the personal and painful. "That argument you had with Horace, Doug . . . he made some incredibly raw statements. I wondered if there was any truth to them."

Doug didn't have to ask which statements she meant. "Who wants to know?" he asked. "The journalist or the friend?"

Friend. It had a nice sound to it. "Sometimes it's hard to separate the two," Cassie admitted. "But I was asking as a friend. I would never use anything personal without your explicit permission."

"I know you wouldn't." Doug switched off the air-conditioning and put down the window in order to rest his elbow on the door. Early evening was his favorite time of day. "Horace didn't take away my mother because I never had her in the first place," he said. "I don't think she's capable of—of *belonging* to anyone in the way that husbands and wives or parents and children do when there's love and commitment in the relationship. As far as Buffy goes, what you heard was typical Miesley bravado, designed to stab me hard and stay around to fester. Buffy didn't like him. He'd tried his best to charm her without success, and he never forgave her for it. The line about my mistress . . ." Doug shook his head, finding the term archaic. "I have no idea who he was talking about. The women I've dated since Buffy died have all been people Horace either knew or eventually met, and I suppose he could have slept with one of them, but it isn't anything that matters to me."

"And his threat to take away control of the company from you? Does that matter to you?" Cassie asked.

"I don't take it seriously," Doug answered. "Both of us know he could probably do it if he put his mind to it, but I doubt he would make the effort. He's too wrapped up in the Padres right now. In fact, I think that on some level he would rather lose than win. It triples his opportunities to make life miserable for everyone connected to the franchise."

Doug was being ironic—Miesley *hated* to lose—but Cassie saw a germ of truth in the idea. Miesley liked to humiliate people. He enjoyed making them feel small. That being the case, she wondered how Doug had tolerated the man all these years. "You could have done anything you wanted to do, been anything you wanted to be," she said. "Why did you settle in San Diego? Why did you go to work for Miesley? He's egomaniacal, abusive, mean-spirited . . ."

". . . Brilliant, visionary, dazzlingly intuitive, encyclopedic in his knowledge of the industry . . ." Doug's expression was sober, telling Cassie that he'd meant every word he said. "I don't like the man, but I realized by the age of twenty that I admired what he was doing and wanted to do the same thing. Somehow it got so far into my blood that no other choice was possible. Horace wasn't lying when he said he'd taught me everything I know and handed me the business on a silver platter. His motive might have been to perpetuate his own image, but still, I benefited enormously. And the plain truth is that if he'd been running the central city project, the preliminary problems would have been settled two months ago. The deals would have been more favorable to the company, and the bottom line would have been healthier. But in the process, people would have been trampled, important considerations swept under the carpet, and bitter resentments incurred. Horace wouldn't have given a damn. I do. I care about fairness, and the people I deal with know it. I couldn't get away with the stuff Horace manages to pull. But even if I could, I wouldn't, because I don't want to be worshiped in public but hated in private. Horace considers that a deplorable weakness."

"Then I feel sorry for him, or I would if he weren't such a bastard."

Doug smiled at that. "You're giving bastards a bad name, Cassie. Some of us aren't so bad."

Some of you are wonderful, Cassie thought, but had the brains not to say so aloud. If there was anything calculated to make Doug Hunter run as fast as possible in the opposite direction, it was an open declaration of love.

The evening was delightful, the nicest Cassie had spent in years. Everyone helped with the dinner, which they ate out on the patio. Afterward they stayed outside to talk, not seriously because the four of them weren't close enough yet, but wittily and cleverly.

Melanie was in top form, telling stories culled from a career's worth of on-set disasters. Cassie, a little jealous that Melanie could make Doug laugh so easily, told anecdotes about researching her book and huckstering it nationwide. The two men kept exchanging looks that labeled the Ford sisters loonier than a pair of sun-crazed camels, but they obviously enjoyed the show.

"Don't look so damn superior," Cassie finally said to Doug. "I know for a fact that things don't always go perfectly even for *you,* Mr. Hunter, and if you don't have enough of a sense of humor to laugh at yourself . . ."

"Who said I don't?" Doug rose to the occasion, managing to come up with a couple of funny, self-deprecating stories. Melanie played the role of the wide-eyed straight man, setting up Doug's lines to perfection.

"I can't get over it," she said as she and Cassie carried some dishes into the kitchen. "I've never seen him so relaxed. He even acts like he approves of me."

"Why shouldn't he? Anyone can see that you make Edward happy." Cassie sighed. "I only wish it were that easy to get him to approve of *me.* . . ."

"Cassie . . ."

"I know, I know. He's never going to take me seriously, and I'll wind up getting hurt." They'd talked about this more than once on the evenings that Cassie and Jessica had come for dinner. "But it's my life, Melanie, and I happen to be in love with him. No risk, no gain."

"I suppose so, but still . . ." Melanie stifled a yawn. "Still, I worry about you, Cassie." A second yawn erupted, more insistent than the first. "I'm sorry, honey, but I've got to get some sleep. These early calls are killers."

Cassie and Doug left about ten minutes later, but neither of them wanted to go straight home. Cassie was too cautious to say so, but Doug had convinced himself that all that talk about friendship was really true. His thoughts were on how comfortable he'd felt that evening and how relieved he was to find himself liking Edward's wife. "Let's take a walk on the beach," he suggested. "It's too nice a night to go back inside."

They drove to the coast and parked the car by the side of a road that ran parallel to one of the public beaches. The breeze was quite a bit stiffer by the ocean, but Cassie didn't mind the cold. She took a deep breath of the salty air, feeling a heady mixture of excitement and happiness. Making love would have been the perfect end to a night like this, but she refused to be disappointed if it didn't happen. She and Doug had come so far already.

They headed to the shore and took off their shoes. They didn't actually walk in the ocean but on the damp sand, near enough to catch the tail end of an occasional wave. Cassie felt enveloped by the wonders of nature: the sight of the bright moon, the sound of the surf, the smell of the air. It was both peaceful and magnificent.

Doug was the one who broke the silence. "I've never seen Edward so content. He doesn't even seem to be worried about not getting his work funded yet." He paused. "What I'm trying to say is . . ."

"I know." Cassie smiled to herself. "Maybe you were wrong about my sister."

"There are no maybes about it. I was wrong, period. Anyone can see she adores him." Doug shook his head. "It amazes me. He says they can't go out to dinner without half a dozen people bothering her for autographs. She works the most god-awful hours imaginable, so *he* does most of the cooking. Edward, who up until a month ago could barely warm up a TV dinner, is suddenly another James Beard. He's had to unlist his phone number, put up with drunken men making passes at his wife in restaurants and total strangers asking her advice in department stores, and tolerate a very limited amount of time with her, but he's happier than he's ever been in his life. I couldn't begin to cope with the things he puts up with."

"But they love each other very much," Cassie said softly.

Doug didn't need for her to spell out what she meant. People who wanted to be together made adjustments, allowances and compromises. "I suppose I had too much of it as a kid," he murmured. "One of my earliest memories is of being taken out to dinner by my mother. I couldn't have been more than three or four at the time. It was a Hollywood hangout, the kind of place where people go to be spotted, and she'd dressed me in a suit with short pants and a bow tie so I'd look cute for the cameras. She hadn't had a decent role in years, but she was having an affair with a studio head, and she'd convinced him to get her back into the public's good graces. I was part of the campaign. I remember her calling me her date, and that I was frightened of the photographers' flashbulbs. I was shy as a child but very photogenic. Good fan magazine material. There were a lot of carefully orchestrated outings after that, but I never really got used to them."

Cassie said she could understand why and kept on walking. She knew Valerie well enough by then not to be surprised by the callous way she'd used her son, but still, her heart ached for him. She understood, of course, that he was talking more about him and her than about Melanie and Edward or him and his mother, that he was warning her that he wasn't about to share his life with someone who yearned for the limelight.

Still, there was an unmistakable sexual tension in the air. When she shivered from a gust of wind and hugged herself to warm up, he gave her a look that set her heart racing. She stared back, offering whatever he wanted to take, but he simply shifted his gaze to the sand. A few seconds later both of them stopped and, by unspoken mutual agreement, started back toward the car.

Cassie couldn't bear it. She longed to be in his arms. If their relationship hadn't been so new, so fragile, she would have taken a chance and said so. Instead, after they'd gone about twenty feet, she gave a surprised yelp of pain and stumbled. On occasion she could be almost as good an actress as her sister was. Doug dropped his shoes and reached for her before she could tumble onto the sand. Still carrying her sandals, she clutched his shoulder for support. She felt him stiffen, but he didn't let go of her.

"Are you all right?" he asked hoarsely.

She lied like a trooper. "I stepped on something sharp—a rock or a shell."

"Is your foot bleeding?"

She dropped her shoes and ran her fingers over the bottom of her foot. "No. It seems to be okay."

"Good." Doug released her and backed away. "We should be getting back. . . ."

"Why?"

"You know why."

Cassie didn't answer him. She simply put her arms around his neck and kissed him.

He took a deep breath. "For God's sake, Cassie . . ."

"It was your idea, not mine. A walk on the beach in the moonlight . . . It's so romantic here. You must have known that, Doug."

She was right. Doug had known it even before he'd opened his mouth to suggest it, which made him wonder if he'd been out of his mind at the time. Sure, he'd wanted Cassie's company for a while longer, but he'd been insane to think he could be alone with her without something like this happening.

He removed her hands from his neck and said firmly, "That doesn't mean it was a good idea. It wasn't. We're going back to the car, Cassie." Much to his relief, she didn't continue to argue.

There were questions that Cassie wanted to ask, questions like "How much longer is this going to go on?" and "What's the point of refusing what both of us want so badly?" She didn't bother because she knew what answers she'd get. She loved Doug for his decency and sensitivity, but at that moment, she wished he had a little bit more of the careless womanizer in him.

He unlocked the door on her side of the car and held it open for her. By the time he'd slid into the driver's seat she knew she wasn't going to let the subject drop. It didn't matter that forcing the issue was the wrong way to handle him. She knew she could seduce him. She was sure that once they slept together they would remain lovers . . . until she left San Diego or until the physical thrill he felt wore off.

He started up the car, but before he could move the stick shift she covered his hand with her own and told him she wanted to talk to him. With a resigned sigh, he switched off the engine and turned to face her.

Cassie was in no mood for melodrama. Her emotions were too close to the surface for that, ready to spill out if they got into one of those horribly serious discussions about what each of them felt and wanted out of life. So she grabbed him by the front of his shirt, a fistful of fabric in each hand, playing at being aggressive. He instinctively recoiled when she leaned forward, but there was really nowhere he could go. She wound up all but resting on his chest, her lips only inches from his own.

Smiling, she asked ingenuously, "Before I left on my book tour I saw my doctor, and do you know what he told me?"

Doug turned his head to the side. "Cassie, listen to me. . . ."

"He told me—" she brushed her mouth across his cheek "—that I was a healthy woman—" she ran her tongue up his jawline to his ear "—in the prime of life—"she sucked on his earlobe and felt him catch at his breath"—who desperately needed a lover."

"Doctors don't give that kind of advice," he mumbled, and gave a halfhearted push against her shoulders.

More confident now because he hadn't rejected her out of hand, she took his face in her palms and turned his mouth to her lips. "I'm accepting applications. He has to be, oh, about six foot two, a hundred eighty pounds, brown hair, brown eyes you could lose yourself in. . . ."

"Dammit, Cassie . . ."

"Terrific at kissing and, uh, let's see now, willing to be tied up and enthusiastic about letting me experiment on his body." She took his lower lip between her teeth and playfully nipped him. "Do you know anybody who fits that description? Because if you do, I won't deny him a thing. Not a single thing."

There was no way Doug could listen to that kind of talk without being affected by it, and the kissing and biting made it that much worse. Still, he'd given the subject a lot of thought, and he'd decided how it should be, and nothing could be allowed to change that. Angry at Cassie for taunting him with what he ached to have but had to refuse, he shoved her away with almost brutal abruptness and twisted around to face the door. There was a limit to how much he could take.

"Forget it, Cassie," he said. "I'm not going to get involved with you. A sexual relationship is out of the question. Either let it go or there won't even be a friendship between us. There won't be anything at all."

"You wanted to make love to me," she answered, making it into an accusation. "You're dying to, even now!"

At the end of his tether, he jerked around and exploded, "Yes, dammit, I want to make love to you, but what does that prove? Didn't you *hear* me down on that beach? Didn't you understand what I was trying to tell you? It isn't going to go anywhere between us, Cassie. We're all wrong for each other. . . ."

"I disagree. Maybe you're not like John, but . . ."

"All right. I'll rephrase it. *You're* all wrong for *me*. Is that clear enough for you? I can sleep with you every night for the next two months and love every minute of it, but it's not going to change that essential fact. I'm not going to fall in love with you. I don't want to spend my life with you. Get that through your head, Cassie, because nothing you do can change it!"

Doug restarted the car and viciously put it in gear. Cassie did what most women would have done at a time like that: she burst into tears. It wasn't only the finality of his rejection, or even its cruel bluntness, but the stupidity of her own behavior. Two weeks of progress had been shot to pieces. She should have been more patient. The thought that he might have meant what he said ripped her to shreds.

Doug didn't waste time on long cuts. He drove straight to the freeway and north to the Rancho Santa Fe exit. He couldn't see Cassie's face because she was looking out the side window, but he could hear an occasional sniff or sob. He felt rotten about making her cry. He wished he'd been more gentle with her. He was perceptive enough to know exactly where all that sound and fury had come from, all that hypocritically self-righteous anger. He'd been trying to convince himself as well as her.

The naked truth was, he was scared. He felt too much already. He didn't think it could work. He didn't want the pain if it didn't work, for either of them.

He was hoping that she would slam out of the car and run into the house when they got home, but she didn't make it that easy for him. She simply sat there, motionless except for the slight trembling of her body that told him she was still crying.

Feeling guilty and helpless, he said, "I'm sorry, Cassie."

She didn't answer.

"I shouldn't have yelled at you. What happened was entirely my fault."

Still no answer.

Her silence rattled him. He couldn't understand why she didn't answer him or, failing that, simply leave. "Please, Cassie, say something. At least turn around so I'll know you're okay."

That, at least, got some response out of her. She straightened up in her seat and stared out the front window. Her face was wet with tears and very grave. She'd finally stopped crying, but she was shaking even more than before.

"If you could just think about it rationally you would see that I'm right," he said gently, and proceeded to make a speech about how different they were and about how their relationship would fall apart the moment it was subjected to the normal stresses of everyday life. The only problem was, he didn't give a damn about any of that.

Somewhere in the middle of his speech she'd turned to meet his eyes, but all she said when he was finished was, "I don't want to lose your friendship. Promise me you won't start pretending I don't exist. I couldn't bear that."

"I promise," he said, and thought, *She's crazy about you, Hunter, and you know damn well she's gotten under your skin. You're living in a dreamworld if you think you can be her friend without also becoming her lover.*

She looked relieved. "I was afraid you would . . . well, never mind." She leaned forward and, with clumsy nervousness, kissed him quickly on the mouth. Then she reached for the door. Her husky "Good night" was almost inaudible.

He grabbed her by the wrist before he had time to

talk himself out of it. "Dammit, Cassie, I can't make any promises—about the future, I mean."

She gave him a wary look. "I never asked you to."

Too much more of this and he was going to break out in a cold sweat. "It's just—I don't want to hurt you. I don't want to hurt either of us."

"I know that," she answered.

"What I said before, about not falling in love with you—it wasn't true. I don't know what I feel, but it's not just physical."

She nodded. "Oh."

"So will you—would you want to spend the night with me?" When there was no immediate reply, he hurriedly added, "It doesn't have to be tonight. I know how much I've upset you."

A slow smile spread across her face. What the smile did to his rate of respiration should have been outlawed. "Tonight will be fine," she said, "but only if I can tie you up."

He couldn't help laughing. Shaking his head, he said, "Oh, no, lady. I'm not falling for *that* one again. Get over here and let me kiss you. You've kept me waiting long enough."

Doug couldn't have said who actually reached out first, but within moments they were in each other's arms. Though he wanted to devour her, he somehow found the self-control to be thorough but very sweet about it. When he gently broke the kiss, she clung to him like a hurting child, resting her head on his shoulder. It made him feel incredibly protective of her.

"When you saw your doctor, did you happen to mention your astonishing fertility?" he asked, caressing her hair. "Because if you didn't, there's a drugstore I need to visit."

Cassie blinked back tears. He was so tender, so wonderful, that she could hardly believe he was real. She slid her hand up his thigh and decided that if he *wasn't* real, the apparition had amazingly convincing substance to it. Teasing him, she said, "It's a good thing I took care of all that, because you're in no shape to wait."

He kissed her again to show how right she was. Sweetness gave way to passion, and passion to straining, red-hot urgency.

Somehow they tore themselves away from each other and made it out of the car. They walked arm in arm to the guest house, moving quickly so they wouldn't be tempted to stop along the way. The future was the last thing on Cassie's mind at that point. All she could think about was the way she felt when Doug touched her. She wanted to hold onto that excitement and let it build till her blood was on fire, and only let go when she couldn't stand another second of it.

She ran into the bedroom ahead of him and had stripped off her shirt by the time he caught up. As she stepped out of her slacks, she said, "It's so nice to have a whole house to ourselves. Where should we make love, Doug? The rug in front of the fireplace? The Roman tub? The hammock on the porch?"

"Do you have something against beds?" he asked with a smile.

She watched him start to undress. "Beds are dull. A man like you needs a challenge." She paused to think of something suitable. "I've got it. We'll make a test of your staying power."

"My staying power, huh?" He kicked off his shoes. "You've got to be kidding."

"No, I'm not. We'll go from room to room . . ."

"Impossible. I'm not letting you out of this bedroom."

"Oh, yes, you are." She gave him a devilish smile. "There are ways to prolong a man's pleasure, sensual tricks they use in the East . . ."

". . . And guard from outsiders. I know, I know." Doug frowned. "Dammit, Cassie, if I thought you'd done that stuff with anybody else . . ."

"I haven't. You were my first experiment. But before you get smothered with pleasure, you've got to catch me." She took off, giggling, as Doug stepped out of his pants. The truth was that he could have stopped her out in the hall, but he played the game and allowed her to make it out to the porch. Blocking the doorway, he finished undressing and then walked to the hammock and lay down.

"Over here," he said, and cocked his little finger at her.

She stretched out beside him and offered her lips, thinking that it was heaven to be in his arms. She still had her underwear on, but the bra didn't last very long. Within moments he was caressing her naked breasts, massaging the nipples into aching readiness. She ran her fingers down his side, teasing his buttocks and inner thighs until he grabbed her hand and put it where he wanted it. Her playful stroking seemed to push him over the edge. There was a clumsy impatience to the way he yanked at her panties, but she lifted her hips and helped him get them off, wanting him just as much as he wanted her.

It was the first time she'd known the raw excitement of being held naked against him, and all she could think about was having him inside of her. He clasped her hips and eased himself on top of her, showing her how he wanted her to move. She wasn't sure just which of them he meant to tease with the slow-paced thrusts that stopped just short of taking her, but it wasn't long before she'd opened her legs in silent pleading and wrapped them around his hips. She strained against him in a fruitless effort to deepen his strokes. Her arms, which were coiled around his neck, tightened convulsively.

He raised his head and murmured against her mouth, "You said something about my staying power. . . ."

"It was a joke. Please Doug, make love to me."

But instead of coming closer he inched his way down

her body till his teeth closed over her nipple. Cassie blindly reached out for him, but he was too far away to touch. And then he was sliding onto his side and his hand was slipping between her legs.

Cassie moaned his name as he started to caress her. He seemed to have a sixth sense that kept her balanced on the edge as he pleasured first one part of her body and then another, always knowing when to draw back. He was toying with her the way a well-fed cat toys with a mouse, but she couldn't bring herself to stop him. She was covered with a sheen of perspiration by the time he rolled out of the hammock and lifted her into his arms.

She expected him to go straight to the bedroom, but he didn't. He put her down on the rug in front of the fireplace instead. The sensual fog Cassie had been trapped in started to lift. She decided that he had no right at all to have so much self-control when she'd been so close to exploding. She aimed to make him pay for it.

He stood over her, staring down at her body as though he wanted to memorize every inch of it. She reached out her arms to him and parted her thighs, then watched him step between her legs and sink slowly to his knees. Only moments later he was raising her hips and thrusting himself against her.

He entered her very slowly, no longer teasing but trying to be gentle. The care he took wasn't really necessary because she was more than ready for him, but she knew he was thinking about how long it had been for her, and she loved him for having remembered.

After half a dozen slow, deep thrusts, he withdrew, sat back on his heels and smiled wickedly. "Don't get too excited, angel. I'm going to make you wait at least twenty more minutes." She couldn't tell whether he was joking or really serious.

It didn't matter, though, because he'd called the shots long enough. As he eased himself back into her, fully on top of her this time, she went over what Kineko had told her. At the time she'd been fascinated but a little skeptical; now she couldn't wait to try it. Doug gave a grunt of surprise when she slid a hand between their bodies, but he didn't try to stop her—not even when her fingers sought him out, applying an intimate pressure. The only thing that changed was the way he was kissing her. His mouth got noticeably rougher.

Doug had known full well that there was no way on earth he could last twenty more minutes, but he'd wanted to string Cassie out for as long as he could. He wanted to excite her so much that she'd forget every other man she'd ever been with. He wanted her writhing with pleasure and moaning for release. And afterward, he wanted her soft, cuddly and feminine, languid in his arms, staring at him in silent adoration. He'd had no reason to think those things wouldn't happen, because she was stunningly responsive to the slightest touch and kiss.

Then he'd felt her fingers pressing against him, the nails digging in a little with each thrust he made. The way she was touching him heightened his excitement, but it also confused him. He wanted her more and more but felt farther and farther away from having her. And then he remembered her smiling words about prolonging his pleasure, and thought, *It's that bloody book of hers. What in hell is she doing to me?*

His movements got a little desperate. She squeezed him even harder, making him feel violent pleasure mixed with gut-wrenching frustration. In the end those twin emotions were so overpowering that nothing existed except a driving need for satisfaction. But satisfaction lingered just out of reach, taunting him like a teasing witch.

Cassie felt the moment when Doug's self-control shattered, but his aggressiveness didn't frighten her. She was just as aroused as he was, and she was having the devil's own time holding back. She almost giggled with relief when he panted a forceful but incoherent protest and grabbed her hand, pinning it to the floor. The giggle died in her throat in the heat of the crazy excitement that followed. The explosion she'd been holding just under the surface burst free and took her in thrall. It was like a series of rolling, sharp-edged waves, drowning her and piercing her at the same time. The sensation was so intense that for long moments afterward, she could barely manage to breathe.

She felt Doug stop moving but was totally unaware that she was rigid beneath him, her face screwed up in apparent agony. When she finally opened her eyes she found him looking at her as if the world had fallen to pieces around his feet. Still out of breath, she asked, "What's wrong? Why do you have that expression on your face?"

"I'm sorry. But whatever you were doing . . ." Grim-faced, he rolled off her onto his back and stared up at the ceiling. "Please let me make it up to you, Cass. Just tell me what you want me to do."

It took her a moment to figure out what he was sorry about, and once she did, she started to laugh. Curling up against his side, she said, "You have a woman named Kineko to thank. I'll have to introduce you to her some day." She nuzzled his lips. "It was wonderful."

He frowned. "But I completely forgot about you. You didn't finish."

"Of course I did."

"I didn't feel you," he said, sounding suspicious.

"Men!" Cassie groaned. "Really, Douglas, I should know. Although I must say, it gives a woman a feeling of real power to excite a man so much that his normal awareness of things sort of clicks off."

"That sounds like Vonda talking." Doug sat up and reached down a hand to Cassie. "If you want to play that role again, we can pretend that I've paid you your three hundred dollars and you're here to cater to my whims. At the moment I want a cold glass of wine and a hot bath. You, of course, will remain available at all times. You can call me when you're ready."

Cassie did as she was told, joining him in the Roman tub. They talked until the water was lukewarm and the wine was gone. Cassie told Doug about Tawny's late-night rides, and he replied that she'd been riding around in the moonlight since her teens and was probably only crossing the property. She had keys to both gates. What Cassie really wanted to know was what Doug felt for the woman, and she got a fair indication of the answer when she suggested that Tawny might be having an affair with Chris Patterson.

Doug gave a careless shrug. "She wouldn't be the first. The guy is catnip to anyone female, including my own mother. But . . ."

"Your mother?" Cassie interrupted, incredulous. She hadn't seen so much as a hint of anything sexual there.

"Sure. Why do you think he sticks around? Valerie started sleeping with him before he even came to work here. He's since been replaced—she won't say by whom—and now she treats him like a favorite puppy. Pocket money, car expenses, clothing—she's always slipping him little extras. But getting back to Tawny . . ." He paused. "She generally likes them smarter, but Chris is supposed to be one hell of a stud, so maybe there's something to your theory."

"Would you mind it if there were?" Cassie asked.

Doug cupped her breast, looking a little distracted. "Me? Why would I mind?"

"Because you used to be lovers," she answered impatiently, and took away his hand. "Maybe you still are. You were down in Acapulco together."

"Ah! I see. You're demanding an exclusive relationship."

"I didn't say that." Cassie was afraid to make a demand like that, but it was, in fact, what she wanted.

Annoyed with Doug for dodging her questions, she started to get out of the tub.

He put his hands on her waist and hauled her back, not stopping till she was straddling his thighs. "Oh, no, you don't! After all the money I paid for you, you're not going to put me off. Come closer. I want to make love to you again."

He moved his hand down her belly, covering the soft blonde curls below. Cassie tried to push it away, but he wouldn't let her do it. "I'm not making love with you till you tell me about Tawny," she insisted.

"I'm not telling you about Tawny till you're exactly where I want you," he replied, grinning at her.

In the end he won, caressing her into submission. Then he slid inside of her and moved her slowly up and down till she didn't care about Tawny Timberlake in the slightest. She could have killed him when, with typical male perversity, he stopped, settled her back on his thighs and said solemnly, "Two years after Buffy died I looked at Tawny and decided she was the perfect woman. I'd known her since she was a kid, and we'd been friends from the time she was old enough for me to consider her an equal. I thought she was everything I wanted and needed. After six or seven months together I hadn't changed my mind, which made the fact that I wasn't in love with her all the more puzzling. We ended the affair two months ago, but the friendship is still intact. One more thing, Cassie. Maybe *you* don't demand an exclusive relationship, but I sure as hell do. Is that clear?"

Cassie had found it hard to concentrate on what he was saying, because he'd kept stroking her belly and thighs the whole time he was talking. "If I'd known you were going to be so bossy I never would have gotten mixed up with you," she said with a satisfied smile, and guided him back inside her. In no time at all, both of them forgot about everything but each other.

Chapter Eleven

*O*nce, in the middle of making love, Cassie whispered feverishly, "I never knew it could be like this." Then she laughed, suddenly realizing that she'd stolen Deborah Kerr's line to Burt Lancaster in *From Here To Eternity*. Doug, catching on immediately, told her she'd obviously had too much exposure to Valerie Hunter and Hollywood.

Doug might equally well have skipped the jokes and answered with the same exact words, because they were just as true for him. What he actually did was to cut off her next remark with a hard kiss and keep on making love to her. Cassie was like an addictive drug: the more of her he had, the more he craved. His physical infatuation with her was so intense that he was willing to give her almost anything she wanted just to avoid arguments that would waste away their time together. He couldn't conceive of indulging her indefinitely, but for once in his life he wasn't thinking about consequences or the future. He was taking things the only way he could: one day at a time.

Cassie saw only Doug's actions, not the anguish buried deep underneath, and told herself that her life couldn't have been better. The book was going well. Jessica was having a wonderful summer. And Doug Hunter was everything she'd ever wanted in a man.

She came to believe he could do anything he set his mind to, even tolerate being in the limelight. After only a little prodding, he'd agreed to join Edward and Melanie for dinner at the city's hottest new restaurant. The gawkers and autograph seekers hadn't been far behind, but Doug had taken them in stride. The four of them had been out to dinner together several times since then, always with the same result. It invariably started with Melanie, but there had been a lot of publicity about Cassie in the local media and Miesley was never out of the headlines for long. No matter how low a profile Doug tried to keep, somebody eventually recognized him and questioned him. They asked about everything from the identity of his father to his problems with the central city project to Horace's very public quarrels with Sam McGuire, but he answered with patience and politeness. The interruptions were annoying, but not so constant or disruptive that the two couples couldn't enjoy their meals.

After a number of cancellations and reschedulings, the reporter and photographer from *Spotlight* magazine finally moved into the house. They arrived on a Wednesday and planned to stay through the weekend in order to cover a large party Valerie was giving in Cassie's honor. Cassie expected Doug to treat them with that frostily reserved civility he'd turned into a high art, but he didn't. Though he was far from effusively friendly, he tried to be cooperative. When there were questions he didn't want to answer, his refusals were always polite and to the point.

In fact, Cassie only wished he'd been as cooperative

with her as he was with *Spotlight* magazine. At first,
afraid he would accuse her of using their personal
relationship for professional ends, she had avoided
asking him about his childhood. But then she'd decided
to treat him like any other source and had pursued him
with her usual aggressiveness.

Getting him to talk was like pulling hens' teeth.
Every now and then she'd get a glimpse of the shy child
he'd been, or the defensive, quick-tempered adolescent, but he rarely dealt in specifics. As far as he was
concerned, the autobiography was Valerie's baby, and
he wanted absolutely no part of it.

Valerie, meanwhile, was delighted to be back in the
national spotlight. The party she was giving had started
as a small luncheon to introduce Cassie to San Diego. It
had mushroomed into a six-hour open house to publi-
cize the book, complete with invitations to half the
country. Fortunately for Valerie, she had the catering
staff of a first-class hotel at her disposal and a home
straight out of *Architectural Digest* available.

Doug didn't say so, but it was the kind of function
he'd spent his entire adult life assiduously avoiding.
People never said anything substantive at these affairs,
but bored you to death with endless chatter about how
successful they were. Doug only stayed around to
mingle because Cassie would have been annoyed with
him if he hadn't. He pretended he was listening when
he wasn't and pretended to enjoy himself when he
didn't.

Valerie, on the other hand, was in her glory, basking
in the approval of her L.A. rat pack, the genuflecting of
Miesley's numerous business associates, and the flat-
tery of the local politicians and business leaders. She'd
given *Spotlight* an exclusive on covering the party in
exchange for the promise of a cover story, and she
loved the fact that the photographer was constantly
trailing around after her, snapping her picture. At one
point, the man tried to talk Cassie and Valerie into

putting on swimsuits and posing on floating lounge
chairs in the pool, their hands held high with glasses
filled with Miesley's champagne. Cassie eventually
agreed to the toast, but she kept her clothes on and
remained on dry land.

Cassie got almost as much attention as Valerie did
and thoroughly enjoyed it, except insofar as it kept her
from studying everyone as closely as she would have
liked. Several of Valerie's guests had written autobiog-
raphies of their own, and Cassie had read them all.
Watching Doug talk to a former glamour queen named
Diana Deveraux, she suddenly realized that *he* must
have been the "virginal son of a friend" whom the
woman had told of seducing and educating. Doug had
been an exceptionally mature fourteen at the time,
Diana almost twenty years older. The account had been
amusing to read, with its frank explanation of how
she'd teased away his shyness and scruples and cor-
nered him in his bedroom late one night. The two of
them talked for quite some time, with Doug acting
pleased to see her.

Dr. Foster Timberlake and his wife, Andrea, were at
the party also, but not their daughter Tawny. Cassie
assumed she was on duty that day. She'd seen Tawny
only the week before, galloping toward the back gate at
a pace that was nothing short of hair-raising. Four days
later they'd actually met when Tawny and her father
came by the house to pick up Horace and Chris and
take them to the ball game. Tawny had seemed happy
and relaxed that afternoon, showing no sign of the
previous week's recklessness.

More than anyone else, though, Cassie kept her eye
on Horace Miesley. He'd been grumbling about the
party all week, except, of course, in the presence of the
pair from *Spotlight,* and spent almost the entire time
pulling people in and out of his office. The office had a
door leading directly out to the courtyard where the
party was being held, so it wasn't hard to monitor the

comings and goings. Politicians, civic leaders, employees of the Miesley Development Corporation, executives with the Padres—all of them were summoned and then dismissed, invariably looking either weary or angry or both by the time they walked out the door. Cassie would have loved to sneak inside and listen to those conversations on the intercom, just to learn what was going on.

At about six o'clock Miesley emerged to help himself to something from the constantly replenished buffet tables, staying outside for the better part of an hour. Cassie had tried to interview him on three separate occasions, but he'd always claimed he was too busy. Now, however, he seemed to be in a jovial mood, so when he finished a slice of pie and headed back to his office, she followed right behind him.

"Horace, I have the distinct impression you've been avoiding me," she said as they walked inside. She closed the door and sat down in a chair beside his desk. "I have to warn you that I'm as tenacious as a bulldog when it comes to my work, so you might as well give in and answer my questions."

Miesley had never been less than charming to her, nor was he now. "My dear Cassie, you're nothing like a bulldog. One look at you and a poor man is bewitched into telling you everything he knows. But there simply hasn't been time, and much to my regret, there isn't time right now."

"We could make a start," Cassie suggested.

"And deprive these people of your company? I wouldn't hear of it. And I must get back to work, my dear." Horace reached for the already open can of beer on his desk. It had obviously been there for quite some time, since he hadn't been in his office for almost an hour. He took a sip, then grimaced. "My God, this stuff is even more bitter than usual. Do you suppose it deteriorates in the open air?"

Cassie laughed at that. "If it does, I hope you'll stop

selling it at the stadium. People get irritated enough when the team loses without subjecting them to lousy beer. Why don't you let me get you a fresh can from the refrigerator, or better yet, something nonalcoholic?"

"You're an angel of mercy, but no thank you." Horace took a long swallow. "The stuff grows on you after a while. Unfortunately, I'm still waiting. Now if you would excuse me . . ."

He picked up a manila folder, acting as though he were alone in the office. Prepared to wait him out, Cassie settled back in her chair and watched him. He continued to sip the beer and sort through papers, paying no attention to her. After about ten minutes he reached into his pocket and took out a handkerchief to dab at his forehead. It was a little warm in the room, and he'd begun to perspire.

"I'll make you a deal," Cassie said. "I'll get you a glass of iced fruit juice in return for five minutes of your time. Just five minutes, Horace. That isn't so much to ask."

He smiled at her. "How do you know I won't lock you out of the office?"

"I'll take my chances," Cassie answered. The bar was crowded, so it took a couple of minutes before she could ask for the glass of orange juice. Horace hadn't locked the door, but was standing near his desk when Cassie returned. He backed up as soon as she'd closed the door and reached for the arm of his chair. Then, swiveling it around into position, he dropped heavily into the seat.

"Are you all right?" Cassie asked. "You look a little pale."

"I'm fine. Just—a little pressure. A pill—should help." He reached into his pocket, taking out a cloisonné pillbox. After fumbling with the catch for a moment, he removed a small white pill, a nitro, Cassie assumed. His coloring remained unusually pale, even after the pill had had a chance to dissolve under his tongue.

Cassie held out the juice, but he shook his head. "In a moment, my dear. Just set it on the desk."

Cassie did so, saying, "You don't look well at all, Horace. I think Foster should have a look at you."

"It's nothing. It will pass in a moment." He picked up the glass and sipped the juice, but when he went to put it back on the desk he missed the top entirely and it spilled all over the floor. Cassie's first thought was to clean it up, but then she noticed the beads of sweat that had suddenly formed on his face and the way his hand was shaking, and jumped out of her seat. "I'm going to find Foster. . . ."

He clutched his chest. "Like an elephant . . . Crushing me . . ." Cassie heard a moan of pain as she ran to the door.

The first person she saw was Lisa Hunter. "Your grandfather is very sick," she said. "Could you find your father and Dr. Timberlake for me? I'm going to phone for an ambulance. . . ." A soft thud attracted her attention. Horace had gotten up and tried to walk, only to collapse onto the floor. Cassie had been thinking in terms of angina—Horace had a history of that— but was now afraid it was an actual heart attack. "I'll start CPR if I need to," she added quickly. "Have them get the paramedics, Lisa."

Doug came running into the office about twenty seconds later. Cassie was down on the floor with Horace by then, checking him over. He was breathing on his own, but the breathing was labored and his pulse was irregular. The pain appeared to be excruciating. Doug didn't ask questions, but reached for the phone. By the time Tawny's father came in a minute or two later, Miesley had lost consciousness and stopped breathing, and Cassie had started CPR. Foster immediately got down on the floor to help her.

The paramedics arrived in just over ten minutes, and Cassie gladly let them take over. CPR was taxing to begin with but nothing short of exhausting when you held somebody's life in your hands. Valerie was in the room by then, but Doug had kept everyone else out. Electrodes were attached to Miesley's chest and a phone hookup to the hospital established. Cassie had seen enough medical shows to understand what the jagged pattern of rapid up-and-down lines on the paramedics' monitor meant. His heart was in fibrillation. She was asked to leave the room at that point, but she knew what would happen. They would work on him until they restored normal heart function and respiration, or until they were sure it was hopeless.

A camera flash went off in Cassie's face as she stepped out of the office, and the reporter from *Spotlight* started firing questions at her. She tried not to let it annoy her. He was only doing his job, the same way she would have if she'd been in his shoes. She answered as best she could, her arm closing around Jessica's waist when Jessie came over to stand beside her. Afterward they sought out Edward and Melanie. Shock was beginning to set in, and Cassie wanted to be with her family. Chris Patterson, of all people, had firmly taken charge and was tactfully urging everyone to leave the party. Lisa, who'd been trailing around after Chris, eventually came over to Edward. She looked a little lost and burst into tears when he took her into his arms.

The five of them went inside to wait. By the time Doug came into the living room and silently shook his head, everyone had left but the Timberlakes, Edward and Melanie, the members of the household, and the two men from *Spotlight*. It would have taken a dozen sticks of dynamite to dislodge the latter, who'd been tactful enough to station themselves next door in the dining room, out of sight but not out of earshot.

"What happens now?" Edward asked Doug.

"They called the sheriff's department about five minutes ago. The patrol deputy should be here soon. I imagine he'll want to speak to you, Cassie. It's just a formality."

Cassie nodded. "Somehow I never expected a heart attack. I know he had angina, but I honestly thought he was exaggerating how bad it was. I mean, he was always complaining about *something*—" She stopped in mid-sentence, suddenly very cold, and looked toward the dining-room door. Then she walked up to where Doug was standing and said in a low, urgent voice, "There's a beer can on Horace's desk. Don't let anyone throw it away."

"He was drinking it before he died?"

"Yes. He complained about the taste. I didn't think anything about it at the time, because he's *always* complaining about the taste, but you never know. Maybe there's enough left in there to test it."

A few minutes later Cassie was repeating her story to the deputy sheriff, and half an hour after that, to a homicide investigator. His name was Sergeant Joseph Mendes, and he listened very thoughtfully to her account of what had happened. She had the chilling feeling that it wouldn't be their last conversation.

The homicide team checked the room for evidence, taking the Dudweiler beer can, and the police photographer took pictures of the body. A little while later somebody from the coroner's office showed up. Cassie was a little numb. She'd never had anyone die right in front of her, much less die from poisoned beer . . . assuming the beer had indeed been poisoned. They would know in a couple of days, when the autopsy and lab reports came back.

Valerie was in her bedroom by then, along with Andrea and Foster Timberlake. Foster had persuaded her to take a sedative, but Cassie wasn't sure she'd really needed one. Mendes had spoken to her at length, but she'd emerged from the interview looking calm and controlled. For all they knew she was already planning her next marriage.

Chris had driven the girls to a movie in order to take their minds off the whole business, but neither had seemed particularly upset by the time they'd left the house. Cassie decided that Lisa's initial reaction had owed more to the natural shock of seeing someone in the household die than to any great affection she had for him. The truth was that he'd had almost nothing to do with her.

The reporter and photographer from *Spotlight* had eventually left, more or less thrown out the door by a determined Doug Hunter. They'd announced their intention to check into a motel and had made it clear that they planned to stay in San Diego at least until the coroner's report came out.

That left Edward, Melanie, Doug and Cassie in the house. After checking on his mother, Doug suggested that the four of them go down to the cottage to unwind. He made coffee while everyone talked, carrying it over to the dining room along with some slices of cake. "Do you know how many people would have liked to kill him?" he said as they all sat down. "Hell, there must have been at least a dozen at the party alone."

"Do you really think it was murder?" Melanie asked.

Doug sipped his coffee. "Frankly, no. The angiogram he had last year didn't show any dangerous blockage, but heart attacks are unpredictable. It seems pretty farfetched to assume someone killed him just because he complained about the taste of his beer."

Cassie looked around the table. "Maybe so, Doug, but it's still a real possibility. Those men from *Spotlight* must be salivating at the thought of it. I'll bet they'd love to put his picture on the cover, with a caption reading 'Murder in San Diego.'"

Doug had been so preoccupied with the endless details created by any life-and-death emergency that he'd forgotten about the gentlemen of the press. It was bad enough to have a pair of so-called journalists sniffing around his home and constantly invading his privacy without contemplating the sensationalized story they would now be sure to write. He was suddenly angry with Cassie for agreeing to have them around in the first place, although nobody could have known the dramatic turn that events would take.

Cassie, however, didn't seem the slightest bit troubled by the prospect of more publicity. "It's a good thing that Mendes is approachable," she went on. "I'd have a real problem on my hands if he were one of those cops who thinks that *his* theories are the only ones that count."

Doug didn't like the sound of that at all. It was one thing for Cassie to poke and prod for the sake of a good biography, and something else entirely for her to stick her nose into a murder investigation.

"I think you should explain that statement," he said.

Cassie had been looking at Melanie, but the ice in Doug's voice quickly drew her attention. He hadn't used a tone like that since the night they'd argued in his car. She hadn't liked it then, and she didn't like it now.

She didn't want to quarrel, though, so she kept the irritation off her face. "After all I've learned and seen, I have no doubt that I can help him. And naturally I plan to keep a close eye on the investigation, because I'll be putting it into the book."

"Keep a close eye on it?" Doug repeated. "And what would that entail?"

Melanie jumped into the fray before Cassie had a chance to answer. "Hey, you two, it's ridiculous to get into an argument about it *now!* For all we know, Horace died of natural causes. There probably won't even *be* an investigation."

Doug paid her as much attention as an elephant pays a gnat: exactly none. "I asked you a question," he said to Cassie. "I'm still waiting for an answer."

Cassie's temper started to simmer. He was talking to her as though she were a naughty, balky child. "What do you think it entails? I'm a professional. I'll try to talk Mendes into letting me go along with him when he talks to people, but if I can't, he's going to get a lot of visits and phone calls from me. And I certainly intend to follow up with questions of my own, when I think it's appropriate."

"The hell you will!" Doug said. "You're not a policeman—"

"I'm a journalist," Cassie snapped back, "and it's a free country."

Doug gave her a hard stare but didn't say a word. Cassie suspected that the only thing keeping him quiet was the presence of Edward and Melanie. Edward was obviously getting the same message, because he stood up and motioned for Melanie to join him. Melanie was visibly reluctant to leave but finally walked around the table to kiss Cassie good-bye. "Call me if you need me," she murmured. Cassie didn't answer her.

Cassie waited in the living room while Doug walked Edward and Melanie to the door. He was tight-lipped with anger when he returned, demanding, "What does your sister think I'm going to do to you? Hit you?"

"I'm sure she doesn't," Cassie said evenly, and sat down on the couch. "I've told you before, she worries about me too much." Doug started pacing around the room like a caged panther. With a sigh, Cassie patted the empty cushion next to her on the couch and said, "Come on, sit down. Let's talk this over."

Doug sat but looked no less agitated than before. "There's a limit to how much I can put up with," he said. "I've gone along with interrupted dinners and reporters following me around and being polite to people I don't give a damn about, but enough is enough. I refuse to let you stick your nose into a homicide investigation.

"Dammit, Cassie, it's bad enough you insist on

writing about topics that range from sordid to danger-ous, but now we're talking about murder! And if somebody out there was desperate enough to do it once, there's no guarantee he won't try it again. You're going to stay out of it."

Cassie had never known Doug to be so irrational. There was a flip retort on the tip of her tongue, but she quickly bit it back. He'd had a trying day. As she had so often in the past, she fell back on humor to defuse a situation that threatened to explode out of control. "Hmm, you might have a point. I'll tell you what, Doug. I'll be really careful about what I drink from now on. Definitely no Dudweiler beer, unless it's a fresh can."

"I don't think that's funny." Cassie realized that Doug had gone back to tried-and-true methods of dealing with people, too. In his case that meant icy correctness. "In my opinion, Cassie, your actions are totally irresponsible. You have an eleven-year-old daughter to consider, but you still insist on taking unnecessary risks."

Cassie could hardly believe her ears. He was the last person in the world to lecture her on that subject. "You think *I* take unnecessary risks? Only last week you were telling me how you were prancing around on some girder five stories above the ground on that hospital addition your company is building. . . ."

"It was perfectly safe. I've been doing it since I was sixteen."

"Maybe *you* think it was safe, but I don't. And in case you've forgotten, you happen to have an eleven-year-old daughter, too, Doug. So I don't see the difference—"

"Then you're deliberately being obtuse," he inter-rupted curtly. "Nobody was about to murder me for inspecting a problem with my own project, Cassie. And I'll tell you something else. I don't run off for months at a time to research some crazy article that the world could easily do without, and I don't shove my daughter in front of an audience and expect her to perform, and I don't display myself like a piece of meat just to make a few extra bucks. I told you this would never work out."

Cassie wasn't about to dignify those statements with a response. At the same time, though, she wanted to give Doug a chance to calm down, think about what he'd said, and apologize. Killing time, she walked to the dining room table, gathered up the empty cups and plates, and carried them into the kitchen. She was loading them into the dishwasher when a new thought struck her. Maybe he was worried about his mother being accused. People just weren't themselves when fear gripped them by the throat.

When she came back into the living room she remarked very calmly that Valerie had been introducing her to people for almost the entire time that Horace was out of his office and that if Valerie had ever gone inside, she certainly hadn't noticed it.

At first Doug looked at her as though he didn't know what she was talking about, and *then* he looked at her as if she'd lost most of her marbles. "I wasn't concerned about my mother," he said. "She had no reason to want Horace dead. Her marriage suited her just fine. And if she's been feeding you a line about wanting to marry her current lover, whoever he may be, I wouldn't pay too much attention to it. She's been telling that to reporters for years—always off the record, of course."

Cassie wasn't about to admit how gullible she'd been. She only wondered how many other lies Valerie had told her. Forcing her thoughts back to Doug's accusations, she said, "So you're angry because I'm irresponsible and exhibitionistic and self-destructive. It's okay for you to take business trips and work impossible hours, to manipulate the local media and politicians in order to get what you want, even to do things that anyone with half a brain would know are dangerous, but it's not okay for me."

"All those things are part of my job. I don't have a choice. You, on the other hand, do have a choice, not only in what topics you choose to write about but in whether you work at all. God knows you don't really need to."

Later Cassie would ask herself whether some deep-seated streak of masochism had compelled her to stay. At the time, though, she told herself that every man in the world had a little male chauvinism in him and that it was childish to storm out of the house because of words that had been spoken in the heat of anger.

A little too hurt to pretend that she wasn't, she said quietly, "You're entitled to your opinion, Doug. I'm going to bed now."

"Here?" he asked.

"Of course, here." Cassie always slept in his bed, at least till one or two in the morning. Not a night had gone by that he hadn't wanted to make love with her.

"I don't see the point," he answered. "Either we have a relationship with a little give and take in it or we don't have a relationship at all."

"You're telling me that I have to forget covering the murder investigation even though it's germane to my book. You're saying that if I don't, you won't be willing to see me anymore." Cassie paused. "Please don't give me ultimatums, Doug."

He gave her an impatient look. "Who said anything about ultimatums? I'm concerned about your safety. I'm simply asking you to be sensible about this."

"Sensible by whose definition?"

"By *my* definition, obviously. I'm the one who's going to worry about you."

Cassie walked up to him and put her arms around his neck. It was hard for her to do given the forbidding expression on his face, but she didn't know of any other way to put an end to their quarrel. At least he'd admitted he cared about her.

"Darling, please," she said aloud. "It's been a long

day. Both of us are upset and tired. Let's go to bed now. We can straighten this out in the morning."

He didn't soften a bit. "Will you change your mind about tagging around after Mendes?"

She shook her head. "No. It's my job."

"Then we'll have nothing to talk about, will we?" He gently removed her arms from his neck and turned away from her.

It was the first time in Cassie's life that a man had ever walked out on her, and for the first few moments she couldn't believe he was being so unreasonable. Then the pain began to seep through and, not long after that, the anger she'd been fighting for the last fifteen minutes. She didn't want to cry but found she couldn't help it.

Doug had gone into the kitchen, so she had to raise her voice to be heard. "I don't try to tell you how to do your job, and you have no right to tell me how to do mine! My work is just as important to me as yours is to you. And I don't say that what you do is frivolous, either, or—or crazy." She took a deep breath, struggling to get the next sentence out. She was very vulnerable where Jessica was concerned. "And don't you dare say I'm a bad mother. I'm not. My daughter is—she's a happy, well-adjusted child. There's nothing wrong with letting her talk to a reporter for ten minutes. And the Valkenbergs are a damn sight better as guardians than this—this screwball assortment *you* depend on!" She waited a minute and when there was no answer shouted, "So you can take your self-righteous opinions and shove them, Doug Hunter!"

Doug winced at the force with which she slammed the front door. For five long minutes he simply stared out the kitchen window, thinking about Horace and who might have killed him. Inevitably, though, his thoughts returned to Cassie. He was sitting with a double scotch by then, angry at everything and everyone in the world, including himself.

He couldn't imagine what had possessed him to hit below the belt that way. Whatever else he thought about Cassie, he couldn't fault her as a mother. Jessica *was* happy and well-adjusted. The Valkenbergs *did* provide a more suitable second home than his mother did. And he could hardly object to Cassie allowing the girl to answer a couple of innocuous questions when his own daughter had told a dozen different interviewers how it felt to be Valerie Hunter's granddaughter.

Any way he looked at it, he'd made a total mess of things. He sighed and poured himself another scotch. Why was Cassie so unreasonable? There were a million things to write about in this world, so why was she attracted to all the bizarre ones, the ones that would turn her into a celebrity? And why did she have to get mixed up with a murder investigation?

The thought made his blood run cold. No matter how much of a bastard Horace had been, ordinary people didn't go around poisoning other people's beer. Sociopaths did.

If there was one thing he didn't need in his life, it was a woman who got mixed up with sociopaths. His thoughts drifted back three years, and it was as though the blood and pain and guilt were closing in on him all over again. He couldn't go through it again. It was a matter of simple self-defense to cut Cassie out of his life before things went any further.

He picked up the bottle of scotch and walked into the bedroom. The bed looked empty without Cassie lying there waiting for him. He pictured her in her own bed, crying her eyes out, and felt even worse. He never should have started it in the first place.

It was long after midnight when he finally fell asleep. The scotch hadn't solved any of his problems, but it had certainly numbed the pain.

Chapter Twelve

The autopsy and lab reports confirmed what Cassie had suspected almost from the beginning: Horace Miesley had been murdered. The coroner had found normal therapeutic levels of the two drugs prescribed by his cardiologist in his blood, as well as a relatively low percentage of alcohol. But in addition, a drug marketed under the brand name "Cardioprim" had been found in both his stomach and his bloodstream. Taken in normal amounts, the drug was effective in inhibiting angina symptoms caused by artery blockage or spasm, but it could also, in rare cases, precipitate a myocardial infarction. An overdose of the magnitude ingested by Miesley wouldn't have killed the average patient, but it *would* have increased the probability of undesirable side effects—including an MI. To nobody's surprise, the independent lab that had analyzed the dregs of Miesley's beer had found a heavy concentration of Cardioprim mixed in with the remaining liquid.

The drug was legally available only by prescription,

but a search of the Miesley residence produced no pill bottle, and an area-wide check of pharmacists turned up no doctor's authorization. As Mendes remarked to Cassie when she stopped by his office on the Friday after the murder, a whole host of people might have had access to the drug, from those who worked for the manufacturer to various medical professionals.

"Any suggestions about where I should start?" he asked. He often teased her about having acquired a partner, but in fact seemed to appreciate her help.

Cassie, of course, had recognized the name Cardioprim as soon as she'd seen it in the coroner's report. It was the drug that Miesley had asked Tawny for over a month before. "I think you should have a talk with Dr. Tawny Timberlake, Foster Timberlake's daughter," she said, and explained about the conversation she'd heard. Then she added, "My gut feeling is that Tawny gave Miesley the pills, that the murderer found out about their existence, and that he or she removed them from Miesley's medicine cabinet and put them in his beer. But I didn't want to mention Tawny until you'd checked for a prescription. The problem is, if Miesley was nagging *her* for the drug, he was probably nagging other people, too. And she wasn't even at the party."

"You mean you didn't *see* her at the party," Mendes corrected.

Cassie didn't argue the point. "That's true. She could have gotten in and out of the house through the back. She wouldn't have even needed her car, since the two pieces of property adjoin one another."

"Did she have any reason to want to kill him?" Mendes asked.

Cassie had to laugh at that. "She might have been one of the few who didn't, Joe!"

With a smiling shake of his head, Mendes started thumbing through his notes, looking for the Timberlakes' unlisted phone number. After a brief conversation with the housekeeper, he told Cassie that Tawny was at the hospital and, according to the housekeeper, had been feeling a little under the weather lately. "I have orders not to upset her. Do you want to tag along? I think you might be able to help. A friendly face and all that."

He didn't have to ask twice. They drove downtown, locating Tawny in the hospital cafeteria, drinking a cup of coffee. She was paler than Cassie had ever seen her, with bluish circles under her eyes, and seemed to be close to exhaustion. There was no way she couldn't have known the details of Miesley's murder, because the murder had been front-page news on Wednesday after the lab report was released, and it had been the talk of the city ever since. Indeed, when Mendes summarized the results of the autopsy and his own investigation for her, she sat there looking blank, as though it was too much of an effort to react.

"I guess you've been busy," Cassie said when he'd finished.

She shrugged. "It's always busy around here."

Mendes straightened up, suddenly the hardened professional. "On the other hand, Dr. Timberlake, maybe your exhaustion is emotional. You're wondering if I know that you gave Horace Miesley the pills that eventually killed him."

Her face got even paler. "I didn't . . . I was at the hospital that day . . ."

"You left the hospital late that afternoon. You drove to Rancho Santa Fe . . ."

"No. You don't understand. . . ." She stood up and, without another word, indicated that they should follow her out of the cafeteria. It was only when they reached the tiny room where she'd slept the previous night that she completely broke down. Collapsing onto the bed, she buried her face in her hands and sobbed uncontrollably.

Cassie waited until the sobs gave way to quiet

weeping and then sat down next to her on the bed and
put an arm around her shoulders. "He asked you to get
him the pills and you didn't want to do it. I was right
there in the room, Tawny. What made you change your
mind? Did he threaten you somehow?"

Tawny nodded, still weeping into her hands. "We
had a terrible fight. He said—he said he would never
see me again if I didn't get him the pills. He wouldn't
let me in when I came over the next night. He—he
wouldn't even take my phone calls, Cassie. Oh, God!"

"So you gave in," Cassie murmured. She couldn't
understand how she'd failed to see the obvious.

"I had to!" She tore her hands away from her face.
Her eyes were haunted by grief and pain. "I loved him.
I can't remember a time when I didn't, but he never
paid any attention to me—I mean, as a woman—till I
started dating Doug. I know what people say about
him, but it's not true. He was wonderful to me." She
yanked a gold chain out from under her blouse. There
was a large gold nugget set with diamonds dangling
from the end of it. "He gave me this. He was—he was
sweet and tender. Nobody knew him like I did." Her
voice took on a defensive edge. "And who was I
hurting? Everybody knew he and Valerie hadn't slept
together in years. She's had a million lovers—even my
own father. And it's not as though I ever asked him to
leave her for me. . . ."

The crying started all over again. At that point
Mendes took over. Maybe he'd decided that Tawny
wasn't any murderess, because he was gentle and
patient. Once he'd finally calmed her down, she told
him that the capsules were physician's samples that
she'd noticed in a friend's office. She'd asked for them
on impulse, still reluctant to give them to Horace, but
had finally given in when he'd promised he would only
take them after talking to his regular doctor about it.
Deep down, though, she'd been afraid that he wouldn't

bother, and her guilt was almost unendurable. Cardioprim was not the kind of drug you handed out without arranging to monitor the patient's reactions.

There was a part of Cassie that wanted to rush right up to Doug the moment he got home and say, "You see? Your precious Tawny Timberlake, supposedly the perfect woman, the embodiment of common sense and stability and propriety, was having an affair with a married man twice her age! She was even stupid enough—and weak enough—to allow him to emotionally blackmail her into giving him the drug that wound up killing him!"

Of course, she did no such thing. She and Doug didn't even talk about the weather these days, much less about anything more serious. He'd set the tone on Monday by retreating into stilted formality, and Cassie had been forced to accept it. Their only real conversation of the week had taken place on Wednesday night, when he'd come into her bedroom to offer a stiff apology for his comments about her fitness as a mother. Her efforts to keep him in the room and warm him up a little never stood a chance of breaching that brittle, invisible wall of his.

She'd coped with his rejection the only way she could: by throwing herself into her work. It turned out that Valerie Hunter wasn't nearly so cavalier about Horace's death as she'd once implied she would be. On some level, she was sorry he was gone. With funeral arrangements to make and business matters to attend to, she hadn't had much time for Cassie, but they managed some five or six hours together in that first week after Horace's death.

Cassie had gotten into the habit of delivering nightly dinnertime reports on her conversations with Joe Mendes, but on Friday she saved the briefing until later in the evening, when the girls were in their room listening to tapes. The adults—Cassie, Valerie, Doug and Chris Patterson—had gone into the family room to have their coffee, and there was a Padres game on the television. Cassie noticed that the players were still wearing black armbands over their sleeves.

"I went over to Joe Mendes's office this afternoon," she began. Doug gave her a cool, so-what-else-is-new look and turned his attention back to the ball game, but Valerie picked up on something special in her tone—satisfaction, or maybe even excitement.

"Something's finally happening," she said. "What is it, Cassie? Does Joe have a lead on the pills?"

"Yes. We found out that Tawny gave Horace some physicians' samples of Cardioprim, and since they aren't in the house, I think we can assume they wound up in his beer." Cassie filled in the details, but in deference to Valerie skipped any mention of Tawny and Horace's love affair. In the middle of her explanation Doug and Chris finally stopped watching the ball game and started listening to what she had to say, Doug looking grumpy, Chris a little nervous.

"The central question," Cassie went on, "is, who knew he had the pills? Besides Tawny, that is."

"Poor little thing," Valerie clucked, sounding genuinely sympathetic. "Do you know that it never occurred to me that he was sleeping with her? But of course, he was always terribly discreet. He had his ways of getting whatever he wanted from a woman, I can tell you that. I suppose she thought she was in love with him."

Cassie admitted that she had. "She looks terrible, Valerie. She blames herself for his death."

"Then she's not a suspect?"

"Not at this point, no."

"I see. Well, all I can tell you, Cassie, is that I had no idea he'd gotten a hold of those pills. I haven't been in his bedroom in months, much less prowled around in his medicine cabinet."

Cassie looked at Chris. "And you? He was always asking you to get him things—medicine, a beer, a sweater, even to answer the phone when he was sitting right next to it. You must have known about the pills, but you haven't said a word to anyone. Why not, Chris?"

Chris looked extremely uncomfortable. "Okay, Cassie, I *did* know about them, but I didn't chuck them into his beer. I didn't have any reason to kill the guy."

Cassie took a shot in the dark. "Didn't you, Chris? You were mentioned in his will to the tune of fifty grand. You had a grudge against him for forcing you to pitch or lose your job, something that cost you your career. It wouldn't have been hard to look up the name of the drug in Horace's PDR. And if you'd done that, you would have known that it can occasionally be fatal. In high enough doses, who knows? I'd say you not only had a motive, but an obvious opportunity."

Doug was looking at Chris now, giving him the kind of measured stare that lesser human beings than himself might find extremely intimidating. Sweat broke out on Chris's forehead.

"I didn't have anything to do with it," he insisted. "I swear I didn't, Doug."

"Then what are you so afraid of?" Doug asked.

Chris wiped his face with the bottom of his shirt. "About a week before he died—it was a Monday, I think—Horace told me to go to the medical-school bookstore and buy this monograph for him—something about heart disease. He had his PDR on the desk, and he pointed to some stuff about that drug, Cardioprim—the section that says 'Warnings'—and he told me he wanted more information. So I asked him if Goldman had prescribed it, and he said yes, that there was a bunch of pills in the medicine chest on the top shelf, and he described them in case he ever wanted me to get him one." He looked at Valerie. "I was having dinner with a couple of the guys last Thursday—it was an open date—and we had a little too much beer to drink, you know how it is, and they started complaining. About, uh, about . . ."

"Horace," Valerie finished calmly. "It's all right, Chris. All of us know he wouldn't have won any popularity contest with the players. So?"

He shot her a grateful look. "I said something about the pills. About the side effects, and how the stuff could either cure you or kill you. Oh, God, Valerie, I'm sorry. I was just joking around. I was ticked off 'cause he'd given me a bad time about being a little late to pick him up from work that day. I was just letting off a little steam, you know?"

Valerie gave him a reassuring smile. "Did you suggest it wouldn't be a bad idea if somebody slipped an overdose into his beer, darling?"

"No. I said, 'Maybe we'll all get lucky and he'll take too many of the damn things some day.' That was all. I swear it was."

"Then the next logical question," Doug said, "is who was at dinner with you."

"Aw, Doug, none of those guys would try to—"

"Who?" Doug repeated forcefully.

Chris listed the names. While it was possible that any one of the four might have driven to the house after Sunday's ball game in time to drug the beer, it didn't seem particularly likely. None of them had anything much to gain except for the removal of an owner who was constantly carping about the team's performance.

Cassie sat there trying to think of who else might have known about the pills. There was always the housekeeper, but she kept to herself and spoke very little English. Mendes had interviewed her, just as he'd interviewed the other members of the household, but that had been before the coroner's report had come in.

"Whoever put the pills in Horace's beer had to have done it while he was outside eating," she remarked. "The murderer also had to have known that there was a good chance Horace would actually drink the beer, even though it would be warm by the time he got back inside."

Valerie had a mocking half-smile on her face. "Then again, my late husband's, shall we say, *frugality,* wasn't exactly a secret, Cassie. We've been going on about Dudweiler beer for years now." She sighed. "I suppose you'll have to tell the good sergeant about Chris, won't you."

"I'll take care of it in a minute," Doug answered, and added to Chris, "He'll obviously want to speak to you, but I think it can wait till morning."

"In that case, we'll say good night." Valerie stood up and held out her hand to Chris. "Come, darling, give me one of your special back rubs. I'm dreadfully tense."

Chris sat there for a moment longer, looking agitated, but then took Valerie's hand and let her lead him out of the room. Cassie had to wonder just what she had in mind: a therapeutic back rub or a more intimate form of comfort.

It was the first time in days that Cassie and Doug had been alone together, but he quickly moved to end that, saying he would call Mendes from the cottage. Wanting to detain him, Cassie followed him over to the sliding-glass door and remarked, "Miesley was holding meetings all afternoon that day. He might have argued with whoever ultimately killed him."

She could tell that Doug was annoyed by her growing involvement in the whole business but didn't let that stop her. "Look, Doug, I realize there was no love lost between you and your stepfather, but still, you should want to find his killer. Obviously the members of this household know a lot more about Miesley's affairs than Mendes does, and any way we can help him . . ."

"You don't want to help him, Cassie, you want to play Woodward and Bernstein. Joe can't make a move without finding you two steps behind him."

Cassie didn't deny it. "He happens to appreciate my advice. Besides, I think the whole thing is fascinating."

"And imagine how many books you might sell!

'Best-selling Author Solves San Diego's Murder of the Year.'" Doug gave a disgusted shake of his head. "Play your cards right, and a story like that might get you a spot on '60 Minutes,' or even a TV movie of the week."

"That's not why I'm doing it, but so what if it does get me publicity? Would it be such a crime to enjoy it?"

"Some of us have better things to do with our lives. Good night, Cassie." Doug slipped out the sliding-glass door and stalked across the courtyard toward the cottage.

It wasn't like Doug Hunter to be sarcastic, which might have been why Cassie slammed out of the house and stomped her way to the tree house. She was furious with the man. He treated her as though she were a cross between a reporter for a sleazy supermarket tabloid and a publicity-mad Hollywood starlet who would take off her clothes and hang off the side of the Empire State Building if she thought it would get her a little ink.

Half an hour later she was still in the tree house. She was still angry, too, but her thoughts had taken a more personal turn. She was thinking about the subject she'd been avoiding all week: her relationship with Douglas Hunter. It was like opening the spillway on a dam. There were things she wanted to say to the man, and it simply wasn't good enough to say them in her head, over and over and over again. She should have said them on Sunday night, but he'd gotten her too upset to think straight. Fifteen minutes later she was pounding on his door, wound up so tight she was shaking.

He was dressed in a lightweight navy robe when he finally opened the door and was holding a glass of liquor. Cassie asked if she could come in, but it was a demand, not a request.

Doug wanted to say no and shut the door in her face, but good manners precluded it. One didn't refuse to talk to one's lover—*former lover*, he silently corrected. He'd been in the bedroom he used as an office, but he'd been doing more drinking than working. The reason for the glass of scotch was Cassie—specifically, why he continued to give a damn about her when she was so totally and thoroughly unsuitable.

Now, seeing her standing there, the reason was crystal clear. Not a night went by when he didn't miss her. He was still as emotionally obsessed with her as ever.

He opened the door and stepped aside, allowing her to precede him into the living room. Always the proper host, he offered her a cup of coffee or a glass of wine. She brusquely declined both. Neither of them sat down.

"You and I are not that different," she announced. "Neither of us had the most normal childhood, in the sense of growing up with the security of a loving nuclear family. I'd be the first to admit that you had it worse than I did—my mother was warm and caring, even if she worried too much and went from being high to low to high again for no reason I could ever figure out—but the point is that both of us have scars. Both of us married young, both of us had children young, and both of us lost the people we loved tragically and much too soon. I'm not going to stand here and tell you that I bounced right back like a rubber ball after John died, because both of us know that it's not true. But I *did* bounce back, Doug. I put the past behind me and I moved on. I try to run out and embrace life, not just sit around and let it happen to me. You don't. You were knocked around and imposed on as a kid, so now you play it safe. You admit a small number of people into your charmed circle and keep the rest of the world at a distance. But there must be a part of you that longs to do the opposite, or you wouldn't be attracted to *me*."

It wasn't a picture Doug much cared for, and he didn't accept its validity. Still, he wasn't about to bare his soul and rebut her remarks on a point-by-point basis. "I prefer to keep my private life private. I prefer to conduct my business affairs in a quiet, dignified way, with as little publicity as possible. That doesn't make me passive or mired in the past. If we're going to stand here and psychoanalyze each other, then maybe I should ask you what's lacking in *your* life that you crave so much outside attention. I could also point out that you must want someone stable and conservative, or you wouldn't be attracted to *me*, but I'm not going to do that. Sex is a basic human urge, and you don't need Sigmund Freud to explain it."

"And that's all you think is between us? Just—sex?"

"What else has there been time for?"

Cassie knew he didn't believe that any more than she did, but still, it hurt. She walked to the couch and sat down, using the time it took to get her emotions under control. "If that's the way you feel, why not keep going to bed with me? Why worry about what I get myself mixed up in?"

"I can't do that. You seem to think you're in love with me. I don't want to hurt you more than I already have."

It didn't escape Cassie's notice that he hadn't answered her questions. She pointed out that the only reason they'd stopped sleeping together was because they'd argued about her involvement in the murder investigation. His scruples about hurting her had had nothing to do with it.

"It underscored how different we are," he insisted, sounding impatient. "It brought me to my senses. I've got work to do, Cassie, so if you wouldn't mind leaving . . ."

"I certainly *would* mind leaving. I'm not going to let you stand there and tell me you don't care about me. I know you do. You told me you do! Dammit, Doug, we were *serious* about each other. The feeling wasn't just from my side and it wasn't just sex. I wasn't trying to tell you how to live your life . . ."

"You were dragging me into yours, and I hated every

minute of it. For God's sake, Cassie, just leave it alone."

"No!" Cassie jerked to her feet, close to tears now. "If you don't like the public part of my life I won't involve you in it. As far as the murder investigation goes, I'm not going to do anything dangerous. I don't understand why you refuse to see that *I* have to decide how to do *my* job!"

Doug had learned to control his temper when he was still an adolescent, but the consequence of keeping a tight lid on it all the time was that when it exploded, it went off like a Bicentennial fireworks display. "Is that what you think it's all about? Telling you how to do your job?" He didn't give her time to answer. "It's about wanting another child and knowing that the child's mother won't be around half the time to take care of it. It's about competing for your attention with everyone from a half-drunk fan who thinks you're really a hooker to some slick Eastern reporter who's more interested in getting you into bed than in writing about your work. It's about knowing that I'd always take second place to the glory of the next best-seller."

"Doug, that's ridiculous—"

"Just shut up!" Doug hadn't told anybody to shut up in at least ten years now, but he was far beyond the end of his tether. "You wanted to know how I feel, so why in hell don't you *listen* for a change? I think about you running around with Mendes and I go crazy. My wife was murdered, Cassie. *Murdered!* Do you understand what that means? Do you have any conception of how I felt, to see her horse come back without her . . . To go out looking for her, panicked that she might have gotten hurt . . . To find her lying by the side of the road . . . her clothes ripped . . . stab wounds everywhere I looked . . . To have her die in my arms before I could get help . . . To know that we'd argued over *nothing*—some stupid charity dinner I didn't want to go to—and she'd ridden off angry and wound up like that and maybe it was all my fault . . ." Doug looked at the ceiling. "Oh, God, I can't stand this." His voice was hoarse with tears. He rubbed at his eyes, impatient that he'd lost control of himself, and then gave Cassie an angry look. "Go ahead and say it: It's my hang-up, not yours. You can't be expected to turn your life upside down because of my neuroses. Okay. Point taken. End of discussion. But I've had one wife die in my arms and I can't—I *won't*—run the risk of living through it again." He started out of the room, then stopped abruptly and turned around. "And just for the record, Cassie, you don't know a damn thing about my child-hood. You don't know that my father killed himself when my mother wouldn't marry him. You don't know about women like Diana Deveraux who get their kicks from toying with a defenseless kid's emotions, or about the parade of housekeepers who were supposed to take care of me when my mother wasn't around but usually didn't, or about all the lies I learned to tell for the sake of how things were *supposed* to look. You don't know anything, Cassie!"

Cassie stood there, rooted to the living-room floor, her only reaction a jerk of alarm at the slam of the bedroom door. She was almost too shocked to move. His wife's death—she hadn't understood the horror of it. John had died, too, but not slowly, and not in her arms. Valerie's version of his father's death had nothing in common with what she'd just heard, and to listen to the woman talk, she'd been as devoted a mother as it was possible to be, given the demands of her job. While Cassie hadn't been gullible enough to swallow that one whole, she'd never pictured Doug as abused. He'd grown up in Beverly Hills, for God's sake.

She took half a dozen steps toward the bedroom, then changed her mind. Doug was right. She *didn't* know anything about his childhood. He was doubly right. There had scarcely been time enough, or trust enough, to learn. It was little wonder he'd refused to talk to her, given how traumatic the past had been. She began to realize that the differences between them were far more serious than she'd ever imagined. Certainly they couldn't be cleared away with a polite wave of the conversational wand.

She looked at her watch. It was just past ten. Distraught and disoriented, she felt she had to talk to Edward and Melanie. Edward seemed to be the only person Doug confided in, the only one who could help her understand him, and Melanie—Melanie loved her. She needed someone who loved her right now.

She called them from the main house. Melanie answered the phone, becoming concerned when Cassie had trouble getting out a simple statement: that she was coming for a short visit. Melanie wanted to come to Rancho Santa Fe instead, but Cassie wouldn't hear of it. "I need to get away from here," she said. "Your house is more private. With Miesley's stupid intercom system, I always have the feeling that someone is going to listen to whatever I say."

"All right, but calm down first and take your time driving over here. I have the day off tomorrow, so we'll have all night to talk. I want you to plan on sleeping here, Cassie."

Cassie agreed, taping a note to her door in case Jessica got up before she returned. She knew she was distracted—she almost forgot to close the gates after she'd driven through them—so she went especially slowly on the curving lanes of the neighborhood. But it was a beautiful night, with no traffic to speak of, and by the time she came to the main road she felt much more relaxed.

She took the freeway down to the last university exit and then headed toward the coast. It was a route that would take her across university property, past the Scripps Institution. Perhaps because it was so quiet along the two-lane back road, her mind wandered back to the argument she'd had with Doug. Driving became automatic; she'd taken this route a dozen times before. Her attention was only jerked back to the roadway when a white-jacketed figure darted into her path.

Cassie braked hard and yanked at the steering wheel to avoid hitting the girl, seeing two or three other people out of the corner of her eye as the car swerved to the side. She tried to control the skid, but it was hopeless. Neither the brakes nor the wheel would respond. The last emotion to pass through her mind was relief, not panic. At least she was wearing a seat belt.

Chapter Thirteen

𝒟oug Hunter had a splitting headache. He'd dulled it with aspirin around midnight the night before and had finally fallen asleep, only to have it hit him like a flying sledgehammer when he woke the next morning to the sound of a ringing telephone. He groped for the receiver, checking the numbers on the clock at the same time. It was six twenty-five.

He grunted something approximating "Hello" into the mouthpiece and waited. The voice on the other end of the line—Edward's—apologized for calling so early and told him to take a few moments to wake up. Not surprisingly, a Saturday call at that hour of the morning had about the same effect on Doug as a barrel of ice water poured over his head.

Something was wrong. He knew it without being told. A roiling nausea assaulted his stomach, joining the ceaseless throbbing in his head. "All right, I'm awake," he said. "What's going on?"

"It's Cassie, but she's going to be okay. She—"

"What do you mean? Isn't she up at the house?" Doug scarcely heard the "okay" part of it. He reacted the way a wild animal reacts to sudden and acute danger: with a soaring pulse rate, intense alertness, naked fear.

"She's in Scripps General, Doug. All we know for sure is that she wound up smashed against a tree a few miles from my house. She was on her way to see Melanie at the time. The police called us from the hospital. They let Melanie in to see her earlier this morning, but it was only for five minutes. Cassie was conscious but woozy—not quite with it. Melanie had trouble understanding what she was saying. The only thing she remembered is not being able to control the car. And there was one more thing, Doug. She made Melanie promise to tell you to check out the intercom line. Do you have any idea what she was talking about?"

"No." Doug dismissed it from his mind. All he cared about was Cassie's condition, and Edward was avoiding telling him the details. A picture of Buffy burned its way into his mind. She was lying on the ground, the life seeping out of her, and he couldn't do a thing to save her. "Cassie—how badly is she hurt? Is she on the critical list?"

"No, no, nothing like that," Edward answered. "She'll be fine, Doug. No visitors except Melanie until we hear otherwise, but—"

"Dammit, Edward, just answer the question. How bad is it? Brain damage? Internal injuries?"

"Just take it easy, Doug. I'm not trying to soften any blows. Cassie is going to be fine." Edward was using his most soothing tone of voice, the one he'd used when they were kids and Doug had gotten riled up over something. "She's got a concussion, some normal confusion about the accident, and cuts and bruises. There's no evidence of broken bones or serious internal injuries. Fortunately, she was wearing a seat belt. We'll have a more complete report later in the day. They'll hold her for observation for twenty-four to forty-eight hours, and if things go the way they expect, she'll be released tomorrow or Monday. In the meantime, tell Jessica what's happened and reassure her that Cassie will be all right. Melanie and I will be over as soon as we can. Melanie is sleeping right now, and I don't want to wake her up. We were at the hospital most of the night.''

Edward was holding something back. Doug knew it and it scared him half to death. It took a threat to muscle his way into Cassie's hospital room and look for himself before Edward finally admitted that Melanie had broken down and cried after leaving Cassie's bedside. There had been a lot of flying glass, although none, fortunately, to any vital spot, and Cassie had needed over forty stitches to close up the resulting cuts. Edward added that the wreckage had apparently been spotted by a passerby, who had called the police emergency number from a phone booth. The only local address in Cassie's wallet had been on one of Edward's business cards. The police had immediately tracked down his home number and called him up, which was a good thing because Melanie was already becoming concerned that Cassie hadn't arrived yet.

After hanging up the phone, Doug gulped down another couple of aspirins and got into a hot shower. He believed that Edward had told him the truth about Cassie's condition, but he was still very worried. He was also feeling very guilty. He'd upset her, and she'd gotten into her car and she'd smashed it up. And then he remembered her comment about not being able to control it, and the blood drained out of his face.

It was a brand-new car. Why hadn't she been able to control it? Had the brakes or steering failed? Had somebody *arranged* for them to fail? It was like the past was rising up and kicking him in the stomach. It had been a one-car accident. You didn't wind up plastered against a tree without a reason.

Only a handful of people both knew about Cassie's involvement in the investigation and had access to her car: Chris, Tawny, his mother. It didn't make sense. But even if Doug didn't know what was going on, he *did* know he'd taken as much from Cassie as he intended to take. The lady was going to stay out of this whole crazy business in the future, even if he had to lock her in his room and throw away the key.

Jessica and Lisa were in the family room watching cartoons when Doug walked into the main house. He took Jessica aside and broke the news about Cassie as calmly as he could, but all the reassurance in the world couldn't have prevented the inevitable: Jessica burst into hysterical tears and wouldn't be consoled. Having lost her father already, she was terrified at the prospect of losing her mother.

Doug had never been so glad to see anyone as he was to see Melanie Ford. He and Edward had breakfast together while Melanie talked to Jessica. His opinion of Edward's wife had steadily improved over the weeks since the wedding, but it wasn't until she walked into the breakfast room with Jessica that he started to love her. The girl's face was streaked with tears and she was clutching Melanie's hand like it was the only source of comfort in a hostile world, but she was also smiling. Doug saw the strength of the bond between the two and wondered how he could have been so wrong about anybody as he'd been about Melanie Ford.

Not wanting to alarm anyone, he kept his theories about the accident between himself and Joe Mendes. Mendes promised to track down Cassie's car and check it over, then get back to Doug as soon as possible. It was only after Mendes went off to talk to Chris that Doug remembered Cassie's preoccupation with the intercom system.

The intercom had been installed when the house had been constructed, but that was before Valerie Hunter had even met Horace Miesley. It was hardly unusual to have a system like that in a large luxury home. Doug tried to puzzle out what Cassie had been thinking of. You could use the system to page someone, or to talk to someone in another room, or simply to listen in, as Buffy had sometimes done with Lisa when Lisa was a baby and they'd come to spend the day.

Listen in. He didn't put it past a paranoid megalomaniac like Miesley. He suddenly realized what Cassie was talking about, grabbed Edward, and started looking.

Cassie was frustrated and annoyed when the nurse kept smiling and nodding and paying absolutely no attention to her, at least until she figured out that it wasn't entirely the nurse's fault. For some reason, the woman didn't understand what she was saying. As far as Cassie could tell there was nothing wrong with her mind, so that left the shot they'd given her—a painkiller, obviously. Her whole body ached, but it was a dull kind of ache and should have been much worse given the shape she was in. She knew how bad she was without being told, because she remembered the quickly disguised horror on Melanie's face when Melanie had first walked into the recovery room. Still, Cassie wanted to see for herself.

She slowed down, enunciated every syllable clearly, and managed to make herself understood. The nurse tried to sweet-talk her out of it but eventually produced the mirror Cassie wanted and held it up to her face. The Bride of Frankenstein stared back at her. It could have been much worse, though. At least the most serious cuts were on the side of her face.

Later that day there were more doctors and more tests. Cassie waited till the drugs wore off and she was more coherent, then called the house and asked Chris to put Jessica on the phone. It was a difficult conversation—lots of tears, lots of fear. At times Cassie couldn't even understand what Jessie was saying, because she was crying so hard. She finally managed to convince her that it wasn't the same as Daddy, that she would never walk out of the house some bright morning and simply never come back. Melanie, who took the phone next, told Cassie not to worry, that they would take Jessica back to their house with them and let her sleep in their bedroom that night.

Then Melanie handed the phone to Doug, who told Cassie he was concerned about her and asked when he could see her. She put him off, feeling much too tired to cope.

"Maybe tomorrow, then," he said, and added softly, "I love you, Cass."

Cassie couldn't answer him. She said good-bye and hung up the phone, falling asleep within five minutes.

A few hours later they moved her into a private room. Melanie came by around dinnertime with get-well cards from the girls and some homemade chicken soup. Jessica, she reported, was doing much better. At that point the plastic surgeon who had stitched up Cassie's facial cuts came by, mirror in hand, to explain her prognosis. Though he didn't promise she'd be as good as new, he did make a smiling reference to future television appearances. Cassie wasn't particularly concerned about how she would look on TV—she was still in the happy-to-be-alive-and-in-one-piece stage—but Melanie cross-examined the poor man. Exasperated, he finally invited her to stop by his office and look at his collection of before-and-after pictures, which demonstrated quite conclusively that cuts had a way of healing, bruises of fading, and swelling of going down.

When the two women were alone again, Melanie sat herself back down and dramatically announced that so much had happened since the night before, she scarcely knew where to begin. Cassie suggested, "At the beginning, Mel."

"Good idea," Melanie said with a grin. "You journalists have such penetrating minds!"

Cassie rolled her eyes. "So?"

"So first of all, Doug figured out what you were talking about when you mentioned the intercom, and he hustled Edward away from me, and the two of them started sniffing around the house like a pair of trained bloodhounds. You know the walk-in closet in Miesley's bedroom?"

"Not intimately," Cassie said. "I've never really had the pleasure."

"Umm. I don't suppose you would have, unlike poor Tawny. Anyway, it has a common wall with Miesley's office, Cassie. The floor in there is carpeted, but if you lift the carpeting up, there's sort of a trapdoor underneath, built into the floor. And underneath the trap, in the crawl space beneath the house, is a whole automated taping system. It's sound-activated from Miesley's office, or you can turn it on manually from the closet and set it to pick up any room in the house via the intercom system. There were probably fifty cassettes stacked up in there. Everyone is dying to know where the rest of them are stored."

It was exactly what Cassie had expected to hear. "I missed all the excitement," she said a little sadly.

"Well, not really. Mendes was talking to Chris at the time, and he wound up taking everything along with him. Obviously there might be evidence on those tapes. Doug is over at Mendes's office right now, listening to the tapes to help identify who Miesley was meeting with."

"That's all so far?" Cassie asked, and couldn't stop herself from yawning. Between painkillers and normal fatigue, she'd been weaving between wakefulness and sleep all day long.

"Isn't it enough? I'm telling you, Cassie, the case is as good as Watergate. But I can see that you're tired. I'd kiss you good-bye but I'm afraid it would hurt wherever I pressed. Edward sends his love." Melanie paused. "Doug sends his love, too, and I think he really means it. He was a little hurt that you didn't want to see him, but I explained about women and vanity."

"That wasn't it." Cassie closed her eyes and yawned again. "I need to do some thinking. I'd rather not see him until I'm sure of what I feel."

"But you love him," Melanie said. "Or was last night so terrible that you don't feel you do anymore?"

"It's nothing like that," Cassie answered. "It's just that I finally had to admit that Doug Hunter knows himself a lot better than I do, Melanie. He's not going to change. I have to decide what to do about that."

Later that night, Cassie would remember the old saw about fame having its price. As far as she could see, that price was paid not only by the person who was famous, but by everyone who was close to him. She'd enjoyed her brush with celebrity and realized that she'd probably been jealous of Melanie all these years, but in her case the price of fame was proving horribly high.

She was released from the hospital late Sunday afternoon. In perhaps the biggest anticlimax of her life, she had turned on the radio about three o'clock that day to hear that Sam McGuire had voluntarily surrendered to the police in connection with the death of Horace Miesley. She'd liked the man and felt sorry for him, but she also felt sorry for herself. All the action had taken place while she was stuck in a stupid hospital bed.

Cassie heard the details from Edward, who came up to her room to help her check out while Melanie waited in the car with Jessica. According to Edward, McGuire and Miesley had had a stormy, bitter meeting on the day of Miesley's death. Not only had they argued about the Padres; they had argued about Valerie Hunter. McGuire had told Miesley that he was Valerie's lover and that he intended to marry her, and Miesley had replied that Valerie could sleep with whomever she

wanted as long as the man in question didn't entertain
fantasies about her getting a divorce. There was no
chance of it, he'd said, because Valerie would never
give up her position as his wife, certainly not to marry a
dumb jock who didn't know anything but baseball—
and was a failure even at that. McGuire, sounding
almost complacently confident, had answered that he
was different—that for the first time in her life Valerie
was really in love with someone. In the end, an enraged
Miesley had told a taunting McGuire that he wanted
the affair to end, and that if it didn't, he would not only
fire McGuire but see to it that he never got another job
in organized baseball. He'd stopped just short of
accusing McGuire of dipping his hand into the company
till, and McGuire, irate, had stormed out of the office.

When confronted by Mendes with the details of the
conversation, McGuire had admitted that he'd heard
about the pills from one of Chris's friends and decided
on the spur of the moment to drop them into the can of
beer. Then he'd left the party. He wasn't clear about
what he'd hoped to accomplish, but it didn't appear
that he'd expected Miesley to actually die. To become
ill, yes; to suffer, yes; to be frightened, yes; but not to
actually die. Given his confused and highly emotional
state, a charge of first-degree murder was unlikely.

Listening to the whole story, Cassie saw McGuire as
victim as well as victimizer. The loss of Horace Miesley
was probably a net gain for the world as a whole. Still,
Miesley wasn't another Hitler, and McGuire was going
to have to pay for his actions.

"How is Valerie taking it?" she asked Edward.

"At first she exploded. Said she never wanted to see
McGuire again as long as she lived. But Valerie being
Valerie, within half an hour she was calling up Mendes
and asking him to bring her the tape. She was listening
to it for the third time when Melanie and I got to the
house this afternoon. By the time we left to pick you up
she was saying that a good lawyer might be able to get

Sam off easy—with a light or even a suspended sentence. He was under intense pressure at the time, and Miesley was threatening to frame him for larceny, to ruin him. Maybe it pushed him over the edge. Maybe he wasn't rational at the time he drugged the beer. As far as the future goes . . ." Edward shrugged. "With Valerie Hunter, who can tell? Up till now she's played the role of the devoted wife and has protected Miesley's reputation, but if she wound up married to McGuire it wouldn't be the first time she'd defied convention to do what she wanted. Look at her decision to have Doug. In her circumstances an abortion would have been easy to arrange, but she adamantly refused."

Edward's remark reminded Cassie of one of the questions she would have asked him two nights before, if she'd ever made it to his house. "Edward, did Doug ever tell you the real story behind his father's death? Valerie claims he deliberately lied to her about being sterile and died in an accident on the set, and Doug says he begged her to marry him and committed suicide when she refused. Frankly, it sounds like two different scenes from two different soap operas."

Edward hesitated before answering, because he generally didn't discuss other people's lives. But then the matchmaker in him took over, spurred on by Melanie's undeniable influence. She'd convinced him that Cassie and Doug would be good for each other. "There are a few things you need to understand first," he said. "Number one, Doug is a complicated person." He saw Cassie's smile, realized he was stating the obvious, and went on, "His relationship with his mother is a complicated relationship, and you can't understand Doug without knowing about Valerie. She isn't a monster, Cassie. She was never an abusive mother, just a selfish and careless one. She loved Doug as much as she could, but she was just as much a victim of her childhood as he is. She was so intent on protecting herself from any further pain that she didn't have the strength to protect her son the way she should have. He understands that and he forgives her for it, but it's had a lasting effect on him. He needs a little more love and a little more caring than the rest of us do. As far as his father goes—his name was Gerry, by the way—he and Valerie had been seeing each other for about two months when Gerry started pressing Valerie to marry him. She refused, but she didn't end the affair. One night he got a little drunk and admitted, or rather, pretended to admit, that he was only half a man because he couldn't have children. He told Valerie he was terrified she would eventually leave him for someone who could. I assume he figured that if he got her pregnant she'd have no choice but to marry him, but he didn't know Valerie Hunter. Afterward, of course, he tried to have it both ways. He didn't have the guts to admit what he'd done, so he offered to marry her even though the child wasn't 'his.' She told him to get lost. As far as his death goes, there's no doubt that he took a heavy risk that day, but he was a stuntman. No one will ever know if it was suicide or an accident."

In other words, Cassie thought, the truth of the matter was somewhere between the two versions she'd heard. She'd more or less expected that, but thanked Edward for everything he'd told her. The conversation had made her that much surer of what she wanted to do.

A nurse came in with a wheelchair and walked by Edward's side as he pushed Cassie down the hall to the exit and out to the car. Jessica, who was waiting by the car door, burst into tears the moment she saw Cassie's face and ran out to meet her. Cassie soothed away her shock, even getting a giggle out of her when she joked about putting a paper bag over her head till she looked more presentable.

Melanie opened the back door and started to help her out of the chair, but Cassie waved her away. Her energy was flagging by then and she could have used some assistance, but for Jessica's sake she stood up and slid into the backseat on her own. She couldn't help dozing off during the trip home.

Doug was waiting on the other end. Without a word, he lifted her out of the car and carried her into the house. They passed Joe Mendes on their way through the living room, making Cassie wonder aloud if the man ever took a day off. She was surprised when Doug answered that he was waiting to speak to *her*.

Mendes followed her into her bedroom, where Doug settled her gently into bed. Jessica had come in also, as had Lisa, and Cassie gave them a few minutes of reassurance before shooing them out. Like most children, their primary concern was that their world should stay pretty much as it had always been. Once convinced of that, they were satisfied to resume their normal routine.

Doug closed the door after the girls had left, staying in the room while Mendes talked to Cassie. After a polite inquiry as to how she was feeling, he got to the point. "Doug tells me there's a possibility that someone tampered with your car. We took a thorough look, but there wasn't much left to work with. If there was any physical evidence there, we couldn't find it."

Cassie had no idea what he was talking about. "There was nothing wrong with the car, Joe." She looked at Doug. "Whatever gave you that idea?"

"You said something to Melanie about it early yesterday morning. And it was a one-car accident. How did you wind up plastered against a tree if it wasn't a mechanical failure?"

Cassie remembered Melanie's first visit to the hospital, but only hazily. "I know I said something about the intercom, but I don't think I told her anything about the accident. I couldn't remember anything but losing control of the car and skidding into the tree at that point. There were some kids fooling around by the woods, and one of them ran in front of my car. That's how it happened. But wasn't that in the police report? I mean, I assumed they were the ones who phoned for help in the first place."

Mendes was much too thorough not to have checked it out. He told Cassie that the call had been made from a public phone booth, by a man representing himself as a passerby. She could only assume that the kids had been too scared to come forward. Maybe they'd been drinking or smoking dope. Certainly they'd had no business being in the woods at that time of night, much less running around in the roadway.

Doug walked Mendes to the front door, feeling like an overimaginative jackass. He didn't generally jump to conclusions on such minimal evidence, which meant that he'd believed what he'd *wanted* to believe. It would have made it so much easier to go back to Cassie and tell her he'd been right, that she'd risked her life for no sane reason and that if she'd only listened to him in the first place none of this would have happened.

It wasn't that simple now. He knew he'd overreacted and he knew how much he wanted her, but he also knew that he could never cope with long absences and a celebrity life-style. And if that made him a hopeless neurotic, so be it.

She was lying there with her eyes closed when he slipped back into the bedroom. It twisted his stomach in knots to look at her face, not because the swelling and cuts were so ugly but because he hated the thought of her being in pain. He wanted to take care of her, probably too much so. He understood that too much concern could sometimes smother a person.

She opened her eyes and gave him a sleepy smile. "I've ruined your day, haven't I! You were all set to chew me out for risking my life and now you can't do it."

He gave her a sheepish look and pulled a chair over

to her bedside. "What can I say? You know me too well."

"Oh? I thought I didn't know you at all. I thought there hadn't been time. I thought there was nothing between us but a sexual attraction that you wished would go away."

Doug figured he had that one coming. He lifted his shoulders in a helpless shrug, saying, "I was obviously wrong. No offense, darling, but right at the moment you look like something from *Night of the Living Dead*, and I still think you're beautiful. Either I'm blind or I'm in love."

"With all these stitches I would have said *Bride of Frankenstein*," Cassie answered, "but still, if I'd known that getting myself smashed up would have such a dramatic effect on you, I would have done it sooner."

"That's not funny, Cassie," Doug scolded.

"Yes, it is," Cassie retorted. "The patient is always right. Tell me how much you love me, Doug. It will help me get better faster."

"You're sure you're not in too much pain to hear it?" Doug asked teasingly.

"I'm sure," Cassie answered.

He took her hand and leaned closer, his expression sobering. "I'm crazy about you, Cassie. I've felt that way from the beginning, and both of us know it." His voice grew husky with emotion as he continued, "You've brought sunshine and moonlight into my life. I don't want to go back to how it was—safe but gray. The world is twice as alive when I'm with you. But darling . . ." He shook his head and stared at the floor.

Cassie waited a few moments, then prompted, "Go on, Doug."

"I don't want to lose you."

"I'm not going anywhere." Cassie gave his hand a weak squeeze. "Especially not in this condition."

"That's not what I meant." Cassie could see the anguish on his face. She started to assure him that

things would work out, but he cut her off with a
nervous rush of words. "I've done a lot of thinking over
the past couple of days about what I can and what I
can't live with, and I want you to understand how I feel.
You seem to have chosen a certain path, and I know all
about the direction it leads in. High-profile projects.
More public recognition and media attention with
every book that you do, until you're more celebrity
than journalist. The pressure will build from inside,
making you feel that each book you write has to say
more, sell more copies, add to your reputation. One
day you'll turn around and the public part of your life
will have crowded out the private part. I don't want to
be crowded out, Cassie. God knows I don't want to
stifle you, but you've got to understand that I need to
come first. I'll bend as far as I can, but when I tell you
that I've reached my limit, you've got to accept it as
final. Because as much as I'd like to believe that both of
us can have it all, I know that we can't—not and stay
together. So maybe you should find yourself a man who
loves the limelight and doesn't mind the invasion of
privacy that goes along with it, a man who's secure and
self-sufficient enough to cope with what you want.
Maybe I'm all wrong for you."

"I've got the man I want," Cassie answered. "By the
way, that speech of yours about sunshine and
moonlight—it was lovely, Doug—was it a formal proposal of marriage?"

Bemused, Doug muttered, "It can't be this easy. On
Friday night—"

"On Friday night," Cassie interrupted gently, "I
hadn't seen the face of the man I love contorted by the
pain of a traumatic childhood, and I hadn't coped with
the fears of an hysterical child. It makes you think,
Doug, about what you really want out of life. I was such
a baby when I married. All I wanted was to be the
perfect wife and mother. And then I started writing,

and a whole new world opened up to me. But it caused problems I'd never anticipated. John didn't like it when I worked during the time he was at home, so I stopped doing it, deadline or no deadline. He didn't want me to travel, so I never chose a topic that would take me too far from home. Naturally I resented it, and naturally I felt guilty about resenting it. After he died, and once I'd moved to San Francisco and had gotten myself back together again, I realized I felt the most wonderful sense of freedom. There was plenty of money and Jane was always happy to take care of Jessica, so I could write about anything I wanted, go anywhere I wanted. It's a very heady feeling, to be your own person, to enjoy your first taste of success. You said I'd chosen a certain path and maybe I had, at least tentatively. But that doesn't mean I can't stop, go back to the fork in the road, and make a different choice. I was so lonely before I met you, Doug. After a single night together, I fell so hard I was reeling, but it took time for me to realize how safe and secure you make me feel. I've realized a few other things over the past day or so. I've frightened people I love, and I don't want to do that again. And I like writing more than I really understood. I like explaining things to people, giving them a glimpse of worlds other than their own. I like it more than a dozen appearances on television or a thousand requests for an autograph. I even like it more than the best-seller list. If I have to choose, I'll choose writing and you and the girls over the brass ring, Doug."

"But you'll miss it," he said.

"Not as much as I would miss you. The important thing is that *I've* made the choice. If conflicts come up about something I want to do, we'll talk them out. Not hurting you and Jessie is more important to me than any story could possibly be."

Doug stroked her hair very gently. "If I could put myself into a different package for you . . ."

"Don't say that." Cassie didn't want him to feel guilty or to feel that she was making some grand sacrifice for him. "I love you the way you are, and I'm smart enough to know that if you were very much different, you wouldn't be the same person and I wouldn't have fallen in love with you. I'm a great believer in chemistry, darling, unlike you, I think."

"You've converted me," he admitted, and then sat there grinning at her. He was suddenly happier than he'd ever thought possible, especially three years before.

Cassie would have smiled back except that she was too busy yawning. "I'm so sleepy. It's these stupid painkillers. Are we done talking?"

Doug wanted the *i*'s dotted and the *t*'s crossed. "As soon as you agree to marry me. Preferably right away, so you can move into my house and enroll Jessie in the local school."

"I can't believe it's September already. But we'll, uh, we'll have to talk to the girls first." Cassie heard the slur in her voice and forced her eyes to stay open, fighting sleep. There was just this final thing. . . . "They seem to get along so well . . . but marriage . . . it's such a change . . . they might hate the idea—"

A pair of high-pitched giggles pierced the silence, drawing the adults' attention to the intercom. Before either Doug or Cassie could get out a word, Lisa said, "Hi, Mom!" and Jessica said, "Hi, Dad!" Then, in a singsong duet punctuated by more giggles, they added, "We promise we won't fight *too* much!"

Doug laughed softly. "They don't *sound* like they'd hate it."

"There's no such thing as privacy in this house," Cassie complained. "If you don't get your mother to rip that thing out I'm never coming here again."

"I'll suggest it," Doug said, "but you know my mother. Nobody ever made Valerie Hunter do a damn thing that she didn't want to."

Cassie closed her eyes, smiling to herself. "Including having you. I'll have to remember to thank her for that."

Doug kissed her on top of her head, but he didn't leave the room right away. He wanted to watch her for a while longer, to make sure he wasn't dreaming.

a fabulous $50,000
diamond jewelry collection

ENTER

by filling out the coupon below
and mailing it by September 30, 1985

Send entries to:

U.S.
Silhouette Diamond Sweepstakes
P.O. Box 779
Madison Square Station
New York, NY 10159

Canada
Silhouette Diamond Sweepstakes
Suite 191
238 Davenport Road
Toronto, Ontario M5R 1J6

SILHOUETTE DIAMOND SWEEPSTAKES
ENTRY FORM

☐ Mrs.　　☐ Miss　　☐ Ms　　☐ Mr.

NAME _____ (please print) _____

ADDRESS _____　　APT. #

CITY _____

STATE/(PROV.) _____

ZIP/(POSTAL CODE) _____

RTD-A-1

RULES FOR SILHOUETTE DIAMOND SWEEPSTAKES

OFFICIAL RULES—NO PURCHASE NECESSARY

1. Silhouette Diamond Sweepstakes is open to Canadian (except Quebec) and United States residents 18 years or older at the time of entry. Employees and immediate families of the publishers of Silhouette, their affiliates, retailers, distributors, printers, agencies and RONALD SMILEY INC. are excluded.

2. To enter, print your name and address on the official entry form or on a 3″ x 5″ slip of paper. You may enter as often as you choose, but each envelope must contain only one entry. Mail entries first class in Canada to Silhouette Diamond Sweepstakes, Suite 191, 238 Davenport Road, Toronto, Ontario M5R 1J6. In the United States, mail to Silhouette Diamond Sweepstakes, P.O. Box 779, Madison Square Station, New York, NY 10159. Entries must be postmarked between February 1 and September 30, 1985. Silhouette is not responsible for lost, late or misdirected mail.

3. First Prize of diamond jewelry, consisting of a necklace, ring, bracelet and earrings will be awarded. Approximate retail value is $50,000 U.S./$62,500 Canadian. Second Prize of 100 Silhouette Home Reader Service Subscriptions will be awarded. Approximate retail value of each is $162.00 U.S./$180.00 Canadian. No substitution, duplication, cash redemption or transfer of prizes will be permitted. Odds of winning depend upon the number of valid entries received. One prize to a family or household. Income taxes, other taxes and insurance on First Prize are the sole responsibility of the winners.

4. Winners will be selected under the supervision of RONALD SMILEY INC., an independent judging organization whose decisions are final, by random drawings from valid entries postmarked by September 30, 1985, and received no later than October 7, 1985. Entry in this sweepstakes indicates your awareness of the Official Rules. Winners who are residents of Canada must answer correctly a time-related arithmetical skill-testing question to qualify. First Prize winner will be notified by certified mail and must submit an Affidavit of Compliance within 10 days of notification. Returned Affidavits or prizes that are refused or undeliverable will result in alternative names being randomly drawn. Winners may be asked for use of their name and photo at no additional compensation.

5. For a First Prize winner list, send a stamped self-addressed envelope postmarked by September 30, 1985. In Canada, mail to Silhouette Diamond Contest Winner, Suite 309, 238 Davenport Road, Toronto, Ontario M5R 1J6. In the United States, mail to Silhouette Diamond Contest Winner, P.O. Box 182, Bowling Green Station, New York, NY 10274. This offer will appear in Silhouette publications and at participating retailers. Offer void in Quebec and subject to all Federal, Provincial, State and Municipal laws and regulations and wherever prohibited or restricted by law.

SDR-A-1

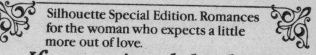

READERS' COMMENTS ON SILHOUETTE SPECIAL EDITIONS:

"I just finished reading the first six Silhouette Special Edition Books and I had to take the opportunity to write you and tell you how much I enjoyed them. I enjoyed all the authors in this series. Best wishes on your Silhouette Special Editions line and many thanks."

—B.H.*, Jackson, OH

"The Special Editions are really special and I enjoyed them very much! I am looking forward to next month's books."

—R.M.W.*, Melbourne, FL

"I've just finished reading four of your first six Special Editions and I enjoyed them very much. I like the more sensual detail and longer stories. I will look forward each month to your new Special Editions."

—L.S.*, Visalia, CA

"Silhouette Special Editions are — 1.) Superb! 2.) Great! 3.) Delicious! 4.) Fantastic! . . . Did I leave anything out? These are books that an adult woman can read . . . I love them!"

—H.C.*, Monterey Park, CA

*names available on request